## Mail-order lovers finally meet face-to-face...

His eyes, dark as gleaming jet, seemed to drill right through her. As if they had the ability to penetrate to her true identity.

Maybe that's exactly what he was doing. Cathryn held her breath, waiting for his challenge, certain that he was about to deny her. To her relief, he nodded slowly.

It was her turn to express uncertainty. "Ben?"

"Yeah." He stroked his square jaw. "I lost the beard. Thought maybe you'd appreciate seeing all of me."

And she did, she realized. Because now she noticed more than that pair of black eyes. She was aware of a strong face; thick, dark hair; tall, robust body clad in well-worn jeans. Things that the snapshot had failed to reveal.

And something else. Something she hadn't expected and that definitely complicated the situation.

Ben Adams was potently, disturbingly sexy.

## ABOUT THE AUTHOR

If setting has anything to do with it, Jean Barrett claims she has no reason not to be inspired. She and her husband live on Wisconsin's scenic Door Peninsula in an antiques-filled country cottage overlooking Lake Michigan. A teacher for many years, she left the classroom to write full-time. She is the author of a number of romance novels.

Jean loves both romance and suspense. She believes that combining the two offers the best of both worlds.

## Books by Jean Barrett

HARLEQUIN INTRIGUE
308—THE SHELTER OF HER ARMS
351—WHITE WEDDING

# Man of the Midnight Sun
## Jean Barrett

## *Harlequin Books*

TORONTO • NEW YORK • LONDON
AMSTERDAM • PARIS • SYDNEY • HAMBURG
STOCKHOLM • ATHENS • TOKYO • MILAN
MADRID • WARSAW • BUDAPEST • AUCKLAND

To my brothers, Richard and Jack, and their wives, Sandra and Diane. Hugs all around.

ISBN 0-373-22384-6

MAN OF THE MIDNIGHT SUN

Copyright © 1996 by Jean Barrett

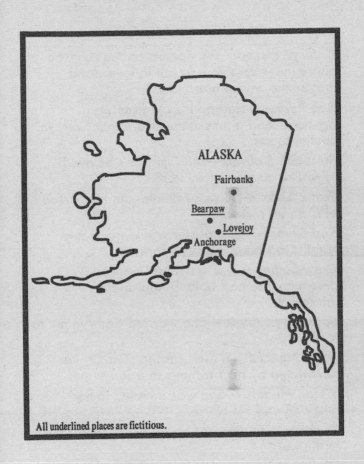

ALASKA

Fairbanks

Bearpaw

Lovejoy

Anchorage

All underlined places are fictitious.

# CAST OF CHARACTERS

*Cathryn McLean*—A woman on the run who chose the wrong time to fall in love...and maybe the wrong man, too.

*Ben Adams*—He had his own secret agenda...and a masculine allure that Cathryn couldn't resist.

*Meredith McLean*—Did Cathryn's beloved lookalike cousin betray her?

*Frank Tesler*—He was relentless in his pursuit of Cathryn McLean.

*Red Quinn*—The mobster would go to any lengths to silence Cathryn forever.

*Gary Bolling*—The assistant D.A. was determined to nail both Quinn and his informant.

*Sourdough Annie*—She warned Cathryn not to trust Ben.

*Hugh Menard*—The crusading senator was devastated by his brother's murder.

*Vivian Menard*—She was devoted to her husband and his cause.

*Zachery*—He was just an innocent child caught in the web.

*Hilda*—Her failing health made her an easy target.

# Chapter One

She trusted nothing now but her instinct to survive. That was why she resisted the temptation of the streetcar rumbling past her with its clanging bell. But, oh, what Cathryn wouldn't give to board that streetcar and sink in exhaustion onto one of its slatted seats! Impossible.

Lingering anywhere, especially in an enclosed situation, was dangerous. Her face must have appeared on every newscast in the city since last night. Recognition was a constant threat.

*Keep moving,* she ordered herself. *Stay on your feet and keep moving. You don't dare risk anything else.*

Cathryn pushed on along St. Charles Avenue, battling fatigue with each determined step. Fear and an urgent need to stay alert had kept her going through the long hours since last evening. That and the relentless memory of yesterday's horror. But she didn't know how much longer she could hold out.

What time was it? She paused to check her watch anxiously. Just after six. Too early to put her plan into action. She'd give it another half hour or so before she found a phone and made her vital calls.

Meanwhile she tried to look as though she belonged in the neighborhood, that there was purpose and direction in her gait. She couldn't afford any suspicious glances. The temperature didn't help, she thought, brushing away the tendrils of caramel-colored hair that had escaped from her thick braid and were sticking damply to the nape of her neck.

The morning air was already uncomfortably steamy, wearing the tang of the nearby river and the earthy, bittersweet odors associated with New Orleans in midsummer. It would be sweltering long before noon.

There! A patrol car circled slowly through the campus of Loyola and Tulane directly opposite her, and headed now for the avenue here. She had almost missed it in her careless preoccupation with the weather.

*Don't panic,* Cathryn commanded herself. *You've been successfully dodging police cruisers all night. See to it that this one isn't the exception.*

Audubon Park was just on her left. Wasting no time, she put the massive trunk of a live oak between herself and the street. An elderly man walking his Labrador gazed at her curiously as she pressed her back against the tree.

"Morning," he greeted her, restraining the dog, who wanted to paw at her playfully.

Cathryn smiled and nodded at him in what she hoped was a convincing absence of guilt. And all the while she was tense with alarm, fearing discovery.

The Labrador and his owner moved on into the depths of the park. A jogger went by, paying no attention to her. She waited for another few seconds, then peered carefully around the thick oak that screened her from the street. The patrol car had emerged from the university campus and was headed toward the Garden District, the direction from which she had come.

Cathryn breathed in relief while reminding herself not to relax her guard. There was no safety for her while she remained in New Orleans. They were looking for her, of course. Every patrol car in the city must be on the watch for her. That was bad enough. Far more terrifying was the realization that someone else wanted her and must also be hunting for her. Someone who would go to any lengths to silence her.

There was no one now she could rely on. She was on her own and desperate.

Time to find that telephone.

She left the park and pressed on wearily along the avenue. She reached Riverbend, and there she found what she needed in a small shopping area situated below the grassy bank of the levee where tugboats and barges congregated. An outside public phone on the wall of a minimart.

Thankful that she could remain in the open, where she lessened the chance of being trapped and caught, she fished a handful of coins out of her purse. She kept her back to the parking lot as she dialed.

A woman answered, "Menard residence."

Cathryn recognized the gentle, cultured voice of the senator's wife. She had met Vivian Menard on two occasions at the senator's campaign headquarters and had found her a kind, handsome woman who was apparently much admired as a hostess in Washington.

"May I speak to Senator Menard, please?"

"I'm sorry, but the senator isn't able to come to the phone just now. Can I take a message?"

"I really need to speak to him personally. It's important."

"May I ask who's calling?"

Mrs. Menard obviously didn't remember her voice. There was no reason she should. Cathryn hesitated, reluctant to disclose her name. But it was the only way to get results. "Cathryn McLean," she murmured.

There was immediate excitement in Vivian Menard's manner, as well as a note of sympathy. "Oh, what a relief! Hold on, Cathryn, while I get the senator."

Cathryn cast a nervous glance over her shoulder while she waited. There was no one paying any attention to her. But this delay worried her. What if calls to the Menard home were being monitored, and even in this very instant her own call was being traced? It was a definite risk, but she owed the senator this call.

The receiver was snatched up, and his deep, mellow voice came on the line with a swift "Cathryn, are you all right?"

"I— Yes, I'm fine, Senator."

"Thank God for that. I've been worried sick about you. We've all been out of our minds with worry since those two officers were found shot, and not a sign of you anywhere in the house. We thought the worst."

"No, I wasn't snatched. I . . . well, I wasn't in the house when it was invaded and they were killed. I'm afraid I disobeyed orders and sneaked out for a few minutes to take care of a necessary errand." He didn't need to know that she had slipped away to use a pay phone at a nearby service station, that she hadn't wanted her police guards to overhear her on the phone in the safe house.

"That was reckless of you, Cathryn, but it looks like it did save your life. Only where have you been all these hours?"

She couldn't tell him. She couldn't bear to recount her appalling discovery of the two plainclothesmen who had been brutally slain in her absence from the house. Nor of how, in mindless terror, she had fled the scene, losing herself in the all-night crowds in the French Quarter. Even in summer the tourists were there in force. In a numbed state she had wandered among them around Jackson Square and along Bourbon Street, an anonymous fugitive in a sea of humanity.

Then, in those melancholy hours before dawn, Cathryn had reached a decision. If that house in Elysian Fields, where they had been hiding her until the trial, had been discovered and breached by the man who wanted her dead, she was safe nowhere in New Orleans. She had to disappear.

Senator Menard must have sensed her pain. "Never mind. That's not important right now. All that matters is you're safe. Cathryn, where are you? We've got to get a police escort to you immediately."

This was difficult. She hated to do this to him. He was a man she deeply admired and respected, a crusader who fought for the rights of the underprivileged. It was why she had worked so industriously for him as a campaign volunteer in support of his upcoming, crucial reelection.

"I'm not coming in, Senator," she informed him quietly.

There was a brief pause while he comprehended her intention. "Cathryn, you've got to come in. You're in danger every minute out there on your own."

"And just how safe was I in that house where they put me? The district attorney's office guaranteed me an invincible protection. Well, they failed to provide it, because Quinn's people managed to find me."

"There must have been a leak somewhere," he admitted.

"Yes, and two officers were slaughtered because of it. That's a guilt I'll live with for the rest of my life."

"Cathryn, I know you're badly shaken, but you've got to tell me where you are. Let me help you, please."

"I'm sorry, Senator. I can't." She wished she could confide to him that it wasn't just herself now she was fighting to save, that her survival was essential to the welfare of someone else. But she didn't dare.

"Cathryn, listen to me—"

"It's no use. I only called because I couldn't just vanish without telling you how sorry I am that I won't be testifying. I know you were counting on me, but . . . well, I'm just sorry, that's all."

"Cathryn, don't do this," he pleaded. "Cathryn—"

She couldn't listen to him. She couldn't weaken. She hung up the phone. There were two further calls she had to make, both of them to the only people who mattered to her now. It was chancy hanging around here to phone them, but necessary.

Afterward she would see about getting a ride out of the city on one of those barges at the levee. It was the only way. They would be watching the airport and the bus and rail terminals. Probably checking every car rental, as well.

She was going into hiding. Her plan was an outrageous one. But in her desperation, without funds and no longer trusting anyone in New Orleans, it was all she had.

THE PROPERTY WAS LOCATED in an exclusive neighborhood on the shores of Lake Pontchartrain. A brick wall surrounded the sprawling house, guaranteeing its security and privacy. The garage sheltered two Cadillacs and a Lamborghini while a sleek cabin cruiser was docked on the lakeside of the grounds. It was an impressive estate, and it had been paid for by every ruthless, illegal operation known to organized crime.

Its owner, Red Quinn, paced the length of his spacious office overlooking the blinding waters of the lake. His lawyer and confidant, Morgan Hurley, waited silently while the beefy, freckled Quinn spewed his rage.

"They screwed up! Went and took out those two cops, and for what? The McLean bitch is still out there somewhere!"

"Take it easy, Red," the lawyer urged smoothly. "You've already been released, haven't you? Without Cathryn McLean, they don't stand a prayer of bringing you to trial."

"Yeah, I'm free! But for how long? She decides to stop being scared and play ball again with the assistant D.A., and I'm right back where I was. Where is she, Morgan?"

The lawyer shrugged. "On the run, of course."

Quinn snorted like a nervous bull. "So she's not trusting the cops to protect her anymore. Maybe that makes her smarter than we figured. I don't like it, Morgan. So what are we doing about it?"

"Waiting for our connection with the D.A.'s office to tell us what we need. They're making every effort to locate her, and as soon as they know something, the information will be passed on to us. Just like before."

"It's not good enough. As long as she's on the loose, I stay worried."

"Relax, Red. We're going to take care of it. I've already hired the man we need. You know who I mean. We've used him before when we couldn't depend on our own people. He's expensive, but he doesn't give up until he gets results. He'll get to her."

Quinn stopped pacing. He gazed out at the lake, his cruel eyes narrowing against the brilliance. "I want her dead, Morgan," he said, his voice a chilling, lethal whisper. "Whatever it takes, I want her dead."

THE TERMINAL WORE a look of bleak desertion as Cathryn left the bus in St. Louis and cautiously checked her surroundings. It was late at night, with only a scattering of people in the drab waiting room. A couple of them were derelicts who had wandered in from the street to use the rest rooms. The others sat on the hard benches, their luggage tucked around their feet as they waited for their buses to be called. None of them was interested in her.

Cathryn had no luggage of her own, other than her purse and a canvas tote bag containing a few essentials. She was dressed in as nondescript a manner as possible. Jeans, a lightweight jacket over a T-shirt and her hair piled under a baseball cap pulled low over her forehead.

Striving to look neither as secretive nor as anxious as she felt, she began to move in a casual manner around the perimeter of the forlorn waiting room. All the while her gaze, watchful and hopeful, checked the corners.

Had she failed to come? Cathryn didn't know what she would do if that happened. Everything depended now on Meredith.

She had reached the vicinity of the lockers when a blond woman emerged from the shadows around the corner. She looked tense and worried as she hurried toward Cathryn.

"Cat," she whispered.

And for a moment that was all either of them said as they clung together in an emotional hug.

"Thank you for being here," Cathryn murmured when they finally released each other.

"Where else would I be when you need me, and we're the only kin either of us has? More like sisters than cousins. That's what we always said. Are you okay, Cat? I haven't been able to do anything but worry since you called me from New Orleans."

"I'm managing. It wasn't easy getting here. After the barge I had to change buses a few times to confuse my trail. What about you, Meredith?"

"I've been careful. No one followed me here. But why should they? There hasn't been anyone who's tried to contact me about you."

"But they will sooner or later. The police won't fail to learn of your existence. I want you to deny that you've either seen me or heard from me. I won't have you involved."

"Cathryn—"

"I mean it. I don't want you at risk. Once I leave here, that's it." She glanced at the big clock on the wall. "I have a little more than half an hour before my next bus leaves. Is there somewhere we can talk safely?"

"There's a coffee shop down there." Meredith gestured. "Practically empty at this hour."

Within minutes they were in a dim booth at the back of the shop, seated across from each other over mugs of coffee neither of them wanted. Cathryn faced the front so she could keep a wary eye on the door. New Orleans had taught her a careful vigilance. She could see that Meredith was saddened by this necessity, as well as by their need to confer in hushed tones.

She leaned toward Cathryn. "There wasn't much of an explanation in the news. Just what did you witness that night? Can you bear to talk about it?"

Meredith deserved to know exactly why she was helping her. Cathryn described the horror as briefly as possible, not just because it was painful to relate but because their time together was precious and needed to be used for matters more imperative.

"I was putting in some volunteer time at Senator Menard's campaign headquarters. They had me working upstairs in a back cubby entering names and addresses in the computer for the mailing lists. It was late when I finished, sometime after ten. There was no one else in the building by then, except for the senator's brother, Francis."

"Who was also his campaign manager," Meredith said. "Isn't that what I read?"

"That's right. I could see him through the glass wall of his office down on the first floor when I came out on the balcony. I started down the stairs when I realized I'd left my umbrella in the cubby. It was a rainy night. I knew I'd need it. I didn't bother putting any of the lights back on. The automatic security lamps were lit by then. Not much of a glow from them but enough to find my way back to the cubby. I groped around for a few minutes before I found the umbrella. When I came out on the balcony again, Francis was no longer alone in his office. He had a visitor."

"Red Quinn," Meredith whispered.

"Yes, Red Quinn. I recognized him right away. He's a well-known mobster around New Orleans. And there was no mistaking that flaming hair, even plastered with rain."

"Why was he there?"

Cathryn shook her head. "I don't know. He and the senator have always been enemies. Senator Menard has been trying for years to see him put away. And that night there with Francis... well, it was some kind of confrontation. They were quarreling, but the door was shut so I couldn't hear their actual words."

"But you could clearly see them," Meredith prompted.

Cathryn briefly closed her eyes. "I can see them now, and I'll go on seeing them for the rest of my life. The two of them standing there in that blaze of light, like it was a stage. And me out there in the darkness, the audience they didn't know existed. Only it wasn't a play. It was real, and—" Her voice faltered. She swallowed, then made herself quickly finish the account. "Red Quinn pulled a gun and he shot him. He killed Francis, then he left the building. And he never knew I was crouching up there on the balcony, or he would have murdered me, too."

Meredith reached across the table and closed her hand around Cathryn's. "I shouldn't have asked you. It must have been devastating for you."

"Not half as devastating as it was for Senator Menard. He and his brother were very close. Francis was dedicated to his causes."

Meredith's expression was rueful. "It's a sorry business."

"Yes, and Quinn is powerful and dangerous. I realized that after what happened at the safe house. He'll never let me on that stand to testify against him, and there's no way I can count on police protection now. If it were only myself I had to think about . . ."

Meredith's fingers squeezed hers. "I know."

Cathryn recovered her composure, and with it her resolve. "Did you bring the letters?"

"It's all here." She produced a thick brown envelope from the depths of her large handbag and placed it on the table between them. "Everything you'll need, including the airline ticket he sent mc."

"He must be pretty eager to have you there when he's willing to pay your flight like this."

"Oh, he's a very decent man, at least by what I could tell from all his letters, or I'd never let you go to him."

Cathryn nodded. "Then I promise you I'll do everything I can not to make him sorry he sent for Meredith McLean."

"I don't question that. It's just that . . . oh, Cat, this is all so extreme! Taking on my identity, hiding yourself in the Alaskan wilderness for God knows how long! Isn't there any other way?"

"Not without funds. All I have is what's here in my purse, enough to take me through another week or so. And I wouldn't have that much if I hadn't cashed a check just before I went into the safe house. I didn't dare to go back to my apartment afterward, just as I don't dare to use a credit card or try to work somewhere to support myself, because any of it would leave a paper trail leading straight to me. And Red Quinn could be the first to follow it."

Meredith's reaction was a rueful one. "It's moments like these that I regret being a schoolteacher in a small town in Missouri, because if I had any real money of my own—"

"I wouldn't accept it. And you know you love the classroom, just as I love—" She broke off to correct herself. "*Did* love being a research librarian."

Regret was pointless, Cathryn realized. All that mattered now were the contents of the envelope in front of her and the potential protection they offered her. She reached for the envelope, opened it and drew out a bundle of letters.

"They're all there," Meredith assured her. "Every one of the letters he sent me over the past eight months since we began corresponding. When you've had a chance to study them, you'll know everything I know about him. The ticket is tucked in there somewhere."

Cathryn flipped through the letters without opening any of them. There was no time for that now, though she did notice the addresses on the envelopes were penned in a strong, masculine scrawl. An encouraging sign?

She glimpsed the airline ticket to Anchorage at the bottom of the bundle. And something else. A snapshot. She slid it from the packet and lifted her eyes questioningly to Meredith, who was solemnly watching her.

"Yes, that's Ben Adams. He included it in one of his letters."

Cathryn gazed silently at the snapshot. It depicted a dark, bearded man posed rather self-consciously on the porch of a log cabin. The animal close beside him looked more wolf than dog. The photograph was an amateur's effort and lacked any real detail or clarity.

"Did you send him a picture of yourself?"

"I'm afraid so. One of those school photos with my kids. But it wasn't that great so it shouldn't be a problem. I mean, if he's expecting *me*..."

"Then why should he believe he's getting anyone else *but* you? And he will before I'm finished. He *has* to."

Cathryn replaced the materials and tucked the brown envelope in her tote bag. Then she faced her cousin. "I have to be sure of this, Meredith. I have to know you don't mind that it's me going to him instead of you."

Meredith shook her head emphatically. "That afternoon when we talked on the phone—you know, just before you got into this awful mess—and I told you about Ben's invitation and how—"

She broke off as the languid waitress drifted toward them to refill the mugs of coffee neither of them had touched. Cathryn smiled at the woman and shook her head.

When the waitress was out of earshot again, Meredith continued. "It's like I said that day. When I answered his ad and we began exchanging letters... well, it was a kind of adventure for someone like me living an ordinary existence in a dull town. You know, the lonely, rugged bachelor in far-off Alaska yearning for female companionship, and me seeing myself as capable of providing it. Okay, so it was damn romantic. On paper, anyway."

"But when it came to reality..."

"Exactly. It wasn't exciting anymore, it was scary. Because suddenly he wants me to join him. Like a mail-order bride. All right, that's an exaggeration. Ben was clear about there being no commitment until we learned whether we suited each other in person. Even so, I realized I couldn't do it. I couldn't go up there and be alone with him in all that wilderness. I've just been too much of a coward to let him know I wasn't coming."

"Now you don't have to," Cathryn said, the determination clear in her voice. "You can tell him you'll be there just as he planned."

Meredith stared at her. There was misgiving in her gaze. Cathryn could see that she was suddenly losing her nerve. "Cat, I don't know. Ben is no fool. Maybe it's crazy to think you can get away with passing yourself off as me."

"Sisters," Cathryn insisted. "We've always said we're enough alike to be sisters. The family resemblance has always been there. All I have to do is change my hair, copy your makeup. I don't have to get any closer than that, just near enough to that image of the woman in the picture you sent him. I can do it, Meredith."

"But what if you end up in a situation where you'll need to produce identity? A driver's license, things like that?"

"It won't happen. And if it does, I'll bluff my way through it somehow."

"I'm not sure. I'm just not sure now that this isn't all a big mistake."

Cathryn grasped both of her cousin's hands on the table and held them tightly. "Meredith, listen to me. It *will* work. I'm going to *make* it work. I don't have an alternative. I have to hide, and where better to do it than in a remote corner in Alaska? There's only one thing that seriously bothers me."

"What?"

"I'm using him. There's no getting around that. I'm using him and I'm afraid that one day I'm going to have to pay the price for that. But I can't let that stop me, because right now Ben Adams is all I have."

Her cousin offered no further argument, but she could see that uncertainty lingered on her attractive face.

Funny, Cathryn thought. Of the two of them, it had always been Meredith who was outgoing and impulsive. She, on the other hand, had been reserved and prudent. Partly because this was her nature, and partly, she suspected, because of what she had had to sacrifice years ago in college. But now it was as if they had suddenly reversed their characters. It was she who was being daring, and Meredith who was being circumspect.

Cathryn wondered if it was necessity that was making her more like her cousin, a borrowing of some of her traits in order for her to impersonate Meredith successfully. It wouldn't be surprising. Not when she knew she needed all the help she could get to bring off this performance.

"I'd better go," Cathryn said.

They collected their belongings and left the coffee shop. Meredith walked with her toward the gates.

"Write to him first thing," Cathryn instructed her. "Tell him I'll be on that flight and that he can meet me in Anchorage."

"The ticket is for a week from now," Meredith said. "Where will you be until then?"

"I'm going to find a cheap motel somewhere that's isolated so I can hole up while I study his letters and do everything I can to transform myself into you. Wish me luck."

"Oh, Cat, are you sure—?"

"Don't. Don't question it anymore. It has to be this way."

They had reached the gate. The bus was there, and the few passengers waiting for it were beginning to board.

Meredith hesitated, then made herself say it. "There is one thing. What you're leaving back in Louisiana..."

Cathryn knew she didn't mean her job, friends or apartment. Meredith was referring to the reason she had sneaked out of that safe house to make her secretive telephone call.

The same call she had made again after talking to Meredith outside the minimart in New Orleans.

"I know. I've thought about it. It's all I *have* thought about actually. Because if Red Quinn or his people ever found out...well, that's really why I have to do this. If I can vanish, and manage to stay vanished long enough, it'll all blow over and I'll be forgotten. And there won't be a risk of anyone finding out about him. Then maybe one day..."

But she didn't dare let herself count on the future. It was too painful to hope for something that might never be possible.

"They're waiting, Meredith. I have to go."

The two women caught each other in a quick, fierce embrace.

"Be careful, Cat."

"It's what I do best these days," she said, managing to summon a parting smile. "Bless you, darling, and don't forget. Tell Ben Adams I'm on my way."

Minutes later, as Meredith somberly watched from the gate, the bus lumbered away into the darkness.

# Chapter Two

The moment was almost here, and she was frightened. Would Ben Adams accept her? She stood in the cramped lavatory at the rear of the droning aircraft, trying to renew her confidence as she gazed critically at the image of the unfamiliar woman in the mirror.

Back at that rural motel in Illinois, Cathryn had been amazed and pleased by her careful transformation. She had cropped her caramel-colored hair, lightening it to an ash blond before copying Meredith's cap of loose, easy-care waves. A sassy style that flattered her face.

Her altered makeup suited her new coloring, along with eyebrows she had plucked and shaped to match her cousin's. It was true that her face was a bit more narrow than Meredith's, but they shared the same straight nose, full mouth and thick eyelashes. She was also somewhat taller than Meredith, but that should present no problem when their figures were otherwise similar.

The changes had agreed with Cathryn, making her seem less drab to herself. Someone who was more interesting. That was what she had thought back at the motel. But now...

Now all she could see were the differences that suddenly looked major to her in her mounting anxiety. Aquamarine eyes when Meredith's were a pure blue. A slight cleft in the chin that her cousin lacked. And Cathryn's biggest concern, a small brown mole below the outside corner of her right eye.

Were any of these problems serious enough to betray her, or was she exaggerating them in her fear?

A polite rap on the door interrupted her scrutiny. She opened it to the friendly face of a flight attendant.

"Sorry for the intrusion, but we're asking everyone to return to their seats now. We'll be landing shortly."

Anchorage. That was the sight the other passengers were trying to glimpse from their windows as the jet descended to the international airport. Cathryn was focused on nothing but the snapshot she had fished out of her purse seconds after she secured her seat belt.

She studied the bearded man in the photo just as intently as she had examined her own face in the lavatory mirror. Striving to invest him with a reality. It was no use. He was no more tangible to her now than when she had pored over his letters in the motel. For all the details of his life he had shared with Meredith, Ben Adams remained to Cathryn an elusive, unknown force.

The best she could hope for, she thought nervously, was to recognize him in the airport.

HE WASN'T THERE.

Cathryn stood in the baggage-claim area, fighting a sense of sudden despair as the last of the crowd streamed away toward the exits. Nearly a half hour had passed since the plane had unloaded at the gate. She had spent most of that time anxiously scanning faces, but none of them had resembled the man in the snapshot. Nor had anyone approached her.

There was no more luggage on the carousel. The area had emptied. She was alone.

She stood there, trying to understand her dilemma. Had there been a mix-up about just when and where he was to meet her, something Meredith had neglected to make clear in her letter? Could that letter have failed to reach him? Or—worst of all—had Ben Adams, suspecting something, changed his mind and decided not to come?

Whatever the explanation, her situation was a serious one. How was she going to survive without him? She had less than fifty dollars now in her purse, and her only possession was the single, inexpensive suitcase at her feet. She wouldn't have that much, or the clothes packed inside it, if it weren't for Meredith's generosity. Her cousin had hidden money for her inside one of Ben's letters, along with a note insisting Cathryn couldn't arrive in Alaska with little more than the clothes on her back.

She couldn't go on standing here being helpless. There was still the chance that a message was waiting for her, perhaps at one of the airline's counters. Hopeful of that possibility, she picked up her suitcase and started toward an escalator to the main floor.

She hadn't reached the escalator when she was stopped by a deep, resonant voice just behind her.

"Meredith McLean?"

Cathryn turned, her heart beginning to hammer in a strange kind of anticipation. As if she was about to make some extraordinary connection.

It was his eyes she noticed first. Couldn't help noticing. They were dark, as dark as gleaming jet, and they seemed to drill right through her. As if they had the ability to penetrate her identity.

Maybe that's exactly what he was doing, because he had the photograph Meredith had sent him in his hand. Frowning, he glanced down at it, then back at her. Cathryn held her breath, waiting for his challenge, certain that he was about to deny her.

To her relief he nodded slowly and permitted a smile, that struck her as oddly reluctant, to hover briefly on his wide mouth.

"I didn't think there would be any way I wouldn't recognize you," he said, "but..." He shrugged a pair of broad shoulders and pocketed the photo.

It was her turn to express uncertainty. "Ben?"

"Yeah, I know." His hand stroked a square jaw. "I lost the beard. I thought maybe you'd appreciate seeing all of me."

She did, she realized. Because now she noticed more than that pair of black eyes. She was aware of a strong face with a Roman nose. Thick, dark hair with a smattering of gray at the temples, though she knew he was only in his midthirties. A tall, robust body clad in jeans and a well-worn sport coat. Things that the snapshot had failed to reveal. And something else. Something she hadn't expected and that definitely complicated the situation. Ben Adams was potently, disturbingly sexy.

Her awareness of this was heightened when he leaned down and kissed her. It was a casual, brief kiss placed beside her mouth rather than directly on it. A greeting that shouldn't have surprised her, considering that the letters he and Meredith exchanged had progressed to a fairly intimate stage. But the contact definitely affected her equilibrium.

"Welcome to Alaska, Meredith."

"Thank you for wanting me to come."

It was a stilted thing to say, emphasizing the awkwardness of their meeting.

He eased the situation with a husky-voiced apology. "Sorry I'm so late. There was a last-minute emergency on the line that delayed my getting away."

She knew from his letters that he was referring to the Trans-Alaska Pipeline, whose construction had first brought him to Alaska and enabled him to buy his cabin. He had stayed on after its completion in a maintenance capacity that permitted him considerable amounts of free time to enjoy the wilderness he relished.

"My section is all secure now," he went on, "so I'm off for the next few weeks. Is that your only bag?"

"Yes."

He took the suitcase from her hand. "Then we'd better head out. It's a long drive to the cabin."

She was breathless with her effort to match his energetic, long-legged stride that carried them out of the building into a dazzling sunlight. The light, together with the sticky warmth that accompanied it, was unexpected, especially since it wasn't much past six o'clock in the morning.

He was aware of her surprise as they moved across the parking lot. "You're in the land of the midnight sun now, Meredith. At this time of the year, the sun rises before four, and heat waves aren't unknown. Here we are."

They had reached a Jeep Wrangler, which looked as though it had seen tough service on the rough tracks of the wilderness.

He turned to her when they were settled in the vehicle, offering a slow smile. Again there was that quality of strange reluctance in the smile, even a degree of impatience. Did he regret having her here after all?

His words, anyway, said otherwise. "I warn you, Meredith, I'm going to do everything I can to make you glad you're here."

There was a seductive huskiness in his promise that unsettled her. She was suddenly aware, for the first time, that she was going off into the Alaskan wilds with this man. That they would share a small cabin, just the two of them alone together. And that he was a total stranger who made the breath stick in her throat.

Cathryn was no less unnerved as they drove off through the city. She was conscious every second of his hard bulk close beside her in the Jeep. This wasn't the Ben Adams she had planned on—the gentle, shy but ultimately cheerful bachelor. This was something else. Something that was...what? Grim? No, that wasn't the right word. *Intense.* Yes, he had a compelling, mercurial intensity that made her wonder how she was going to survive a remote cabin with him.

Maybe he was thinking the same thing, because he kept sneaking glances at her as he drove. Or, she asked herself nervously, was he suspicious after all? She kept fearing that at any second he would confront her with a scowl and a harsh question: "You're not Meredith McLean. What the hell are you trying to pull?"

*Enough, Cathryn. The man is probably just being as curious about you as you are about him. It's only natural.*

But in order to save her battered courage, she tore her eyes away from that dark, almost brooding gaze of his. She distracted herself with the scenery of Anchorage.

The city, sprawled against a backdrop of the Chugach Mountains, was a fascinating contrast of modern high-rises rubbing shoulders with structures that looked like survivors from the pioneer days. There was a raw quality about the place that suggested the bleakness of long winters and the vastness of the wilderness at its door. No doubt about it. Alaska was turning out to be as much of a shock and a mystery as the man who sat beside her.

Cathryn wasn't sure just when she became aware of the gray Jaguar sedan that was tailing them. It might have been there for some time, just another vehicle in the flow of traffic. But it was such a distinctive car that she couldn't help eventually noticing it. Because it was always with them whenever she twisted or turned in her seat to take in the sights.

In time she became certain that it was no accident the Jaguar was there, that it was deliberately following the Jeep. Panic gripped her. Had her enemy somehow tracked her to Alaska?

She waited, trying to remain calm and rational. She wanted to be sure the threat was real. The traffic thinned as they drove north out of the city. Cathryn again checked the highway behind them. The Jaguar was there in close pursuit.

She faced forward and glanced quickly at her companion. Ben was either unaware of the car behind them or not worried by it. But he did feel her tense gaze on him.

"What?" he asked her casually.

She couldn't tell him, not unless it became absolutely necessary. They were passing through a small community, a kind of suburb of Anchorage. The place offered an appealing attraction just beside the highway. She used it as a diversion.

"There. What is it?"

Ben slowed the Jeep to a crawl. "It's a Russian Orthodox church, a leftover from the days when Russia owned Alaska."

Cathryn tried to concentrate on the unique, onion-domed church constructed entirely of logs. The cemetery adjoining it was equally unusual. Vividly painted wooden structures covered each of the graves.

"Spirit houses," Ben explained. "Made by the Athabascan Indians to protect the spirits of the dead."

The oncoming lane was suddenly clear of traffic. The Jaguar behind them surged forward. Out of the corner of her eye, Cathryn glimpsed the driver—an impatient, elderly woman. The car swept by them without a pause and disappeared over a rise. All this time the Jaguar had merely been waiting for an opportunity to pass.

Ben must have sensed her enormous relief. He looked at her curiously. She'd have to be more careful after this. The constant strain that had been with her since New Orleans was making her paranoid. She needed to remember she was in Alaska now and that she was safe. Wasn't she?

THEY STOPPED at a rustic roadside diner that sold miniature totem poles and featured reindeer sausage on its menu. Ben urged her to take advantage of the enormous country breakfast he ordered for them, explaining that there were scant opportunities between here and his cabin, which they couldn't hope to reach before evening.

Cathryn had been too tense to want much of anything on the plane. She suddenly realized she was ravenous.

Maybe it was the satisfying meal she ate or the bracing air of a higher altitude, but she felt much more relaxed when they were back on the road again.

Of course, the scenery could be equally responsible for that. She had never imagined that mountains could be so spectacular. Their massive presence on every side was a reminder of Alaska's awesome dimensions.

"Like them?" Ben asked.

"They take my breath away."

He seemed pleased by her reaction. He pointed to a range far to the north where a snowcapped double peak loomed above the rest. "Mount McKinley," he said. "Visible even from this distance. That is, when the weather cooperates."

They were traveling the Glenn Highway now, and to Cathryn, each vista seemed more magnificent than the last. Wild river gorges, sweeping forests of spruce and aspen, a blue-tinted glacier, alpine meadows strewed with blue forget-me-nots and magenta fireweed.

"It's all so—so *big*," she murmured.

Ben chuckled, drawing her attention to a nearby crag where several horned white animals were poised against the sky. "Dall sheep," he said.

Cathryn was enchanted by them. He promised her she would see many more of them. Alaska teemed with wildlife.

Hour after hour the Jeep wound through the remote backcountry. Cathryn never tired of the scenery, and Ben seemed happy to share it with her. They talked of nothing else. But all the while there was another subject that was waiting to be broached. She was conscious of it thrumming between them like a live thing, provocative and ultimately unavoidable. How long would she remain with him? An extended visit or something more definite, something involving a permanent relationship? A mail-order bride. That's what Meredith had said, and she couldn't forget her cousin's tantalizing words.

Ben must be thinking of the same thing, but he wasn't pressuring her with it. She was comfortable with that. And she was actually able to relax now that Anchorage was far behind them, and the danger she had lived with since New Orleans no longer kept her alert and frightened every minute.

The mesmerizing landscape eventually lulled her into a peaceful sleep, the first she had known in days. Her last, satisfying thought before she drifted off was centered on the man beside her. She suddenly realized that she felt completely secure with him. Strange, considering how on every other level she found Ben Adams alarmingly intriguing.

*ALLURING.* That was the word that had leapt into his mind the first moment he'd laid eyes on her back at the airport. He had thought her alluring. He still did as he glanced at her sleeping beside him, her blond hair all mussed like a woman who'd just made wanton love, her breasts looking lush in her embroidered cotton sweater. He damned himself for the treacherous tightening in his groin.

She was alluring, and she was trouble. *Big* trouble. He felt it in his gut. Had instinctively sensed it ever since he'd been coerced into this job. What he hadn't expected was to be so immediately, strongly aroused by her. That kind of thing was a real mistake in his line of work, a weakness that could result in the worst kind of penalty. He'd already learned that, hadn't he?

There was another reason for avoiding a relationship on that level. It made it tougher to maintain his role, left him susceptible to careless errors. He had already slipped up a bit at the airport. She hadn't questioned his lie about being delayed by an emergency on the pipeline, but his attitude had puzzled her a couple of times.

He'd have to guard against any further signs of reluctance. She mustn't guess his resentment that bordered on bitterness, or she would end up suspecting his identity. He had to remember he had only one objective that mattered. He had to get her to trust him completely. That meant no emotional involvement, though he wouldn't bet at this point that he was going to be able to resist the physical temptation of this situation. Not when she looked like that and with the two of them alone in an isolated cabin.

Problem was she was already suspicious of everything and everyone. Had every reason to be. And she was far too observant. Look how she had been spooked by that innocent Jag. Ironic that it had worried her when the whole time it was the man sitting right beside her she ought to have been worrying about. If only she knew...

Oh, hell, he hated this whole thing. He wanted it finished, with Cathryn McLean out of the way, so that he could go back to his solitary, uncomplicated existence.

He checked his watch and the mileage on the Jeep's dash. Still a good distance to go. Meanwhile, he didn't like the look of those clouds that were beginning to mass over the mountains.

FRANK TESLER WAS breathing hard by the time he neared the clearing. And his feet hurt. It had been a lot farther than he'd anticipated. Uphill all the way, too.

No choice about it. His rented Land Rover would have announced his arrival. He had left it a couple of miles down the rough track. Parked it out of sight behind some evergreens.

Well, it was his own fault he was puffing and sweating. He was overweight. Betty had been after him to shed some pounds. Maybe he'd work on it when he got home. Just because he was thinking about retiring soon didn't mean he should let himself go.

He caught a glimpse of the cabin's roof through the trees. Time to leave the track. He headed into the thick woods, pausing to mop at the perspiration on his balding head and to slap as noiselessly as possible at a persistent mosquito. Alaskan mosquitoes were the worst. He could swear that the last one that had tried to feed on him had been the size of a hummingbird.

Frank knew the value of caution. He approached the clearing from the side, screening himself behind dense undergrowth as he reached its edge. From here he carefully checked the situation.

Nice place, he thought, peering through the leaves at the log structure tucked among the tall spruce. Real homey.

No vehicle in the yard. The place was silent, wearing an air of desertion. Had he come all this way for nothing? He had to be sure.

Keeping himself hidden among the trees, he slowly circled the clearing, alert for any noise or movement. Nothing. All he observed was a flash of blue water below the back side of the cabin. There was a lake down there. He wondered if it offered any worthwhile fishing. Probably did.

In the end Frank risked leaving the trees. Sneaking up on the cabin's front porch, he risked a fast peek through a window. By then he had his hand on his semiautomatic pistol.

There was no one inside. The place looked empty. He tried the door. It was unlocked. Guess there's no reason to bother with a lock way out here, he thought.

At this point he didn't expect any surprises, but he was ready with his piece when he entered the cabin. It was just what he figured. Nobody home and a feeling about the place that it was going to stay that way for a while.

The lack of groceries told him that. That was always a telltale sign, especially when folks weren't handy to stores and needed to keep a stock. He checked the cabinets and the bottled-gas refrigerator. Nope, not a perishable in sight.

Maybe Adams and the McLean woman weren't going to hole up here, Frank thought as he returned to the porch. Maybe he was taking her somewhere else. He wondered just where that might be.

The nearest community was a place called Bearpaw. Not much more than a bump on the road. He had already checked it out. But there was a post office there. Must be where Ben Adams got his mail. He'd go to Bearpaw, then, and look for answers. And if that didn't work... Well, then he'd try something else. Whatever it took. Betty was forever telling him he was the most persistent cuss she knew.

There was the rumble of thunder over the mountains as he came away from the clearing. He hoped he wouldn't get caught in a downpour before he got back to the Land Rover.

THE CRASH OF GUNFIRE! Red Quinn had found her—she was going to die!

Cathryn came awake in a panic, struggling against the restraints that were preventing her escape as a second terrifying explosion rent the air.

"Easy," advised a deep, soothing voice. "It's just thunder and lightning. Sounds like the devil in these mountains."

Startled, she gazed at her companion. Then she realized where she was. Ben's Jeep, and the restraint holding her down was her seat belt. A storm. Only a summer storm.

"Sorry," she murmured. "I guess I was dreaming."

He nodded his understanding without sparing her a glance. The road demanded his attention. They had left the Glenn Highway, perhaps long ago, and were traveling now over an unpaved route through the backcountry. Cathryn could no longer see the mountains. They were obscured by sheets of driving rain.

"It's getting dark. How long have I been asleep?"

"A few hours. It's late enough, but we're losing the light sooner because of the storm."

"How far now to the cabin?"

"Still a way to the turnoff."

"Can we get there before night?"

"If we don't run into a washout. The road isn't dependable in weather like this. Don't worry. The Jeep has survived worse than this."

Cathryn wasn't worrying. His presence close beside her was solid and comforting. They were silent now as he concentrated on his driving. She watched the rain beating against the windshield. For a long while there was nothing else to see.

Then, out of nowhere, an alarming bulk loomed directly in front of them. The headlights, inadequate in the half light and the heavy rain, had failed to provide a sufficient warning. Cathryn, suddenly aware that they were on a collision course with a bull moose, braced herself with a sharp cry.

Ben's curse was equally pronounced as his foot punched the brake. His swift reaction prevented an impact, but the Jeep skidded on the rain-slick, muddied gravel. Had they been traveling at a less cautious speed, the vehicle might have overturned. As it was, it seemed to leap off the road, defying Ben's struggle at the wheel.

There was no shoulder to control them. Nothing but the sudden edge of the road and a curtain of low growth through which they smashed. Then a sickeningly steep incline. Somewhere down its madly bouncing length, Ben managed to bring them to a stop. But the halt was so rough and abrupt that it felt as if they had slammed into a wall.

Cathryn recovered herself after a dazed few seconds and turned anxiously to her companion.

"Ben, are you—?"

She had been about to ask him if he was all right. But she could see by the light from the dash that he wasn't all right. He was unconscious, his head hanging limply to one side. His seat belt was still in place, so he couldn't have smacked into the wheel or the windshield. That last jounce must have flung him sideways, cracking his head against the door-post.

Was he injured? Maybe *seriously* injured? She had to find out. Releasing her seat belt to permit herself a freedom of movement, she stretched across Ben's still form. Gently she lifted and turned his head toward the glow from the dash. She could see it now, a trickle of blood down his left temple.

She spoke to him insistently. "Ben, can you hear me?"

No answer. He remained unconscious. Either that or—

Dreading the alternative, she groped nervously at his neck, seeking a pulse. There! She released a breath of relief as she located a slow but steady beat in the hollow of his throat.

Counting the rhythm to be sure it was within the normal range, Cathryn suddenly became aware that her hand was in contact with his warm, strongly corded flesh. There was the tingling sensation against her skin of silky, masculine hair where his shirt was parted. Seized by a mixture of guilt and confusion, she quickly withdrew her hand.

What now?

The Jeep! She realized then that the engine was still running and that they could be in danger of rolling farther down the incline into Lord knew what. Her hands fumbled around the controls until she found and secured the emergency brake. Only then did she trust herself to turn off the key, though she left the headlights on.

There was no helping it, was there? She had to leave the Jeep. She had to go out there and check their situation because they could still be at risk on this slope.

There was rain gear in her suitcase, but she didn't bother trying to get at it. She found a flashlight in the glove compartment. Arming herself with that, she opened the door and eased herself out of the vehicle. Rain, driven by a strong wind, stung her face. Within seconds of leaving the shelter of the Jeep, she was soaked. It wasn't important. Only their dilemma mattered.

Aided by the flashlight, the headlights and the intermittent flash of lightning, she picked her way down the slope. She didn't go far. Mere yards in front of the Jeep, the land ended in a void. Cathryn stood on the edge of the precipice, and when the lightning flashed again, she found herself glimpsing a frightening drop to a canyon floor far below. They had come within feet of tumbling to their deaths.

Gasping with shock, she swung the flashlight toward the Jeep, expecting it to come loose and charge down the slope with Ben inside it. That was when she saw that the wheels were caught in a deep rut. The rut had saved them, but she didn't trust it.

There were rocks everywhere on the slope. She went back to the Jeep and began stuffing them under the tires. Drenched with rain as she worked, grimacing over every violent clap of thunder, she battled a frantic sense of helplessness.

What was she going to do, trapped out here in a storm with full night coming on? She had to do something because Ben could be—probably was—in need of professional medical assistance. There had been no sound or stir from inside the Jeep.

Cathryn was reaching for the door to check on him again when she heard it—the sound of another vehicle approaching from the opposite direction up along the roadway. For a moment she was too amazed by the miracle to trust in its reality. But the promise of help actually being there in all this remoteness was something she couldn't afford to miss.

Knowing she had to reach the road and signal the driver, that he would never spot them down here otherwise, she clawed her way up the slope. Wild with haste, slipping and sliding over the wetness, she lost the flashlight and didn't stop to recover it. The other car was almost here.

She broke through the wall of undergrowth, shouting for the driver's attention. Too late! The car had already swept by her, its driver never hearing her cries over the sounds of the storm. Without pausing, the vehicle rounded a curve, revealing itself as a green Land Rover in a flare of lightning. Then it was gone.

Cathryn could have wept with frustration. For a moment she stood there, feeling alone and abandoned in the vastness of the wilderness. There was no other sign of life. Even the moose that had caused their accident had vanished. And the Land Rover might have been a mirage for all the good it had done her.

She had to go back. She had to find the vital flashlight. That much she realized. She was turning around when a shadowy figure lunged at her out of the darkness.

# Chapter Three

It had quit raining by the time the Land Rover rolled into Bearpaw. It was almost dark, though. Or as dark as it probably ever got in Alaska at this time of the year, Frank thought. He had already discovered that the sky was never absolutely black, whatever the hour or the weather. It made going to bed an odd experience for an outsider.

Bearpaw hardly qualified as a town. There were less than a dozen houses and a couple of stores. That was about it, except for a tiny post office that served the area. Closed, of course.

As late as it was, however, Frank had a bit of luck. There was a woman out front under a pole lamp fussing over pots of geraniums that had been battered by the storm. He assumed she was connected with the post office.

Edging the Land Rover to the curb, he rolled down his window. "What a shame," he sympathized, referring to the geraniums. "Looks like they were real beauties, too, before they got beat down. Any hope of rescuing them?"

She looked up. She had frizzy hair almost as red as the flowers. "They'll come back," she said flatly.

"It's always a matter of patience, isn't it?" he observed amiably. "Would you happen to know when the post office here opens in the morning?"

"I'd better, since I'm the postmaster."

"Oh, now, that's handy because I figured, you know, that a rural post office always knows its customers and that maybe this one could help me to locate a fellow I've been trying to look up. I was out to Benny's cabin just now, but not a sign of him."

"Benny?"

"That's right." He chuckled. "I suppose I should say Ben. Ben Adams."

She hesitated while he smiled at her guilelessly. If pressed, Frank would show her the impressive identification he always carried, but he hoped to keep it simple and casual. He didn't want Adams alerted.

"There wouldn't be any sign of him," she finally admitted. "Not for a few weeks anyway. We're holding his mail while he's spending some time down in Anchorage."

Frank went on smiling at her while hiding his aggravation. Why hadn't he stopped at the post office in the first place instead of asking for directions to the cabin from that kid at the service station out on the edge of Bearpaw? Could have saved himself a trip and wasted hours. Still, the cabin had needed to be checked out. Anchorage?

"Sorry I went and missed him. Well, maybe I'll see him in Anchorage. Would you know where he's staying down there?"

"He didn't say."

Even if she had an address, Frank didn't think she would reveal it. She was beginning to look as if she regretted telling him the little she had. He'd better not raise her suspicion.

"It's not important. Thanks for your help, and good luck with those geraniums."

Once out of sight around a bend in the road, he pulled over on the shoulder. He was a careful driver and didn't want to risk his concentration at the wheel with the act of unwrapping a stick of gum.

After the gum was in his mouth, Frank sat there for a moment, chewing slowly, enjoying the fruity flavor as he examined the situation.

He'd wondered up at the cabin why Adams and the McLean woman hadn't arrived. They should have been there by then. This explained it. They were staying in Anchorage, apparently not coming up here at all. At least not for a few weeks. He wondered why. Maybe Adams was showing her the sights. Or maybe, just maybe, Cathryn McLean had decided not to get herself cornered in an isolated mountain cabin.

Whatever the explanation, Frank had to find them. Wasn't going to be so easy now. Anchorage was a big place. They could be holed up anywhere. Didn't matter, though. In the end he would somehow get to them.

Easing the Land Rover back onto the road, he headed south. It was late, but he wasn't tired. He'd drive as far as he could, and then he'd park somewhere safe and grab a few hours of sleep.

There was one little thing that bothered Frank as he traveled the long road to Anchorage, all the while working on the gum in his mouth. Adams wasn't supposed to know the woman he'd sent for wasn't Meredith McLean. So if Anchorage *was* her idea, how had she convinced him to remain there instead of settling down all snug and cozy in the cabin? Something not quite right about that.

CATHRYN FELT the wind punched out of her as she went down under the weight of her attacker. For a moment all she could do was struggle for air, unable to cry out or fight back. When she could breathe again, there was no reason to defend herself. The figure sprawled on top of her remained motionless.

That was when she understood the situation. He hadn't lunged at her. He had lurched into her because he'd been dazed. Was still dazed. It was Ben, of course, though she could hardly make him out in the rain and the darkness. He must have regained consciousness, crawled out of the Jeep and stumbled up the slope after her. She feared now that he had passed out again.

"Ben," she called, trying to rouse him.

He didn't stir. Cathryn was conscious of his hard body pressed against hers, of sensations she had no business experiencing under these circumstances. Panic of another kind surged through her. She felt the need to remove herself immediately.

"Ben, wake up!"

He groaned when she shoved at him and, to her relief, rolled over on his back. Scrambling to her knees, she leaned over him, anxious about his condition.

"Ben, can you hear me?"

He didn't answer her for a moment, and then he muttered, "Hear you." There was another pause, followed by a reassuring "Give me a minute. I'll be all right."

She waited tautly, and eventually he made an effort to struggle into a sitting position. When she tried to help him, he growled, "Don't fuss."

Cathryn drew back, allowing him to lift himself. He leaned forward, resting his head against his upraised knees. She wondered if he was going to be sick or whether he was slipping into a state of shock. She tried to remain calm, to deal with him reasonably.

"Do you know where we are and what happened?"

Silence.

"Ben, answer me," she insisted.

"Sure," he mumbled. "You screamed, scared the hell out of me and I ended up losing control of the Jeep. Okay?"

Considering his condition, she had tried to be understanding and forgive him his gruffness. But she wasn't about to go on sitting here in a miserable downpour in the middle of nowhere and meekly take the blame for an accident that was in no way her fault.

"Well, of course," she said sweetly. "And if I hadn't been responsible for making you late to the airport, we wouldn't have been delayed getting on the road. Then that moose wouldn't have been there at that particular second, and I wouldn't have hysterically landed us in this fix. That about it?"

He grunted something and was silent again.

He wasn't being fair and he knew it. But his head was pounding, and he was in no mood to admit that no one was to blame for the situation. Unless it was a resistant Ben Adams that he'd had to take care of before he was able to race to meet her plane. It was Adams who had made him late. This whole thing stunk. Why had he ever let himself be trapped in it?

"Do you think," she suggested dryly, "that it might be a good idea to get out of this rain?"

"Yeah, okay."

This time he permitted her to help him to his feet. Together they made their way in the direction of the Jeep. Halfway down the slope Cathryn stumbled over the flashlight. She picked it up and tested it. It still worked.

"What's that doing there?" he grumbled.

Had he not already suffered a blow to the head, she would have been tempted to conk him with the flashlight. She didn't answer him. They reached the Jeep and gratefully took shelter in the front seats. Ben must have turned off the headlights before he came looking for her. They sat in the dark, listening to the rain on the roof. It was beginning to ease up.

There was silence between them for a long moment, and then he uttered a simple, contrite, "Sorry."

She knew he was apologizing for his temper. "You're forgiven."

"I don't make a good patient," he added.

"I could tell. Are you going to be all right? You were bleeding a little when I checked you."

"Not now, and my headache is clearing. I'll be fine. What were you doing out of the car?"

She told him how she had checked their situation, wedged rocks under the wheels and tried to flag down the Land Rover.

"You did good," he said.

His easy compliment warmed her. "What now?"

"There's no way we're going to get the Jeep back on the road in the dark, and I don't see us sitting here for the rest of the night soaked to the skin. We need to find shelter until morning."

"Where?"

He didn't answer her for a moment. The rain had stopped, and the clouds were already rolling away. The sky wore the faint glow of a summertime midnight in the far north. Cathryn supposed that at this latitude the sun was never far below the horizon.

"You say there's a deep canyon just in front of us?"

"That's right."

He frowned, trying to remember what he had learned of the area during his week of concentrated preparation. There was something about this place . . .

"Come on," he said impulsively, "I want to check it out. I think I know where we are."

"Shouldn't you be resting? Just in case?"

But he was already out of the vehicle and headed toward the precipice. She had no choice but to follow. By the time she joined him, he was planted on the very lip of the cliff and practically leaning out into empty space in order to view the canyon floor. He made her a nervous wreck. What if he turned dizzy again, lost his balance?

"What do you see down there?" he demanded.

She peered into the depths. Without the rain or the clouds, she was able this time to glimpse a river in the murky light. And there was something else showing in patches through the trees.

"Roofs?" she said.

"Roofs," he agreed. "We're looking down on Percy."

"You mean a town?"

"What's left of it. Percy is a ghost town. It was a booming gold operation early in the century. Alaska had a number of them. Then the ore from the river dwindled. It's been abandoned for decades. The point is, enough of the buildings are still intact to offer us a place to spend the night."

"Aside from the fact that investigating a ghost town at midnight doesn't particularly thrill me, how do you propose we get down there?"

"There must be a way. Look, you can see the canyon wall starts sloping down just off to the right there. All we have to do is follow the edge. We need to take cover and try to find a way to get warm. Both of us are wet and miserable."

He had a point. She was shivering in the night air. "But why can't we just stay in the Jeep and run the heater?"

"I don't trust it, that's why. We're on a steep, slick slope, and the rocks and emergency brake might be worth nothing if something starts to slide."

She had to admit it was an uncomfortable prospect. "You win. But at the risk of your snarling at me again, should you be trying a hike like this?"

"I told you I'm fine," he insisted.

Why did men like Ben Adams forever deny any suggestion of even a momentary weakness? Cathryn wondered. Exasperating. "Fine," she mumbled. "You're fine, I'm fine, Percy is—"

"Where are you going?"

"To get my purse and suitcase from the Jeep."

"No suitcase. We don't need any burdens."

She had been looking forward to changing into dry clothes, but she didn't argue with him. "Okay, but I'm not leaving my purse," she said stubbornly.

"You thinking of checking in down there with a credit card?"

She could see his white teeth gleaming in a wide grin.

"You're going to regret that," she promised.

"Probably. All right, let's go get your purse. And the flashlight. At least that's a useful item."

Minutes later, with the Jeep behind them, they were picking their way along the edge of the bluff on a rough, narrow track that was probably an animal trail. Even with the aid of the flashlight, it was a difficult route. Brambles tore at them, rocks and roots tripped them and Cathryn was aware every second of her damp clothes sticking to her unpleasantly. She had wanted Alaska and now she was getting Alaska.

She didn't complain but she did worry. What if Ben had a relapse and passed out on her again? She refused to ask him how he was doing, though. Not after his testy response back at the Jeep. Anyway, he was handling the rugged terrain better than she was.

The real challenge came when the path started to descend toward the river. It would have been a treacherous route in full daylight, but by night Cathryn considered it practically suicidal. It doubled back on itself without warning, and in places was merely a thread overhanging the gorge, inviting a headlong plunge into nothingness.

In one of the worst spots they had to ease themselves down using their hands, as well as feet. Ben, in front of her and waiting to catch her if she missed a hold, chuckled and asked wickedly, "Enjoying yourself, Meredith?"

Funny man.

"Well, if I remember correctly," he persisted, "you did say in one of your letters that Alaska sounded like a romantic adventure."

"I was probably thinking of a salmon dinner on a catamaran cruise. Speaking of water, do I hear it?"

There was an unmistakable gurgle several yards ahead of them. The flashlight revealed a spring oozing from the rock of the cliff face. The action of the water had washed away a portion of the ledge along which they were traveling, leaving a perilous gap several feet in width. There was no way around it.

"This is where I stop being a sport," she threatened, "and crawl back to the Jeep."

"Come on, Meredith. It's an easy jump, and once on the other side we're almost down."

"Got a question."

"Ask."

"Is Percy worth it?"

"You'll never know if we don't get there."

He swung around, leapt the gap with ease and turned to her, hand extended. "See, you can do it. I'm here to catch you."

She approached the gap with uncertainty, thinking that her work as a research librarian had in no way prepared her for something like this. But she was a long way from that tranquil library in New Orleans. She could no more return to her existence there than she could go back alone to the sanctuary of the Jeep. All she could do was go forward.

"Better free yourself of the flashlight first," he instructed. "Here, toss it over."

Aiming carefully, she lobbed the instrument in his direction. He caught it without effort and placed it on a flat boulder so that its beam was focused on the gap. The measure enabled him to use both hands to grasp her.

After making sure the shoulder strap of her purse was securely in place, Cathryn launched herself from the brink. Her nervous leap was more forceful than the gulf demanded. She landed against Ben's chest with an impact that sent them staggering backward. He managed to steady both of them.

He might have released her then. He didn't. His arms were still around her. *Tightly* around her. Neither of them stirred.

"What did I tell you?" he whispered. "Nothing to it."

He was wrong, she thought. It was a risky undertaking and growing more dangerous by the second. Trouble was, she didn't know how to extricate herself from this peril. Worse, she didn't want to.

"Ben?"

"Mmm?"

"Am I safe now?"

"Let's see. You're on this side, standing on solid rock and I've got you."

"That's what I figured. So I'm not safe."

"No," he drawled, "I guess you're not."

That's when he kissed her. A deep, probing kiss that sent her head spinning. She had known from their first meeting that if his mouth ever claimed hers, it would be a sensual, compelling business. She hadn't guessed that it would be a joining of such intensity it would threaten her with destruction.

She was weak and trembling when his mouth finally lifted from hers. She could still taste his skillful tongue, could still feel his clean breath mingling with hers.

"A few more minutes of this," he said, "and our clothes ought to be dry."

She was completely befuddled. "What?"

"Wasn't that steam rising from us?"

She laughed softly. "Probably mist from the river. Don't you think it would be a good idea if we got down there before it turns into fog?"

"Sounds reasonable."

But she regretted her practical suggestion when the powerful body that had been holding her so intimately moved away from her. He recovered the flashlight, and they continued their descent into the canyon.

Neither of them referred again to the kiss they had shared, Cathryn because she didn't trust herself to mention it, and Ben because... Well, she didn't know. Maybe it had meant next to nothing to him. It would probably be safer for both of them if that were the case. So then why did she find this wisdom depressing?

*Better forget that and concentrate on the trail.*

Not that it demanded much attention at this point. There were no further hazards, and the incline was much less challenging. Within minutes they reached the level floor of the canyon. They came through the trees to the edge of the burbling river. Looming in front of them was a great hulking shape that, at this hour and in this place, might have been a crouching monster that ought to have been extinct eons ago.

"What's that?" she demanded.

"A gold-dredging machine, I think. Probably was easier to just abandon it here and let it rust than to try to remove it."

Harmless, Cathryn thought. Nothing to worry about.

She went on reassuring herself with those words as she followed Ben into the remnants of Percy itself. But her chant was far less comforting among the shadowy, sagging structures that fronted the river. What might have been fun to explore under a cheerful midday sun was, in the feeble light of an Alaskan midnight, damn eerie. There was, after all, a reason why they called them ghost towns.

The evidence of desertion was everywhere. Weathered walls, gaping black holes that had once been windows and doors, the odor of neglect and decay.

"Not very encouraging," she said. "Most of these places look like they lost their roofs long ago, and the ones that are still in place...well, I don't think I'd trust spending the night under any of them."

"No, not very sound," he agreed, "except..."

He had been sweeping the flashlight over the faces of the buildings as they progressed along the single street. Now he pinned the beam on the walls of a structure that was in far better shape than the other shells.

"What do you know," he said, referring to a faded sign, "Percy had itself an opera house. Not a very grand one, but it somehow ended up getting preserved. Let's see what it offers us."

"Ben, do you think maybe—?"

But he was already on his way through the open doorway. She had no choice but to hurry after him or remain alone on the spooky street.

She caught up with him in the small auditorium behind the tiny lobby. He was busy with the flashlight investigating the walls.

"Look at the fancy decorations."

Cathryn did look. They were filthy and peeling, though she had to admit they must have been handsome in their day. The only thing that mattered was the place was intact and dry.

"There's a lantern there at the side of the stage." She pointed it out. "Do you suppose it still—?"

Her speculation was interrupted by a loud clattering from behind a curtained doorway at the other side of the stage. Cathryn's heart seemed to leap into her throat. Someone, or *something,* was lurking in the wings.

"Who's there?" Ben challenged the intruder.

They heard only a silence followed by a soft scrabbling noise. The ragged curtains at the doorway began to stir. Cathryn held her breath, expecting an apparition to materialize in the auditorium. She was prepared to hear moans and the rattle of chains.

But something far less appropriate to a ghost town poked through the curtains and stood there regarding them mildly. Cathryn couldn't believe her eyes.

Neither, apparently, could Ben. He looked at the creature in surprise, then at Cathryn. She looked at him. They blurted it simultaneously. "A *llama?*"

The animal snorted at them.

"Just what," Cathryn asked, recovering herself, "is a llama doing in here?"

"Auditioning?"

The buff-colored beast must not have cared for Ben's humor. Head high with dignity, it trotted up the far aisle, clumped through the lobby and disappeared into the street.

Cathryn stared after the departed animal, relieved that it had preferred to escape instead of charging them. "All right, I'll buy a llama wandering around an abandoned opera house. At least, I might in Peru. But Alaska? Even I know llamas aren't native to Alaska.''

''Must have gotten away from somewhere and is living wild now. Let's investigate that lantern. We could use some real light in here.''

Ben, headed toward the stage, had lost interest in the llama. She hadn't. The mystery of its presence worried her. But she didn't press it. By the time she joined him on the stage, he had the lantern down from its wall mount and was checking its reservoir.

''Ah, still oil in it. Now let's see if we can light it.'' While she steadied the flashlight for him, he patted the pockets of his sport coat, eventually producing a lighter. ''Here we go. Left over from the days when I smoked. Hold the lantern for me, can you?''

Within seconds the lamp was lighted and back on the wall, where it cast a comforting glow.

Ben rubbed his hands together in satisfaction. ''I'm going to take the flashlight and poke around backstage. If the llama was wandering around in there, maybe he's turned up something interesting.''

Cathryn wasn't exactly pleased over the prospect of being left alone while he went off exploring, but she didn't argue about it. ''Be careful back there,'' she cautioned him as he vanished into the wings.

There was a battered trunk near the back of the stage. She thought it might produce something useful, but she approached it with misgiving. She half expected bats to fly into her face as she cautiously raised the lid. Instead, she found only a pair of heavy velvet draperies that might once have graced the arch of the stage. They smelled musty, and there was dust along their folds, but the trunk had kept them dry. They would be something warm to wrap around themselves during what was left of the night.

She could hear Ben rattling around somewhere back-stage while she removed the draperies. She was spreading them open when he reappeared.

"Look what I found," he said, pleased with his discovery. "And it's clean. It was wrapped in a plastic sheet. Our bed for the night."

She watched him as he dragged a double mattress from the depths of the wings, flopping it down in the center of the stage.

"Ben?"

"Blankets, too," he said, eyeing the draperies. "We're in business."

"Ben?"

"Huh?

"Don't you think this is all a little too coincidental? A mattress that's still useable, a lantern that still has oil in it and a llama that probably belongs to somebody."

"What's your point?"

"Someone is camping out here."

"Couldn't be. That mattress hasn't been touched in months, maybe years. The plastic wrapping had a layer of dust thicker than Grandma's attic."

"I still say—"

"Meredith, relax."

He demonstrated his advice by dropping down on the mattress, tugging off his boots and tossing them onto the stage floor, where they landed with loud clumps. Cathryn perched gingerly on her side of the mattress and began to remove her own shoes.

Ben sighed. "Comfort at last. Well, almost. I'm all hollow inside. That breakfast we had was a lifetime ago."

"Did you check the lobby? Maybe there's a refreshment stand."

"Did that. They were all out of popcorn."

"We'll just have to substitute, then."

He watched with growing interest as she reached for her purse and began to rummage through its contents. His dark eyes gleamed with eagerness when she removed a paper napkin wrapped around four buttermilk biscuits she had slipped into her bag back at the diner.

"Well, you did warn me it was going to be a long time between meals," she explained. She started to offer him the biscuits, then pulled her hand back. "Wait a minute. I seem to remember you objecting when I refused to leave my purse behind in the Jeep."

"You're going to make me beg for one of those biscuits, aren't you?"

"Me? Never. Never hold a grudge."

"All right, next time I trust you. Guaranteed. Now pass me those biscuits."

She obliged, dividing the biscuits and handing him his share. They ate in silence, seated cross-legged on the mattress.

"Don't look at me like that," she cautioned him when he'd finished his two biscuits. "I don't have any cold beers in my purse. The biscuits were it."

"I was thinking about our clothes. Yours still look pretty damp, and I know mine are. Time to get rid of them and hope they dry before morning."

She stared at him. He was already removing his sport coat. "You mean sleep in the raw?"

"Well, yeah. That's not a problem, is it? We've got the drapes there for covers."

"Uh, I guess that makes sense. I guess we shouldn't be sleeping in wet clothes."

She hated her sudden awkwardness in this situation, her inability to remain composed. If she weren't so inexperienced . . . But that was the trouble. She *was* inexperienced.

It was why the breath stuck in her throat as she watched Ben nonchalantly unbutton his shirt and cast it aside. He wore nothing underneath, making his chest a riveting sight in the mellow glow of the lantern. He was all hard muscles and a wedge of dark hair that narrowed tantalizingly at his belt line.

The breath caught in her throat turned into a lump when he got to his feet and began to shuck his jeans. He noticed her hesitation.

"If you'd rather not do this, Meredith... I mean, if it bothers you to—"

"No, of course it doesn't," she croaked, forcing her gaze away just as the jeans dropped to the floor.

She concentrated then on hastily peeling off her cotton sweater and her slacks. The whole time she kept her eyes lowered, but she was conscious of his shorts joining his jeans on the floor. She would have been fine if his sudden approach hadn't startled her into looking up. He was standing so close she could feel the heat from his body. She found herself viewing a very powerful, totally naked virility.

Flushing, she dragged her gaze to the level of his face and learned that he was equally aware of her exposed flesh.

"What?" she murmured.

He cleared his throat, betraying his own tension. "Just waiting to collect your things so that I can lay them out to dry."

She began working feverishly on her socks, which, in their dampness and her nervousness, resisted her efforts. She was conscious the whole while of his nearness.

She succeeded with the socks, added them to her other garments and shoved the bundle in his direction.

"Aren't you taking off the rest?" he urged.

She knew he was referring to her bra and panties, but this was as far as she was prepared to go.

"No need to. Nylon. They're already dry."

A slight lie, since they were still faintly damp, though not enough to matter.

If he was disappointed, he didn't comment on it. He took their clothes and moved toward the apron of the stage. Cathryn used the opportunity to dive under one of the velvet draperies. Her action afforded her a glimpse of a very shapely male backside as he set their things to dry along the edge of the stage.

She managed to avoid looking in his direction again until he was safely under the other drapery on his side of the mattress.

"The lamp," she reminded him.

"Let's leave it burning. Helps to keep the llamas away."

Not a bad idea, except she had counted on darkness to shield her from those dark, probing eyes of his. The drapery suddenly didn't seem nearly adequate enough.

Cathryn turned on her side, facing away from him. This was better. She could hear him settling down on his half of the mattress, making a nest for himself under his own drapery.

"Night, Ben," she whispered a moment later.

He didn't answer her, and when she glanced over her shoulder, she saw that he was already asleep. The man was understandably exhausted after his long day at the wheel and their ordeal in the rain.

Cathryn curled into a snug position and closed her eyes, hoping to sleep but not expecting to after her lengthy nap earlier in the Jeep. Besides, she was still uneasy about their surroundings. She must have been more tired than she realized, however, because in no time at all she drifted off.

She dreamed. A nasty dream, where—alone and helpless—she wandered the fog-cloaked streets of New Orleans. She was lost and couldn't find her way, and when the fog thinned New Orleans had become Percy. Specters from its past were on the dark street with her. They began to close in from all sides, and each of their faces wore the cruel features of Red Quinn. She began to run, but it was no use. She was surrounded.

She must have cried out. The next thing she knew, she was sitting up on the mattress and Ben was pressed to her side, his arms securely holding her.

"All right, sweetheart," he crooned, his voice still husky from sleep. "It's all right. You were having a nightmare. Must have been a doozy."

She was trembling. She tried to collect her wits, wishing she could tell him about the dream. She couldn't. She was supposed to be Meredith McLean. She wasn't supposed to be on the run from a man who wanted her dead.

It didn't matter. Ben's arms around her were comfort enough. His warm flesh was against her flesh, no barriers between them. The draperies had slipped down to their waists. That was when she remembered she wore only her bra and panties and that he wore nothing.

Ben must have been equally conscious of their provocative situation. His black eyes suddenly wore a drowsy, seductive look in them. One of his hands holding her shifted. She felt his thumb slowly caress the underside of her breast. The thin fabric of her bra might have been nonexistent. Both her nipples instantly hardened.

That was when Cathryn realized that it was not the ghosts of Percy she had to worry about.

"Ben," she pleaded.

"I'm here," he said, his voice raw with desire. "I'm here for you, sweetheart."

He leaned toward her, continuing to stroke her breast with his thumb as he began to kiss her. She was still shaken from his kiss back on the trail. But this was even deeper, far more potent.

Cathryn, fighting for self-control, knew that she had a serious problem on her hands. She was a fool not to have anticipated this moment and prepared herself for it. A man like Ben Adams, a *lusty* man, would never have sent for Meredith McLean if he hadn't expected a total relationship.

All right, she *had* known this moment would occur. She just hadn't counted on it happening so soon. All that had mattered was getting far away from Red Quinn and his goons. She had figured the rest could wait. Well, obviously it could wait no longer.

She had a fast decision to make. She could surrender to Ben's passion, to her own awakened yearnings, and pray there were no serious consequences, or she could end this situation before it was too late.

Ultimately there was no choice, because those consequences already threatened her in the shape of an emotional involvement. She didn't want to be unfair to either of them, anyway no more unfair than she was already being with her masquerade. And if she engaged in lovemaking before either of them was committed to this relationship...

She couldn't. She couldn't compound the lie.

His mouth was on her shoulder now, planting a series of moist, eager kisses.

"Ben, wait," she whispered.

He either didn't hear her or was ignoring her. She began to struggle in his embrace.

"Ben, *no,*" she demanded.

For a few seconds she was afraid he wouldn't listen to her. To her relief, he abruptly released her and leaned back.

"What is it?"

She tried to explain it to him. "It's—it's too soon. Remember what we agreed on in our letters? No pressure on each other about this kind of thing until we knew each other in person and were sure of ourselves."

He gazed at her in silence. There was a hard glitter in his eyes, a dangerous glitter that alarmed her. Then he relaxed, his tight expression softening to a gentleness.

"You're right," he said. "We don't want to make any mistakes."

"I'm sorry, Ben."

He nodded. "We'll wait. You okay now?"

"Yes, fine."

But she wasn't fine at all, Cathryn realized a moment later after Ben had settled down again on the mattress, his eyes closed in sleep. She was worried. Worried that her resistance had amounted to nothing but another lie, that all of it was the result of the mistake she had made years ago, leaving her with so many insecurities about the intimacy of relationships. Would they always interfere like this, prevent her from giving herself freely to a man?

*This* man, she thought, sliding down on the mattress so that she was facing him, his head only inches from hers. She gazed at his sleeping face. It was an appealing face with its dark shadow of beard. There was an ethnic quality about it, something in the features that suggested a Latin or Indian heritage. Maybe both. There had been nothing in his letters referring to such a background. It was another mystery about him.

She didn't count on falling asleep again. She expected to go on being intrigued by Ben Adams's strong face. But a deep sleep claimed her in the end, this time without nightmares.

When she awakened, it was morning. Sunlight penetrated the auditorium from the street, Ben's arm was stretched across her hip and the double barrel of a lethal shotgun was inches from her nose.

# Chapter Four

The bearer of the shotgun was no ghost from Percy's vanished heyday but a sinister reality. Cathryn was terrified.

Eyeing the weapon that remained steadily leveled at their reclining figures, she sneaked a cautious hand in Ben's direction, nudging him insistently. He failed to stir.

"Ben, wake up," she whispered to him frantically. "We've, uh, got company."

He opened his eyes, muttering a groggy, "That damn llama back?"

"Not exactly."

"Then who—?" He lifted his head, saw the gun. "What the hell—"

"Got the full attention of both of you now, have I?" said the voice behind the shotgun. "Then maybe you'd care to tell me what the two of you are doing in my town."

Cathryn was startled by the voice. It was rough in its challenge. It also belonged unmistakably to a woman, a fact that had escaped her until this instant, which was understandable, since the burly figure was clad in stained pants, a loose denim shirt and a prospector's hat crammed over short, iron gray hair. The hat looked as if it might have arrived in Alaska during the gold rush of the previous century. So did the weather-beaten face under its brim.

Ben fearlessly answered the woman with a demand of his own. "You telling us you own Percy, including this opera house?"

"I'm a full-time resident of the town. That makes it as good as my own."

"In other words," he observed dryly, "you're a squatter here, same as us."

She smiled at him, a smile that meant business. "There's a difference, mister. I'm the one with the shotgun."

"Doesn't give you the right to point it at us. Put it down."

Cathryn could see from the woman's scowl, and her refusal to lower the gun, that Ben was clearly alienating her. She began, swiftly and apologetically, to explain their presence.

"Our Jeep went off the road last night, so we took shelter down here. We had no idea someone was living in the town, or we would have asked permission to spend the night." She suddenly realized something. "The lantern and the mattress must be yours, then. Sorry we went and borrowed them."

The woman regarded Cathryn, her hostility diminishing. She shrugged. "They're not my property. Left behind by a couple of guys who camped out here for a week or so last summer. Something about researching ghost towns for a book. Left a second mattress back there like this one. But I guess," she added, gazing meaningfully at their state of undress, "one was all you needed."

Cathryn meant to have a word with Ben about that second mattress, whose existence he had conveniently omitted, but this was the wrong moment. The shotgun was still confronting them.

"I suppose you two have names."

Cathryn hastened to introduce herself and Ben, adding, "Ben has a cabin in the area. That's where we were headed."

"I've heard the name. Work the pipeline, don't you?"

He nodded, relieved that she'd never met the real Ben Adams. But she continued to observe him with suspicion, though her attitude toward Cathryn had softened considerably. Enough, anyway, that she relaxed her hold on the shotgun.

"Well, I'm satisfied. Can't be too careful when you're on your own. They call me Sourdough Annie. A real hoot, huh? Don't ask for the rest. That's all the name you get."

"Sourdough?"

"A sourdough is someone who's been in Alaska for a long time," Ben explained to the mystified Cathryn.

"And if anyone qualifies," Annie said proudly, "it's me. Been kicking around this state for over thirty years."

Cathryn decided that she liked Sourdough Annie. She was a character by any definition. She was also sharp-witted.

"Yeah, I know. I'm an eccentric. Being a hermit, though, doesn't mean I can't offer hospitality when it suits me. In this case it's breakfast, if you two are interested."

Cathryn wondered if the invitation was Annie's way of apologizing for the shotgun. In any case she was too hungry to refuse. "Breakfast would be good," she said.

Ben, too, was famished and made no objection.

Annie grunted her approval. "In that case I'll leave you some privacy to climb back into your duds. When you're ready, follow your noses to the end of the street. My shack will be the one with the odor of frying bacon coming from it."

When she was gone, Ben emerged from the cover of his drapery and went to the edge of the stage to recover their things. Cathryn, hurrying into the clothes he brought her, avoided gazing at his tempting nudity. He might in no way be bothered by it, but she certainly was. Besides, she had to concentrate on an accusation.

"About that second mattress," she said.

"You mean the one you could have been spending the night on all by yourself instead of sharing this one with me?"

"That's the one."

"Never noticed another mattress back there," he claimed innocently. "Must have overlooked it in the darkness."

"Uh-huh."

"Hey, a single mattress made the evening interesting, didn't it? Well, maybe not as interesting as it could have been, but promising anyway. Come on, let's go find out if Sourdough Annie can cook as well as she can handle a shotgun."

"You're sneaky, Ben Adams, but I don't have the strength to argue with you about it. Not until after I eat."

Annie had breakfast underway by the time they reached her shack near the edge of the river. She showed them a privy out back, which they used gratefully, and provided them with the essentials for washing up before they settled at her table.

In spite of the primitive setting, no meal had ever tasted better to Cathryn. The shack was small and bleak, containing the bare necessities, but it was scrupulously clean.

Annie noticed Cathryn curiously eyeing a wide, shallow pan hanging on the wall beside the door. "My batea," she said.

"A what?"

"Batea," she explained. "It's what you use to pan for gold in the creeks and rivers. Separates the sand and dirt from the heavier deposits that carry the gold bits. Not enough out there to support a mining operation anymore, but I get by with what I find."

That was how she existed, then, Cathryn thought. By panning for gold. It apparently suited her, but it had to be an extremely lonely life. Not altogether lonely, however, as she learned a moment later.

Cathryn was working on her second cup of coffee when she felt herself being stared at from the open window at her back. She swung around in her chair to find the head of the llama poked through the opening. Annie crowed with laughter over their startled expressions.

"That's Lulu. She's always looking for handouts."

"Must have been what she wanted last night," Ben muttered.

"Lulu go and visit you? Never know where she'll hang out. Thinks the whole town belongs to her, don't you, girl?"

"Lulu belongs to you, then?" Cathryn said.

"Makes a better pack animal than a burro. Takes me to places that old heap of a pickup out there won't go. Good company, too."

The llama, accepting an apple from her mistress, retreated from view.

"We may have to beg you for a lift in that pickup," Ben said. "Providing, that is, I can't get my Jeep back on the road."

"Tell me again just where it's stuck," Annie said.

Cathryn noticed that the woman's manner was brusque whenever she spoke directly to Ben. He might not be aware of it, but she still didn't trust him. Cathryn wondered why.

Ben described the Jeep's location.

Annie nodded. "Think I know just where you mean. You wouldn't have noticed in the dark last night, but that rut that caught you is part of the old wagon track that was the original road down into Percy. If you can turn your car in the rut and bear left, not right like you went on foot, you'll come to a fork in a couple of miles. The right branch winds down in easy levels to Percy, the left one puts you back on the road."

"Let's hope I can manage to squeeze the Jeep around, because this way sounds easier than trying to gun that risky slope." He scraped his chair back and got to his feet. "Time to climb back up there and see if we're in business."

Cathryn, thanking Annie for the breakfast, started to join him.

"Why don't you wait down here and let me collect you in the Jeep?" Ben suggested. "No need for you to tackle that rough footpath again."

Cathryn hesitated. "I wouldn't mind staying behind if you're sure you can handle it on your own. I hate to leave Annie with all these dishes."

To her surprise, Annie made no objection to her offer to help with the cleanup. As it turned out, she had a reason for wanting to be alone with Cathryn. But Cathryn didn't learn that until after the dishes were washed and put away.

The two women had wandered outside and were standing beside the battered pickup truck, waiting for Ben's arrival in the Jeep. Annie had been thoughtfully silent for the past few moments. Then, in that abrupt manner of hers, she asked, "How well do you know this friend of yours?"

"Ben? Fairly well, I guess. Like I told you over dishes, we've been corresponding for months."

"Not the same thing as being familiar in person, is it?"

"You don't like Ben, do you?"

Annie shrugged. "He's a good-looking devil and maybe he's not too good to be true. Maybe I'm all wrong to have this feeling that there's something there that doesn't add up. Look, just do yourself a favor, girlie, and watch yourself with him."

Cathryn gazed at her, not sure whether to be amused or alarmed.

"One other little thing," Annie added, "and then we'll drop the whole subject. You ever need me, I'm here for you. Even if you have to come on foot, you come."

"I appreciate the offer, Annie, but I think Ben's cabin is miles from here."

"Yeah, I know just about where it is, and by road it is a good haul. But as the crow flies... well, there's a foot trail almost straight to Percy. Comes off the road near where his cabin track joins the main drag. Wouldn't hurt for you to remember that.

"Listen, there's the sound of the Jeep coming down. Guess he had luck turning it."

CATHRYN EYED her companion at the wheel as he drove the Jeep the final miles to his wilderness cabin. She tried to see him through Sourdough Annie's perspective and failed. She couldn't find any solid reason to be suspicious of Ben. Not after last night. Not after the humor he had revealed in their shared banter and his caring warmth following her nightmare.

But she couldn't seem to shake Annie's warning, even when it made no sense. Because it had to be nothing more than the imagination of an elderly woman who had lived by herself for too long and didn't trust outsiders, maybe men in particular.

On the other hand, Cathryn remembered that, beneath his concern and his humor, there was an intense quality about Ben Adams. As if he were at war with himself over something. She had sensed it immediately at the airport yesterday and again on the drive from Anchorage before their accident. Or was this, too, imagination, no more than the result of her terror in New Orleans?

Ben interrupted the long silence between them. "What were you and Annie talking about while I was wrestling with the Jeep?"

She started with a guilty lowering of her gaze. Had he read the direction of her thoughts?

"She told me about some of her experiences in Alaska. I told her they were fascinating enough that she ought to write a book." That much was true. Over the dishes Annie had talked about her varied career.

Ben made no comment. Cathryn concentrated on their imminent arrival at the cabin and tried not to be anxious about remaining in an isolated situation with a man who was still a stranger to her. She also tried not to watch for a sign of that footpath Annie had described to her. But when she caught what she thought was a glimpse of it just before the turnoff to the cabin, she couldn't deny a small satisfaction in knowing it was there.

She was able to put her concerns behind her as they climbed the long, winding track to the cabin. The forest crowded in on both sides, aromatic spruce and thickets of slender birch and aspen. And suddenly they were in a clearing, climbing out of the Jeep, and Ben was showing her his cabin.

"Like it?" he asked.

She did. It was the image of what a northern cabin was supposed to be. Walls of heavy spruce logs, a welcoming porch stretched the full length of its front, an expansive stone fireplace and simple but solid furnishings.

She remembered his telling Meredith in one of the letters that, though the cabin was lit by old-fashioned oil lamps, tanks of propane made possible a range, a refrigerator and a water pump that provided indoor plumbing, a luxury in the Alaskan wilderness.

What he had never described was the layout of the cabin, and it was this that worried her. The place was small, after all. One long room at the front that was living room at one end and kitchen-dining area at the other. Behind that was the bathroom and... She didn't know what the sleeping arrangements were. Would there be a single bedroom with a solitary bed in it that he expected her to share with him?

Ben must have understood her nervousness over the subject. "Relax, Meredith." He steered her into a tiny hallway, pointing to a doorway off one side. "My bedroom." Then he indicated a second doorway in the opposite direction. "Your bedroom."

Cathryn was grateful to him. He hadn't forgotten last night's promise about waiting. But he must think she was a fool. She couldn't help it. Though she risked cheating him by her resistance, there was the greater danger that an early surrender would only delude him further. She had to be sure of the outcome. The trouble was, she had never expected her masquerade to be so emotionally complicated, nor Ben Adams to be so powerful a temptation.

"Of course," he added in that smoky drawl that made her pulse quicken, "if you find the mattress in that room isn't comfortable enough, I'd be more than happy for you to try the mattress in my room. Half of it, anyway."

The hallway was very tight. There was no way for two people to occupy it at the same time without standing so close that they were touching. And Ben was touching her. Pressing against her, in fact. No room for her to back away. Nor had she the will to remove herself.

Her eyes sought his. But his gaze was distracted and wore a questioning, slightly puzzled expression. She didn't understand until his hand lifted, his fingers lightly, thoughtfully investigating the area of her cheek just below her right eye. And then she knew, and her heart seemed to stop beating.

The mole! The small brown mole that had worried her on the plane. The mole that Meredith McLean wasn't supposed to have. He had just discovered it. Was he remembering that it hadn't been visible on the photo Meredith had sent him? That something was all wrong?

Cathryn held her breath, expecting his harsh challenge.

"They once called these beauty marks, didn't they?" he murmured. "They were right."

She felt a rush of relief. It was all right. She was safe. Safe, that is, until he began to brush the slightly rough pad of his thumb slowly, sensually across the mole.

A few more seconds of this, and he would be kissing her again. She couldn't be sure of where it would lead. Maybe to that mattress of his sooner than either of them planned. He didn't realize that she wanted this as much as he did, but she still needed them to know and be sure of each other.

Self-control. She had to exercise self-control before it was too late. She cast around in her mind for some way to defuse the moment. And then she remembered.

"Angel," she said with a suddenness that confused him.

His hand left her cheek. He frowned. "What?"

"Angel," she repeated. "I just realized she wasn't here to greet you. I haven't seen any sign of her since we arrived."

He looked blank for a second and then he understood. The dog. She was talking about Adams's dog. "Angel ran away," he said. "I haven't seen a sign of her in days."

"I'm sorry. I like dogs."

"I think she might have been responding to the call of the wild. She is part wolf, you know."

"I remember that from your letter and the snapshot." Cathryn didn't think he seemed very concerned about the loss of Angel. "Any chance she'll find her way back?"

"Maybe." He led the way back into the living room, abruptly changing the subject. "Would you mind if I left you on your own for a few hours?"

"I don't think so. Is something wrong?"

"Nothing that some intensive shopping down in Lovejoy won't fix. I need to stock up on supplies. I always let the groceries get low before I go out to the pipeline. That way there's nothing to spoil while I'm on my tour of duty."

"Makes sense. But isn't Bearpaw the nearest town?"

"Yeah, Lovejoy is a lot farther. But it's much bigger than Bearpaw, so it has more facilities to choose from. I've even moved my mailbox down there."

Cathryn wondered why they hadn't stopped somewhere for groceries on the way up from Anchorage. Instead of which, he was turning around, almost without pause, and facing another long drive. He must have sensed her puzzlement.

"I know," he said. "But you'll come to see that distances don't mean anything to Alaskans. They think nothing of heading down the road for a hundred miles on a casual errand. And if there is no road to drive on, they'll fly there."

"I've heard that."

"Anyway, I need Lovejoy because there's a mechanic there I trust. I want him to check over the Jeep to make sure nothing was damaged in the accident. When you're this isolated, you have to know you've got transportation you can count on. You're welcome to come with me, Meredith. I just figured after all that traveling, you were ready to stay put for a while."

He was right. She also thought it would be wiser for her to avoid any more towns. At least for the present. "I'll be fine," she assured him. "Gives me a chance to unpack and have a bath."

"I figured as much. Uh, just one thing. Stick close to the cabin while I'm gone, huh? I wouldn't want you wandering off and getting lost on your first day here."

ALL LIES, HE THOUGHT as he followed the road to Lovejoy. Practically everything he'd told her had been a lie.

While it was true that the cabin needed provisions, they could have been picked up on the way from Anchorage. And Bearpaw would have been the logical place to acquire them. But he had to avoid Bearpaw. It was too small, and everyone in it was familiar with Ben Adams. Lovejoy was just big enough and far enough away that there was less risk of questions he didn't want to answer.

Nor did the Jeep require a mechanic, but there were telephones in Lovejoy. And he couldn't have her with him while he used one. Besides, he had to keep her away from other people as much as possible. That damn Sourdough Annie was already suspicious of him.

The phone was a necessity. He had to obey orders and check in with the man who had hired him, report that Cathryn McLean had arrived and everything was under control.

Except everything wasn't under control. He was still fighting his treacherous desire for the woman. He had almost lost the battle last night in Percy. Probably would have if she hadn't called a halt to the whole thing. She was still suffering from New Orleans, of course, afraid to let down her guard. And she was shy about sex, which was surprising for a woman of her looks and maturity.

Just as well, he thought. Her resistance would help him not to fall for her. Fatal in his kind of work. There had been another woman he'd cared for, and in the end—when she'd been sacrificed—a part of him had died with her.

He had to go on reminding himself that Cathryn Mc-Lean was nothing but a job. A target whose trust he had to win. Once that objective was achieved, the rest was supposed to be easy. He just had to remember to control his weakness.

Didn't help that he couldn't seem to shake the image of her last night: stripped down to bra and panties, all soft and luscious. The memory alone made him go hard. Made him wonder how long he could maintain this frustrating masquerade.

He glanced at his watch. It was still early. He should be able to make it to Lovejoy and back before midafternoon. He hadn't liked leaving her, but the cabin was remote. She'd be all right on her own for a few hours. She thought she was safe now, with nothing to worry about.

CATHRYN FELT SECURE for the first time in days. She was finally hidden away in the wilderness, confident that the threat of New Orleans was thousands of miles behind her and that Red Quinn couldn't reach her in this place. Everything was going to be fine. There was only her relationship with Ben to think about, and in time they would work that out.

It was in this state of optimism that she busied herself around the cabin. She had her bath, unpacked her belongings and stowed them away in closet and drawers, all the while familiarizing herself with a place that might eventually become her permanent home. The cabin was snug and friendly. She could see herself living here, a mail-order bride in reality. Too early, though, to count on something like that.

It was past noon when she investigated the kitchen and found only a limited stock of canned goods. They would have offered her some form of a lunch, but she wasn't interested after Sourdough Annie's enormous breakfast. She would wait for Ben.

Restless now, Cathryn went outside and explored the clearing. On the back side of the cabin, where the land sloped away through the trees, she caught a tantalizing glimpse of blue water. There was a lake down there, and it was a lure she couldn't resist. She had promised Ben not to wander away from the cabin, but she preferred to think the lake didn't count. Not when it could be reached by a direct path from cabin to shore.

She was glad of her decision when she descended the hill and came to the edge of the lake, which must have been a mile or so in length and embraced several wooded islets. The sight of shining blue water against the backdrop of snow-frosted mountains was breathtaking. And she was alone in all this splendor.

The path here turned and followed the shore. She began to stroll along it, not planning to explore it for any rash distance. She had traveled less than a dozen yards when she realized that she was mistaken about her solitude. A figure suddenly trotted into view ahead of her.

Cathryn came to a standstill, gazing nervously at the creature. Why hadn't she listened to Ben and remained at the cabin? Now she was on her own out here and confronting what might be a dangerous animal. Defenseless, she did the wise thing and kept perfectly still.

The wolf, too, was motionless in front of her, regarding her warily. It demonstrated no evidence that it considered Cathryn a threat, neither bolting nor snarling a warning.

It seemed forever that they stood there considering each other. It was the sun shining on the animal's thick coat, emphasizing its silvery color, that finally made her remember the photograph Ben had inserted in one of his letters. Realization brought relief.

Angel! Not a wild wolf, but Ben's dog, Angel!

Thrilled that the animal had returned, Cathryn crouched down on the path until she was level with the dog. Slowly extending one hand and careful not to startle her, she called to her softly.

"Here, Angel."

The dog's ears lifted as she recognized her name. She dropped back on her haunches, interested but undecided.

"It's all right, girl," Cathryn coaxed. "I won't hurt you. Come on, Angel, let's go back to the house."

For a moment she thought Angel would approach her. Then, trading curiosity for caution, she turned and plunged through the trees. Reluctant to abandon her effort to reclaim the dog for Ben, Cathryn got to her feet and followed.

There was another thread of a path where Angel had left the shore trail. She followed it up the steep slope and glimpsed the dog ahead of her. Angel paused and looked back, as though she were worried, and then she streaked out of sight.

When Cathryn reached the spot where the dog had disappeared, she discovered that the hill here sharpened into a series of mossy ledges. It was under the closest ledge, where the overhang formed a shallow cavern in the rock, that Angel reappeared.

Fallen stones were piled on the sandy floor of the hollow in what might or might not be a naturally oblong arrangement. The animal was stretched out on this bed of stones, panting slowly as she watched Cathryn with suspicious concern.

When Cathryn knelt down just outside the cavern, Angel whimpered softly.

"What is it, girl? What's wrong?"

The dog stirred and whined but continued to occupy the stones. As though she were guarding something. Except there was absolutely nothing here to guard.

Cathryn spent another few moments trying to persuade Angel to come to her, but the dog refused to leave the cavern. Deciding in the end that it was wiser to leave her recovery to Ben, she got to her feet and headed back to the cabin. She hoped that in the meantime Angel wouldn't vanish again.

SHE WAS SEATED on the front steps, waiting impatiently, when the Jeep finally pulled into the clearing. An eager smile on her face, she left the porch and went to meet Ben as he climbed from the vehicle.

"Looks like maybe you missed me," he said with a pleased grin.

"You wish. Come on, I've got something to show you."

"The groceries—"

"Can wait for a few minutes. I just hope my surprise is still there."

"What's going on? Where are we going?" he demanded, mystified as he followed her around the cabin and down the hill toward the lake.

"Something nice," she promised. "You'll like it."

"Have you been out exploring? Thought I—"

"Don't fuss. I didn't go far. Here, this way."

She led him along the shore toward the place where the path branched inland to the cavern. When they came to the turning, Angel was blocking the way.

"Look," Cathryn said, "she's come down to meet us."

She stepped aside on the narrow trail so that dog and master had a full view of each other. But the excited reunion she had been anticipating didn't occur. Angel didn't bound into Ben's outstretched arms. Ben didn't issue a shout of gladness.

Animal and man confronted each other for a long, silent moment. Then, hackles raised and teeth bared, Angel growled menacingly at her owner and began to back away. Cathryn was stunned.

"Ben, what's wrong with her? She wasn't this way before. She wouldn't let me get close to her, but she wasn't unfriendly."

"I don't know," he muttered, wearing a scowl. "Let her alone. Come on back to the house."

"But—"

"Meredith," he said, plainly irritated, "she's part wolf, remember? The wild side makes her unpredictable sometimes. Forget it."

"Look, she's headed back to the ledges." Angel had turned and was slinking off through the trees. Cathryn explained how she had followed her to the cavern under the overhang. "Shouldn't we go after her?"

"She's all right on her own. And don't go up there again poking around," he warned her. "It can be dangerous. There are rockfalls."

"Ben, it's Angel. Don't you even care?"

"Right now I care about getting those groceries unloaded and put away. The dog will come back when she's ready. Are you coming?"

He left her no choice. She followed him back to the cabin, puzzled by the whole thing. Angel's reaction to Ben just didn't make sense. If she didn't know better, she would think that he had abused the dog in some manner.

# Chapter Five

Cathryn awakened with a sense of alarm. For a moment, still fogged with sleep, she didn't understand what was wrong. Then a faint movement behind her warned her that she wasn't alone in her room.

Turning quickly on her back, she discovered a figure looming over her. She couldn't see his face in the shadows, but there was enough light from the open door that she could tell it was Ben.

This was her third night at the cabin, and to her knowledge, he had never entered her bedroom before this. What was he doing here now?

"What is it?" she whispered nervously, struggling to sit up.

"Sorry if I startled you," he said. "I've been calling you, but you were dead to the world."

"It's all this pure Alaskan air," she muttered. "Better than any pill." Not to mention her feeling of well-being since arriving here. She noticed then that he was fully dressed. "Haven't you been to bed at all?"

"I fell asleep over my book in the living room. Then I went outside for a bit to stretch my legs."

"In the middle of the night? What time is it?" She glanced toward the window and saw that it was the darkest hour of the short northern night.

"Late," he admitted. "After midnight."

"Why were you calling me? Is something the matter?"

"I want you to get up and get dressed. And, no, there's nothing for you to worry about. But there is something I want you to see."

"Can't it wait until morning?"

"Absolutely not. Come on, you can sleep all you want afterward." This time she detected a note of mischief in his voice.

"You're crazy," she grumbled.

"And you're missing the opportunity of a lifetime."

"That special?"

"Guaranteed," he promised. "Get moving. I'll wait for you on the porch."

Five minutes later, having donned jeans and a light jacket against the chill of the evening air, she joined him outside. She saw that he had a flashlight in his hand.

"Where are you taking me?"

"No more questions. If we don't get going, we'll miss it."

Exasperated by his obstinate mysteriousness, but also intrigued, she accompanied him around the cabin and down the path that led through the woods to the lake.

He stopped her just before they emerged from the trees near the shore. "I want you to close your eyes now," he directed, "and let me lead you the rest of the way."

"Ben—"

"Trust me. It's worth it."

He was like an eager boy with his surprise. "All right, but if you're planning to drown me—"

"We'll keep it dry. And no peeking."

Reluctantly she obliged him. He took her by the hand and guided her carefully in the direction of the lake. She could hear the gravel of the beach crunching under their feet. Then she felt the planks of the little pier where he kept a small outboard.

"Now?" she asked when he brought them to a standstill at the end of the short pier.

"Not yet. Wait until I tell you you can open them."

He helped her to sit down on the edge of the pier, her legs dangling toward the water that she could hear lapping softly against the piles. She felt him lower himself close beside her on the boards.

Just when she was no longer able to bear the suspense, he reprieved her with a soft, "Now you can look."

Lifting her head, Cathryn opened her eyes, stared for a moment in silent wonder, then gasped with grateful pleasure.

"Like it?"

"It's awesome," she whispered, feeling suddenly humble.

Above the majesty of lake and mountains, the evening sky was shot with banners of light that shimmered in a fantastic array of colors. Yellow, green, red and violet arced across the vastness in restless, shifting waves.

"It's rare to see the northern lights at all at this time of year," he said. "And to have them this brilliant . . . the conditions must be just right."

"Thank you," she said, touched that he had wanted to share this dazzling spectacle with her.

They went on watching the display in a companionable silence. And Cathryn thought about Ben Adams. She thought about other intimate moments they had experienced together these past few days and what she had learned of this man that had somehow not been expressed in his letters. Things of tenderness and humor. Things that she loved about him.

"Better than fireworks, isn't it?" he said.

"Yes," she agreed.

But there was all the rest, as well, she remembered reluctantly. The things that were in conflict with the good moments. It wasn't just that intermittent intensity in him that still troubled and puzzled her. It was other things, little things mostly. Like his inability sometimes to recall where he had put items in his own cabin. He claimed he had cleaned the place just before her arrival, rearranging its contents to make room for her. It did make sense, this explanation of his forgetfulness, so why should it bother her?

Maybe it was because of his disregard of her own errors, such as her occasional failure to respond to Meredith's name. Or the mistakes she knew she must at times be committing concerning the contents of her cousin's letters. He never referred to them. She wondered if he had kept Meredith's letters. And, if so, where?

"Look down at the water," Ben said.

She did and discovered that, because the bursts of light in the northern sky were so strong, they created mirror images across the surface of the lake, rippling streamers that were equally lovely.

Cathryn continued to enjoy the miracle, but on a deeper level her mind returned to the subject of Ben. She had two other concerns about him. Why would a man of his rugged good looks, with so much to offer, need a mail-order bride? When she had playfully asked him about this, he had briefly informed her that men far outnumbered women in Alaska. It was a reasonable explanation, she supposed, but he had no satisfying explanation for Angel's puzzling behavior. The welfare of the dog continued to worry her, but Ben refused to discuss it any further.

"A fascinating mystery, huh?"

Her insides tightened. Had he read her thoughts? "What is?"

"What we're watching. The aurora borealis."

"Oh. Yes, I guess it is one of nature's mysteries."

She relaxed, told herself that she had to stop all these paranoid suspicions. They had no true substance, were nothing more than the residue of New Orleans. Except for one thing.

Cathryn knew that she was not imagining the sexual tension between them. It was very real—and constant. Even now, in this serene interlude, she was aware of his exciting closeness and how in moments it could seize her with an exhilaration that was positively dangerous. But it never blinded her to her persistent feeling that Ben Adams was tormented by something, some demon from his past perhaps that could explain his enigmatic intensity. If so, she prayed that eventually there would be enough trust between them that she could help him to resolve this dark thing. But that couldn't happen until she was honest with him about her own secrets. Until she confessed her deception.

"This is nice," Ben said.

"It *is* nice," she agreed, forcing herself to forget all the rest and concentrate on the luminous phenomenon above them. The performance they were witnessing was too special not to be fully appreciated.

Ben, conscious of her restlessness, thought resentfully that her mind was probably on the damn dog again. Why couldn't she let it alone? Why did she insist on daily putting out food for the animal? He didn't want to see the dog starve, but she was half-wild anyway and could fend for herself. He didn't want her hanging around, growling at him whenever he appeared. She was a threat to him.

And so, he realized, was his constant yearning for Cathryn McLean. He had to keep his distance, try to cool his desire by remembering what had happened in that safe house and how she had been responsible. He had to remind himself that she was only using him. Or at least the guy he was playing, which amounted to the same thing. All he was supposed to do was win her confidence. Nothing more. At least for now.

Hell, face it. What he was supposed to do just wasn't working. She was driving him nuts.

"I can't believe the colors," Cathryn said. "I never knew the northern lights had colors like these."

"Like a rainbow."

They went on watching the curtains of dancing light, sitting there on the pier together and sharing the magic until the glow diminished and faded with the first signs of daybreak. What they did not share was trust.

FRANK TESLER SAT on a park bench overlooking Cook Inlet, idly observing the boat traffic and nursing a can of diet soda. What he really wanted was a cold beer, but he was trying to be good. He had even switched to sugarless gum in an effort to shed some pounds. Betty would be proud of him.

Maybe a weight loss would help his feet. He sure hoped so. Right now they were sore as hell from long hours of tramping over hard pavement.

Anchorage was turning out to be a real bummer. He had spent three days systematically checking out the hotels, guest houses and motor lodges. Had even asked around the bars. No luck so far. Not a clue as to the whereabouts of Adams and the McLean woman. Well, they had to be somewhere, and eventually he would find them.

Problem was, he had to be careful. He didn't want to raise any special curiosity, risk having the word somehow passed to Adams that a stranger was asking questions about him. Frank was experienced and knew how to be cautious with his inquiries, but it was a big city. He could have used help with his search. Only there were no contacts here he was willing to rely on.

He had only himself and his bulldog determination. It all took time. Time and patience. Meanwhile his feet hurt.

There were a couple of kids playing along the waterfront while their father supervised them. Twin girls. Couldn't be more than six years old. Cute as all get-out. Frank watched them with a smile on his round face.

The father glanced at his watch, calling to his daughters. "Come on, kids. Time to pick up your mother."

Their departure reminded Frank that he had to be underway, as well. He needed to get to a phone. New Orleans would be expecting another report from him. They were getting impatient for results. He was equally frustrated that their research had failed to produce any further information that could be helpful to him in his search. You'd think with all their sources down there they could turn up something useful on Cathryn McLean.

He headed for the Land Rover, unable to shake the feeling that had troubled him back in Bearpaw. There was something about all this that didn't fit. A piece that was missing.

CATHRYN WAS ALONE in the cabin this morning. Ben, hoping to land a trout for their supper, was out on the lake fishing. He had asked her to go along, but she had declined with the excuse that she wasn't fond of boats.

That was true, but there was another reason why she had stayed behind. She was trying to write Meredith a letter, and she didn't dare work on it when Ben was in the cabin. Heaven only knew when she would ever get a chance to post it or even if it would be safe to send it. But she owed her cousin some kind of report on her status, and a letter was the only way since a telephone wasn't available. Ben had told her the nearest lines were in Bearpaw and that the cabin was too remote for any cellular phone.

*You're kidding yourself, aren't you?*

Hunched over the kitchen table, pen in hand, she made an effort to concentrate on the letter in front of her.

*Come on, face it. This isn't the reason why you wanted to be alone.*

Cathryn put down the pen and gazed out the window. All right, so she'd been lying to herself. But she didn't like the truth. She didn't like the nagging little voice that had told her that, with Ben out of the way, she was free to investigate that hollow under the overhang.

The image of the place had been haunting her since the first day when she had followed Angel there. Why was the dog drawn to that pile of stones, and why had Ben warned her to stay away from the cavern? Did the rocks conceal something that Angel felt compelled to guard? It was a chilling concept, like a forbidden room in an old Gothic romance.

She was being very silly. It was simply a sheltered place that a half-wild animal was using for its lair. And that was all there was to it, even if this didn't explain Angel's hostile behavior to the man she was supposed to be devoted to.

Cathryn also felt she was being disloyal. She didn't want these suspicions. Not after the magic of the other night. Not while noticing how Ben gazed at her in that melting way whenever he thought she wasn't looking. Not when a casual contact, as they brushed by each other in the confines of the cabin, sent sparks charging through her veins.

*But don't you see that this is your chance to settle it one way or another? All you have to do is go down there, look under those stones and satisfy yourself that there's nothing hidden there. Nothing for you to worry about. And if there is something there...*

It was no use. She couldn't resist the temptation. She couldn't go on with these conflicting feelings. She did have to know.

Scraping her chair away from the table, she took the half-finished letter and tucked it out of sight in her bedroom. Then she left the cabin and made her way down to the shore. There was no sign of the boat on the lake. He must be anchored behind one of the tiny islands. It was safe for her to proceed.

As she followed the path to the cavern above, she wondered if she would find Angel there. Maybe the animal wouldn't let her near the stones. In which case she wouldn't have to worry about what they might be covering.

But the dog was nowhere in sight when Cathryn reached the overhang. The pile of stones in the sandy hollow was undisturbed. She crouched down in front of it, gazing at the mound for a long, indecisive moment. Her determination had suddenly failed her, together with her nerve. She didn't know if she could bring herself to pull the rocks away, if she could bear now to know a truth that might be awful.

*They're just stones. Probably nothing under them.*

Leaning forward, she rested her hand against the hard, rocky heap. Again she hesitated.

"What are you waiting for, Meredith?" came the harsh voice directly behind her. "Go on, drag the stones away. Dig up the sand. That's what you've been wanting to do since you found this place, isn't it?"

Cathryn tensed, afraid to turn around, afraid to see the expression on his face.

"Too bad I came back in for another set of lures. If I hadn't interrupted you, you could have gone ahead in secrecy and satisfied your curiosity. Maybe learned the worst."

She couldn't bring herself to answer him.

"What's the matter? Too embarrassed to look at me?"

She swung around in defiance and found him towering over her threateningly, his face a rigid mask of anger. "You didn't have to sneak up on me like that."

"Is that what you call it? And what do you call what you're doing?"

"Ben, please—"

"Forget it. Just go ahead and do what you came to do. Dig up the grave. Because that's what you think those stones look like, don't you? Maybe they are. Maybe there's a body under there, someone I killed and buried."

Cathryn couldn't bear to admit that this was exactly what she had feared. Only she hadn't dared to name the unthinkable to herself, much less confess it openly now. She was suddenly ashamed of her despicable suspicion. She made what she considered was a vital decision.

"I don't want to remove the stones," she informed him quietly. "Let them stay where they are."

"No?" He hunkered down close beside her. "All right, if you've lost your nerve, then let me do it for you."

He began to tug at the rocks. She placed a hand on his arm, trying to stop him.

"Ben, don't," she begged him. "Let's just forget the whole unpleasant thing. I don't have to know."

"Yes, you do," he insisted coldly, shaking off her hand. "We're going to settle this right now because if we don't, it's going to go on coming between us."

Sitting back on her heels, she watched helplessly as he cast the stones aside, quickly reducing the pile to a bed of sand.

He began to paw at the loose stuff underneath, shoveling handfuls of dry sand out of the way. Within seconds they were assaulted by a powerful odor.

Cathryn stared at him in dismay. He paused, looking uncertain for the first time. Then, mouth tightening grimly, he renewed his effort, scraping away more sand until the thing that had been buried under the rocks was uncovered.

"Maybe you'd better not look," he warned her.

It was too late for that. She found herself gazing at the decaying remains and feeling as though she might be sick.

"My God," Ben whispered.

She knew then that he was as shocked as she was by their appalling discovery.

# Chapter Six

It was a body.

Not a human body. Cathryn was grateful for that much, though for a nauseating moment she feared the bloodied carcass was Angel. Then she realized it couldn't possibly be Angel. The dog had been guarding the pile of stones, already in place. And she had glimpsed the dog only last evening devouring the food she'd been regularly placing for her at the edge of the clearing. Angel would approach the cabin no closer than that.

This animal had been under the ground for at least a week or so. Its rough gray coat was much darker than Angel's. That and the gunshot wound that had killed it were all she could stand to see before she looked away from the vile sight.

Ben, however, was examining the remains more closely. "A wolf," he muttered angrily. "A full-blooded male wolf. The question is, who shot it and put it here? And why?"

Cathryn didn't answer him. He turned his head and found her gazing at him speculatively. The accusation and distrust were back in her eyes. He knew what she must be thinking. That he was only pretending disgust and outrage over the senseless slaughtering of the creature. That he must be responsible for its death and that this was the explanation for Angel's dislike and fear of him.

"I didn't kill the animal and bury it here, Meredith," he promised her softly.

She nodded silently. Damn it, why couldn't she believe him? And why did he care so much that she should?

He began rapidly recovering the wolf with the sand, replacing the rocks over the grave. No, he hadn't shot the animal. But he suddenly realized who probably was responsible.

Cathryn was waiting for him back on the shore path when he finished. He didn't speak to her. He struck out ahead of her along the trail, passing the boat tied up at the pier without a pause or a glance.

"Aren't you going back out on the lake?"

"No," he called over his shoulder as he strode up the hill toward the cabin. "I'm driving into Bearpaw. There's a bar there where the locals hang out. If anybody knows who's been hunting wolves in the area, one of those guys will."

It was a lie. He wanted to find the nearest telephone so he could call Anchorage. He didn't invite her to go along. Couldn't. She didn't ask to join him. She stayed behind on the pier.

All right, so it didn't make sense, he thought as he drove the long miles to Bearpaw. What was the point of satisfying himself with answers when he couldn't share them with her afterward? When she'd probably go on thinking he was some cold-blooded bastard who went around murdering the wildlife for the fun of it?

But then, none of this whole deception made sense to him any longer. Why had he ever agreed to a ridiculous masquerade that was pulling him apart emotionally? All he'd wanted was to be left alone with his grief, and now this woman was in his blood. Worse, he was beginning to fear that all of it was going to end in disaster and that he would be powerless to control it. He knew what that was like. It had happened to him before.

There was a decrepit service station out on the far edge of Bearpaw. He figured it would be safe for him to use the public phone affixed to one of its outside walls. If anyone was curious, and they usually were in these small communities, he would be just another traveler on the road.

The real Ben Adams must have been sleeping late. He sounded as if he'd just gotten out of bed when he answered his call. "Something wrong?" he asked.

"You tell me. I want to know about your dog."

"Angel? I did tell you. She ran off a little while back."

"Well, she's back and acting none too friendly. She won't let either of us near her, me especially. I'm thinking maybe it's because of what got buried under those rocks above the lake. What do you think?"

"Oh." There was a brief silence before Adams continued. "You found the wolf, huh? How'd that happen?"

"Never mind. I just did. Why did you shoot it and put it there?"

Adams was immediately defensive. "Listen, I had no choice. The thing was hanging around the place weeks ago, driving Angel crazy. Probably trying to lure her into the wild. I hear a rogue will do that. I finally got rid of him, only to have him turn up again the other week. I wasn't going to put up with that crap again, so I took care of him and made sure Angel wouldn't try to dig him up. What's the difference? Just another sneaky wolf."

He had decided from the beginning of this operation that maybe he didn't care much for Ben Adams. The guy had started out being agreeable to their switch. Too agreeable, considering he was losing a woman who was supposed to matter to him. Then, just before they'd left for Anchorage, e'd suddenly been reluctant about giving up his cabin, causing the delay that had been responsible for Cathryn's having to wait at the airport. Adams had probably been hoping for more money. He hadn't gotten it.

Now, hearing this story about the wolf, he was sure of it. He didn't like Ben Adams.

"Seems to have made a difference to your dog when she's gone and left you."

"Angel will be fine. Give her time, she'll settle down."

Adams didn't deserve his dog. "Okay, forget it. I'll handle it. Everything all right down there?"

"Fine." His laugh was a suggestive one. "Anchorage is turning out to be fun since I found me some consolation."

He could imagine what Adams had managed to find. A replacement for Meredith McLean. The guy was a jerk.

A FRANTIC CATHRYN RACED around the corner of the cabin just as he swung into the clearing. When he climbed from the Jeep, she met him with a breathless cry. "It's Angel! I tried to help her, but the line is snarled. She's in a panic and wouldn't hold still for me. I couldn't break the line. I was on my way to the cabin for a knife when you—"

He cut her off with a brisk, "Meredith, slow down. You're not making sense. Where is the dog?"

"I told you—in the lake!"

"No, you didn't tell me. But I guessed that much already. You're soaked from the waist down."

"Ben, there's no time for this! I'm afraid she'll drown before we can get her out!"

At this point, appreciating the need for action, he wasted no more precious seconds demanding explanations. "All right, let's go."

She was behind him as he trotted toward the path. Struggling to keep up with his long-legged gait, she filled him in on the situation in anxious little snatches.

"I was relaxing on the pier when I saw her. She was swimming out. Trying to catch a teal that landed on the water. Next I knew, she was caught on something. Yipping like crazy. I waded out to her. She was all tangled in the stuff by then. Twisting to get free. Making it worse."

"Fishing line?"

"I imagine. Something like that, anyway. I held her up, tried to work it loose. But she kept squirming and yelping. Ben, she can't touch bottom. And I don't know how long she can keep afloat."

They had reached the shore by then. Cathryn, fearing the worst, was relieved to spot Angel's head still above the water several yards off from the pier. *Barely* above the water. The animal was tiring rapidly in an effort not to sink against the tug of the fishing line that permitted her to do no more than paddle in tight, endless little circles.

Ben didn't hesitate. He plunged into the water, working his way rapidly toward the dog. Cathryn started to follow him, but he stopped her.

"Get me the penknife, Meredith. Should be in the top tray of the fishing box in the boat."

She turned back to the pier. Of course. Why hadn't she thought of the fishing gear instead of losing time by flying off to the cabin? She appreciated Ben's coolness in the emergency. She admired his restraint even more after she quickly found the knife and joined him out in the cold waters of the lake.

Instead of rushing directly to Angel's rescue and making the animal even more panicked in her distrust of humans, Ben had stopped a few feet away, allowing Angel to accept his presence as he spoke to her soothingly.

"It's all right, girl. We're going to get you out. Just hang on."

He went on talking to the dog with gentle encouragement as he began to edge toward her slowly. Cathryn, creeping forward behind him over the stony lake bottom, held her breath, praying Angel would permit him to approach her.

The animal was either too exhausted to resist him or else in her desperation she sensed that he was a source of help. Cathryn was relieved when Angel accepted him as he reached her. She made no objection to Ben's hand sliding down under her chest to support her.

"Hold still now, Angel," he murmured.

Amazingly she obeyed him as his free hand began to explore the mass of knotted line that had snagged her.

"It's a regular spider web," he muttered. "And one end of the line is caught down there on a sunken log, which is what kept her paddling in circles. I'll need the knife for this."

Cathryn, just behind him, passed the penknife to him and watched tensely as he sawed through the stuff in several places. Within seconds he had cut Angel free of the trap.

"A lot of it is still wrapped around her," he reported, "but we'll wait for the beach to remove the rest."

Cathryn took the knife from him, allowing him to scoop Angel into his arms. She followed as he waded with his load back to the shore. He placed the dog on the sand and crouched beside her to examine her condition.

"Here's the answer to why she was yipping when you tried to help her. Every time the wrong move was made, this damn thing cut into her."

Cathryn dropped beside him on the beach, discovering the wicked points of a three-pronged fishing hook still attached to the line and pressing painfully close to Angel's front paw.

He cursed savagely. "I'd like to get hold of the irresponsible idiot who cut this thing loose and just left it floating out there." Probably Adams, he thought angrily. Who else would have been fishing the lake?

"How can I help?" Cathryn asked as he took the knife from her again.

"Be ready to hold her still. She may not be so cooperative this time."

But Angel, as Cathryn held her head and stroked her comfortingly, never stirred when Ben went to work on her. She lay there quietly with patience and trust, her earlier dislike of him entirely forgotten.

Cathryn, watching him carefully slice and unwind the fishing line, regretted anything she had ever suspected him of with regard to Angel. But her emotions went beyond that as she followed the gentle movements of his strong, capable hands. She experienced something soft and yearning deep inside her, something that tugged at her powerfully. But she wasn't prepared to identify that feeling. It was much too unexpected, much too awesome.

Struggling to sound ordinary as Angel was released from the last shreds of the fishing line, Cathryn asked quickly, "Will she be all right?"

The dog answered that for her. She was suddenly all over Ben, wriggling and licking her gratitude. Cathryn shared in his rich laughter and felt that joyous sensation swelling inside her again.

"You know what she's bound to do next, don't you?" Ben said, trying to lean away from Angel's enthusiastic assault. "She's going to—"

He never got the chance to finish. The dog, fulfilling his prediction, shook herself vigorously, showering him with lake water and sand.

Cathryn laughed at the disgusted expression on his face. "That's right, Angel. Give him what he asked for."

"Get her, Angel!"

And Angel obeyed. Rolling happily on the beach until she was properly coated with sand, the animal launched herself against Cathryn, knocking her flat and covering her with debris.

"You dog!" Cathryn shrieked. "No, not you, love. Your stinker of a master."

Still playful, Angel leapt away with a shrill bark and began to tear around them in excited circles.

"I guess she doesn't object to being rescued," Ben said dryly.

"I'd say that's an accurate observation. She's like a pu— Ben, look. What's wrong with her now?"

Angel had come to a standstill. Her head lifted and turned alertly in the direction of the hill above the beach. She stood there motionlessly for a few seconds, as though she'd suddenly heard or remembered something. Then she swung around and streaked away from them in the direction of the ledges.

"The cavern," Cathryn said. "She's going to the cavern. Oh, Ben, I can't bear for her to go back there after—"

"Angel!" he shouted. "Come back here!"

The dog ignored them. Scrambling to their feet, they chased her.

"Did you find out who shot the wolf?" Cathryn asked him as they climbed the steep slope.

"No," he said, unable to share the truth with her. "No one was admitting anything."

Angel was in view ahead of them as they reached the crest. She had paused at the mouth of the deep overhang. She looked back, checking on them. She didn't seem worried now by their presence. Cathryn, saddened by the dog's attachment to the dead wolf, waited for Angel to dive under the ledge.

"What the— Now where is she going?" Ben demanded.

Not into the cavern, Cathryn thought, equally puzzled as they watched Angel lope away along a thread of a path that cut off to the left of the overhang. She disappeared into the trees.

They followed and came to another place where the ledges formed a deep hollow. This second, narrower cavern was slightly above the first. There was the sound of activity within the dimness that told them Angel had reached her destination.

Getting down on their hands and knees, they peered into the shadows of the den. Angel was there, lying peacefully on her side. She was not alone. A litter of almost full-blooded wolf puppies, four in number and surely less than two weeks old, was already suckling eagerly.

"Well, I'll be damned," Ben murmured in wonder. "You clever girl, you. This is what you've been protecting all along."

It had never been the body of the wolf at all, Cathryn realized. Angel had merely utilized the grave in that other cavern as a kind of blind. Mother love was very strong throughout nature, sometimes impelling animals to use themselves as decoys to keep danger away from their young. With the father of her puppies destroyed, Angel must have sensed a threat to her litter and behaved accordingly.

Cathryn related to that maternal instinct. The practice of decoying was something she could easily understand because—

She didn't trust herself to finish the thought. There was a sudden lump in her throat as she watched the contented dog nursing her puppies.

"I suppose there's no question of who the father was," Ben said, wanting to wring Adams's neck for shooting the wolf.

"I guess you never noticed she was pregnant."

"Dumb, huh?" he said, excusing himself. But he couldn't have known, since Angel had already fled by the time he'd arrived on the scene.

"Well, she does have an awfully thick coat," Cathryn said in his defense. "And she'd never let either one of us that close?"

"Because she was nervous about us. And this is why."

But Angel was no longer bothered by their nearness. Her eyes closed in lazy satisfaction as her offspring continued to feed. Ben and Cathryn, side by side on the ground, went on watching the tender scene.

She was conscious of their sharing a special moment. She didn't realize how special until she felt his gaze on her. She turned her head and was riveted by the longing she read in those jet dark eyes. She felt a similar ache tighten inside her.

"Meredith," he said, his voice gruff with emotion.

And that was all he said. All he needed to say. She swallowed nervously.

Ben got to his feet. "Come on," he urged, his voice still disarmingly husky. "Let's leave Mama with her babies. We've got something else to do."

She was afraid to ask him what and where as she stood beside him. Afraid and at the same time eager. "Like what?" she ventured.

"A cleanup. Look at us."

She was disappointed by his answer, though she appreciated its accuracy. She realized for the first time that both of them were a mess, sopping wet from the lake and plastered with grime from the beach.

"You're right. So, do we race each other to see who gets the shower first?"

"The hell with that. I want a long, relaxing soak in a hot tub. *Together.*"

"Oh," she said breathlessly, then added quickly, "Too bad we don't have one."

"Wanna bet?" There was a wicked gleam in his eyes and a promise in his tone.

"Care to explain that little mystery?" she challenged him.

"More fun to show you."

"Ben—"

"Trust me," he said, leading the way down the hill.

"I seem to remember hearing that before. I think it was the night of the accident down in Percy, just before we confronted assorted ghosts, an indignant llama and a nasty shotgun."

The thing of it was, like Angel, she did trust him implicitly now. She even wondered, after his caring moments with the dog, how she could have ever doubted him at all.

She followed him to the shore, her heart beating with a strange, happy expectancy that was in conflict with her sudden shyness. When he started for the pier, however, instead of turning in the direction of the cabin, her anticipation changed to reluctance.

"Oh, you're not going to propose we go swimming in that frigid lake. Wading in to rescue Angel was one thing, but—"

"I said *hot* tub, remember?" Reaching the pier, he scrambled down into the boat. "Come on, we're going for a little ride in the outboard."

She regarded with misgiving the hand he extended toward her. "Uh, maybe this isn't such a good idea."

"I remember, you're not crazy about boats. Don't worry. It's not far, and I'll stick close to shore."

*Trust, Cathryn. You told yourself you trusted him now.*

"Take a chance, Meredith," he encouraged her.

The gleam was still there in his dark eyes, making his secret objective ultimately irresistible. "I give up. I'm a sucker for surprises."

She accepted his hand, taking pleasure in his firm grip as he helped her into the small boat. She was settling herself on the seat in the bow while he bent over the motor when she remembered something.

"Towels and fresh clothes! I mean, if you're serious about us having a bath out there somewhere—"

"Not necessary. We're going to let nature provide us with all we need."

It was a provocative assurance. She didn't argue with him.

Seconds later the outboard was cutting along the edge of the lake. Once she commanded herself to relax, Cathryn enjoyed the experience. From this open perspective, the mountains and lush forests were even more spectacular, the water a pure, incredible blue.

Within minutes they glided into a sun-warmed inlet fed by a creek emerging from a dense grove of willows. Ben secured the boat on the gravel shore.

"This way," he directed, leading them along a narrow path that climbed steeply through the trees.

She was thoroughly perplexed by now. "I hear the sound of rushing water."

"Right. The source of the creek down there. Here we go."

He held aside the low boughs of a spruce, allowing Cathryn to precede him. Head low, she ducked through the opening. When she emerged on the other side, she found herself in a glade.

The scene was as enticing as a travel poster. Water tumbled from the fern-cloaked ridge above them, cascading into a rocky pool at their feet before spilling away again into the creek below. The slowly swirling pool had all the proportions of a large bathtub. A fine mist rose from its serene surface, like a thin layer of smoke. When Cathryn held her hands over the curling wisps, she felt a low, steady heat.

"It's warm," she said in wonder.

"Hot springs," he explained. "Alaska is volcanic, so they're common in the state."

She smiled at him in delight. "You weren't kidding. We do have our own hot tub. Uh, how do we... ?"

"Take the plunge? Simple."

He demonstrated for her. Kicking off his tennis shoes, he lowered himself into the pool with a carefree confidence. The sight of him, immersed up to his neck while fully dressed, had her crowing with laughter.

"You're crazy!" she accused him.

"I'm being practical," he insisted, paddling around the pool. "My clothes are as dirty as I am, aren't they?"

"You have a point," she conceded, realizing her own clothes were equally grimy. Besides, his method was probably less awkward than stripping down to nothing in this intimate situation. But not as interesting.

"Are you going to stand out there or join me?"

She accepted his challenge, recklessly pulling off her own shoes and easing herself into the pool. The sensation, even with the restriction of clothes, was delicious. A soothing warmth seeped into her body.

"Good, huh?" He stroked around her in lazy circles.

"Mmm," she agreed, closing her eyes as she crouched down to her chin.

They drifted in silence for a moment in the balmy waters. She should have known he had no intention of maintaining the safe barriers of clothing. She heard him stirring, and when she opened her eyes, he was climbing out of the pool.

"That takes care of the laundry," he drawled, his voice wearing a new, husky tone. "Time for the body."

With the same confidence he had displayed that night they had spent in the old opera house, he began stripping away his wet clothing, spreading the garments to dry on a flat, sun-warmed boulder. Cathryn, watching his robust body emerge from shirt and jeans, knew that her flushed face was not a result of the heated water.

He was in no way self-conscious about his sleek nudity. But she was aware of every facet of his tantalizing masculinity. Hard shoulders, hair-darkened chest, strong thighs and above them a blatant virility that made her catch her breath.

When she lifted her eyes, their gazes collided. There was no teasing expression in his eyes now. The gleam that burned in them was earnest, vital. "It's time, Meredith," he said, his voice low and rough with need.

Time for her to shed her own clothing. But she knew he meant much more than that. She also knew he was right. The situation was not just ripe; it was appropriate. It was time for her to become the bride he had sent for.

But she was unable to perform the simple function of removing her clothes. He must have sensed her nervousness, even though he was unable to understand the reason for it.

He came to her then. Sliding into the pool, he approached her with the same unhurried care and patience he had used to woo the frightened Angel.

She rose to her feet, trembling as he advanced on her slowly. He stood facing her, so close now that the heat from his compact body was more potent than the temperature of the water drifting around them lazily. He seared her without touching her, his hot, black eyes making her aware that the shirt clinging to her revealed the contours of her breasts and nipples.

"I'll help you, Meredith. Let me help you."

He lifted the hem of the shirt, began to draw it over her head. She raised her arms to accommodate him. When it was off and slung over his shoulder out of the way, he savored the vision of her naked breasts.

"Beautiful," he said. "You're a beautiful woman."

She gazed at him. Expectant. Eager. And still very nervous.

He began to work on her jeans. She didn't resist him but she didn't assist him, either. Somehow he freed her of the garment, as well as her panties underneath, without unbalancing either one of them. He took her clothes and placed them near his own on the boulders.

Her last defense had been eliminated. She was totally vulnerable when he returned to her in the pool. Even her will was stripped from her when his hands molded the fullness of her beasts, his thumbs slowly stroking her nipples into yearning peaks.

His mouth dipped toward her face, and she waited for his kiss. But it was not her mouth he sought. It was the mole just below her eye that his lips caressed with a sweet, lingering sorcery. From there he trailed a path to her mouth.

Her lips opened to his, inviting the intimacy of his stroking tongue in a deep, prolonged kiss that had her straining against his slick body. They were so tightly clasped that she could feel his rigid arousal surging against her. She fought for self-control.

When his mouth lifted from hers, he searched her face. "It's not there yet," he said.

"What isn't?" she whispered weakly.

"The wildness I want to see in your eyes before I make love to you. The same raw need for me as I have for you. But it will be before we're through."

It was no rash promise. Within the space of seconds, she learned about the sensual magic he could perform. He taught her with his skillful mouth on her breasts, his capable hands between her thighs. None of it was quick or rough. All of it was applied with a care and a tenderness that erased the last of those old, lingering memories of failure and humiliation. It was as if on some intuitive level Ben knew about the disastrous relationship that had left her so unwilling to be involved all these years. He knew, and was determined that she would never be hurt like that again. And she responded to his stirring kisses, his sensitive, probing fingers, with a desire that inflamed her.

"Now," he said, staring into her eyes. "Now I see it."

"Yes," she gasped, ready for him. More than ready. Consumed by a need to have him joined with her in every way.

He answered her urgency, lifting her from the water, placing her on the velvety surface of a ledge thick with moss at the edge of the pool. Only when his body covered hers, hot and suddenly demanding, did Cathryn experience a reluctance.

Ben, feeling her hesitation, drew back. "If you tell me not to go on, Meredith, I won't."

It was all the reassurance she needed. "Please," she implored him, "it's going to be all right."

But it was more than just all right once he was inside her, her body clasping his. More than just good. There was an incandescence about their oneness that filled her with awe. She had never known it could be this way between a man and a woman.

But patience was no longer possible for Ben. Nor for her. She moved with him, matching his compelling rhythms with her own. The rapturous waves that broke over them at last were as molten as the deep rock that fueled the hot springs beside them.

The wonder stayed with Cathryn afterward as she lay peacefully in Ben's arms. Their lovemaking had brought her more than just a profound pleasure. It had freed her of the resistance that had haunted her for too many years. She would always be grateful to him for that.

But there was even more. There was a recognition of that sweet sensation that had swelled inside her as she had watched him gently free Angel from the fishing line. She could name it now. It was the moment when she had begun to fall in love with Ben Adams.

Frightening. Wonderful but frightening.

But why should this admission scare her? What was left for her to worry about? That elusive, mysterious intenseness she kept glimpsing in him?

Cathryn lifted her head to gaze down at him. There was nothing intense about him now. His eyes were shut, his mouth wearing a little smile of satisfaction.

She had a longing suddenly to touch those bold, masculine features, to assure herself there was nothing dangerous here. Her fingers, with a will of their own, began to trace lightly the planes and angles of his face.

He wasn't sleeping. He chuckled when she came in contact with his strong Roman nose. "Gift from an Indian ancestor," he said without opening his eyes.

She remembered thinking that night in the ghost town that there was a suggestion of an ethnic heritage in his looks. "Bet he was a Sioux."

"You'd be wrong. Choctaw."

"Interesting."

He rose up on one elbow, sporting a wickedly sexy grin. "If we're going to do some body exploring here, let's be thorough about it."

She didn't mistake his meaning. "Again?"

He glanced over at their clothes spread on the boulders. "Hey, it's going to be a long while before they're dry. We've got to find something to do until then, don't we?"

# Chapter Seven

It was an unfurnished apartment, newly redecorated and waiting for a renter to fall in love with it. Frank Tesler had admired the place when he broke into it. It was almost as nice as his own apartment back in New Orleans.

That had been hours ago. Nothing to admire now. It was night, and the rooms were silent and dark. Frank had stationed himself behind the window blinds of the empty master bedroom. His carefully chosen position provided him with a clear view into the living room of the apartment directly across the yard from this one in the complex. Sooner or later his objective would appear in that living room.

It was not an easy vigil. His feet were killing him. Blisters now. Painful blisters from pounding too much Anchorage pavement. It helped that he had brought a folding camp stool into the apartment with him and could sit while he waited.

He would have been a lot more comfortable if he could have removed his shoes. It wasn't possible. Once he had scored the hit, there would be no seconds to waste. He would need to be fully ready to get out of the building and under way in the Land Rover parked down the block.

*A little patience,* he counseled himself. *You're almost there.*

He'd be in the air by morning, with Alaska and this job far behind him. Once back home, he would put his feet up and let them heal while Betty waited on him.

All he needed now was to squeeze just a little more luck out of the situation. He would get it, he thought confidently as he helped himself to a fresh stick of gum. It was all going in his favor suddenly. Had to be, after that huge slice of luck this morning.

Days of hunting for Ben Adams, and where had he found him in the end? Behind a traffic light on a busy Anchorage thoroughfare. The shiny Ford Explorer just in front of his Land Rover, waiting for the light to change, hadn't captured his attention. But its license plate had.

Frank had a habit of checking out plates on the road. Not for any professional reason. It was because the best of the vanity plates amused him. Some of them were damn cute. This one had been a disappointment—BN DMS. Nothing clever about that.

He had glanced away in disinterest. Then his gaze had shot back to the plate with excited awareness. BN DMS. Restore the vowels, and it read BEN ADAMS.

A long shot. Maybe the letters stood for something else or nothing at all. Maybe the plate represented another Ben Adams. The Anchorage phone book listed several of them, all of whom he had already checked out.

But something told Frank that he had his man. He'd followed the Explorer and its lone occupant. A dark, bearded fellow somewhere in his thirties. There had been no description of Adams made available to Frank, but the age had to be right.

The Ford Explorer had led him to the complex here on the outskirts of Anchorage. He had watched its driver disappear into one of the apartments. The name meant nothing to him when he cautiously checked the mailbox. Nick Gillette.

Did he have the wrong man, after all, or was Adams merely visiting the apartment? Frank had to know, and that meant taking a risk he didn't like. He'd hunted up the maintenance man for the buildings, displaying his impressive identification. A forgery, of course, but the guy had bought it and answered his questions.

"Yeah, Gillette's the tenant there, but he's away for a few weeks. Letting this Ben Adams from up Bearpaw way use his place while he's gone. No, he's not alone. Not now, anyway. Has a girlfriend in there with him. I don't know her name. I haven't seen her around, but I know she's there."

Cathryn McLean, Frank had thought. It had to be Cathryn McLean.

"Hey, is somebody in trouble?"

Frank had assured him a mistake had been made and that these weren't the people he was looking for. The maintenance man had been distracted then by the arrival of an elderly couple asking about a vacancy in the adjoining building. That was when Frank had learned about the empty apartment before quietly slipping away.

Luck, all right, he thought now as he worked on the gum in his mouth. Only it was the kind of luck you made for yourself with patience and persistence. They always paid off in the end.

The night wore on as he tried to forget about his angry feet. He kept a constant watch on the Gillette apartment with his binoculars. They weren't asleep over there. The lights were on, and he glimpsed Adams a couple of times on his way to the kitchen or bathroom, mouthing something once to the woman who had yet to show herself.

Neither of them ever entered the living room. They kept to what had to be the bedroom. From the look of Adams, who always had a towel wrapped around his hairy body and a grin on his face, they must be exhausting themselves in there.

It was after midnight, and Frank was struggling to keep awake despite the fresh air from the open window, when Adams finally sauntered into the living room. Picking up the remote, he switched on the TV and settled on the sofa. He called something to the girlfriend in the bedroom. Urging her to join him?

This was it.

Alert now, Frank dropped the binoculars and picked up the weapon waiting at his feet. A high-powered, custom-made rifle equipped with a telescopic sight.

Moving into position, he sighted on the doorway of the living room across the yard. He had a clear, unobstructed target. He waited. She was taking her time about appearing in that doorway.

"Come on, come on," he muttered tensely.

He braced himself, finger ready to squeeze the trigger. There was a movement in the doorway. A woman struggling into a robe. Now!

He never got off the shot. He stopped himself just in time with a grunt of surprise. Lowering the rifle, he snatched up the binoculars and trained them on the figure crossing the living room.

No, this wasn't Cathryn McLean! Couldn't be. The woman over there was a brunette, voluptuous but on the heavy side and with coarse features. Nothing like the photograph and description he'd been provided. So much for all that luck he'd been congratulating himself he had earned.

Uttering a violent obscenity, Frank sank back onto the camp stool. Chewing his gum, he tried to work it out. Something was wrong about this whole setup. He had sensed it from the beginning. He just couldn't seem to put his finger on it.

He was still trying to understand it during the following two days as he kept a cautious surveillance on the apartment. Adams and his brunette left the building several times and were never guarded about their appearances. There was no sign of anyone bearing a resemblance to the McLean woman.

Unless Frank's information was wrong—and he'd been assured he could count on it—Cathryn McLean was supposed to be in hiding with Ben Adams while she pretended to be her cousin. Only she wasn't with Adams. So what was going on here? Where was she, and who *was* she with?

He considered grabbing Adams. He knew some interesting ways to make him talk. But that was dangerous. He didn't want the McLean woman alerted before he reached her.

It was afternoon of the second day in the apartment before the possibility finally struck him. Nick Gillette. The guy whose apartment Adams was borrowing. Out of town for a few weeks, the maintenance man had claimed. Out of town where?

That was when Frank remembered the cabin by the lake. Adams's cabin in the wilderness. What if Adams and Gillette had switched addresses? What if the cabin *was* occupied? Occupied by this Nick Gillette, whoever he was, and Cathryn McLean was there after all?

Frank would have to go back to that cabin. It was a long drive, and his blisters were worse than ever. But his feet would have to wait. He wanted Cathryn McLean and he would do whatever was necessary to get her.

*What was wrong?*

Cathryn had been asking herself that question for the past

several days. She was still asking it tonight as she stirred restlessly in her lonely bed, unable to sleep as she listened to the sound of insects in the warm darkness outside her open window.

Ben hadn't touched her since that magic afternoon at the hot springs. Not so much as a casual kiss. She couldn't believe he was in some way angry with her. He was warm and friendly, joked with her constantly. But he avoided any physical contact, even though she tried to indicate without being blatant about it that she would welcome further intimacies.

The trouble was, she had almost no experience with sexual relationships. She didn't know the rules. Had he been disappointed in their lovemaking beside the pool? It didn't seem possible. She could swear their afternoon had been as incredibly rapturous for Ben as it had been for her.

Then what was wrong? She didn't understand. And she was afraid to ask him. Afraid to hear a truth she might not be able to handle.

That wasn't her only fear. There were others that she hadn't considered until now. Like her fear that she might one day endanger Ben because of her association with him. She couldn't bear it if anything happened to him because of her. He was everything she had ever dreamed of in a man and never expected to find in reality.

Love. It wasn't supposed to involve fear on so many levels, was it? But the fear of loss because of her masquerade was worse than all the rest, probably because it was already in progress. She would have to tell him the truth, and tell him soon, but what if he hated her when he learned about Cathryn McLean and her deception?

But not yet. She hadn't the courage to risk it. She preferred to live with the anguish of her guilt. Her recognition of that guilt had been there from the start, but it was so much more intense now that she was emotionally involved with the man she had come to Alaska deliberately to use.

"Forgive me, Ben," she whispered in the darkness. "I didn't plan for any of it to happen this way. Forgive me..."

She turned restlessly on the bed, longing for the man who was just a room away.

THEIR DOORS WERE AJAR. He could hear her moving on her bed and wondered if she was as sleepless as he was. He pictured her lying there in her thin night wear, blond hair all mussed, her body flushed from the warmth of this particular evening. An alluring image that taunted him.

Every nerve ending in his body, rigid with arousal, screamed for him to go to her. He wanted to hold her, bury himself in her sweet flesh and watch the passion for him burn again in her eyes.

Instead, he pounded his pillow in angry frustration.

He couldn't touch her. He couldn't make that mistake again. The outcome could be fatal for both of them, just as it had been for another woman back in New Orleans.

He had already made too many errors. Choctaw. He had really slipped up with that one. Hell, why hadn't he gone on and told her that there was Cajun in him, too, probably Creole, as well? That would have cinched it for sure. Sent her running for her life.

There could be no confessions until she was completely secure with him. And he knew he hadn't won her absolute trust, because she had yet to reveal herself to him. Even then, when he could finally risk an admission of his own, she might hate him. Probably would.

In the meantime he had to guard against losing her. If she suspected anything, there was the chance that she wouldn't stop to ask questions before she disappeared again.

Damn, why hadn't he restrained himself? Why had he complicated this whole mess by making love to her? Worse, much worse, why hadn't he obeyed his self-promise not to fall for her? Now he had to live with this torment.

Cathryn McLean was slowly killing him, and there was nothing he could do about it.

"WHAT HAVE YOU DONE to these feet, man? Deliberately abused them?"

Frank gazed anxiously at the raw blisters on his bare heels, then into the thin face of the man who was examining them. He looked more like a teenager than a qualified M.D. "They're going to be okay, aren't they?"

"The blisters are infected," the young doctor bluntly informed him.

Frank could see that for himself. It was why he'd decided to interrupt his drive to Adams's cabin with this detour into Lovejoy. In the end he had no longer been able to stand the pain, and Lovejoy was the nearest town of any size.

"So you can give me something for them, huh? I have this really important appointment north of here, and I need to be on my way."

"Cancel it. You're not going anywhere for a few days. Not unless you want to wind up with blood poisoning and a trip back to the hospital here for what could be an extended visit. Which I wouldn't encourage, considering the head nurse over there has the disposition of a Toklat grizzly."

"But I can't hang around here."

"Sure, you can. We've got a comfortable hotel in town. You'll love it. Used to be the local brothel. You can rest and stay off those feet there. Before you check in, you stop at the pharmacy down the street. I'm going to give you two prescriptions, and I want to see you back here in forty-eight hours.''

No choice about it, Frank thought dismally as he watched the doctor write the prescriptions. His trip up to the cabin would have to be delayed.

The doctor handed him the slips of paper. "One more thing. You have slippers in your luggage?''

"No.''

"Get a pair. You can buy them at Horner's next door. The kind without backs. You wear them without socks whenever you're on your feet, and you don't worry about how it looks. Any questions?''

Frank had none. He left the office. Cathryn McLean would have to wait. But not for long, he promised himself grimly. He would take her if he had to hobble on his knees to do it.

# Chapter Eight

"You're from the South, aren't you? Somewhere in Louisiana, I bet. Maybe around New Orleans."

Cathryn stared apprehensively at the clerk behind the drugstore counter. Was it possible? Had she fled thousands of miles from home only to end up somehow being recognized?

Seeing her startled expression, the young woman waiting on her laughed. White teeth gleamed in an attractive Native American face.

"I have an ear for accents," she explained, bagging Cathryn's purchases. "A gift for duplicating them, too, I hope. I'm studying to be an actress. University at Fairbanks."

Cathryn regarded the lively, friendly face across from her and relaxed. There was no danger here. "I didn't realize my accent was enough to show."

"I'm right, aren't I?" the clerk persisted.

"Yes, I'm originally from the New Orleans area," Cathryn admitted. After all, there was no reason to hide it when Meredith had come from Louisiana herself.

The clerk chortled, tossing back her long, sleek black hair. "Knew it. One of my teachers said I'm a regular Professor Higgins when it comes to dialects."

Cathryn smiled at her, wished her well in her career and left the counter with her purchases. There was a public phone in an alcove at the rear of the store. But before moving toward it, she checked the street entrance to make certain Ben was nowhere in sight. He was supposed to be getting his hair cut in the barbershop down the block, but she didn't want to risk his wandering in here while she was making her calls.

They had separated after leaving the supermarket. He had been reluctant about that. Come to think of it, he had been hesitant about her joining him at all on this latest, necessary shopping trip into Lovejoy. Probably just because he had sensed a tension in her about the outing, even if he didn't understand it.

This was her first time away from the cabin since her arrival. She had made herself come to Lovejoy today, knowing she couldn't hide up there forever and that there was no real threat in this remote town. Besides, she couldn't stand not phoning Louisiana. She had to know everything was all right.

But first, she thought, reaching the telephone in the alcove, she would call Meredith in Missouri. She had never finished that letter she owed her, and her cousin must be frantic by now.

Meredith answered on the first ring, as though she had been sitting there just waiting for her call. Cathryn quickly filled her in on all the essentials. They had been talking for several minutes when she realized that Meredith didn't sound like herself. She could detect a kind of stress in her manner. An explanation occurred to her.

"Meredith, do you have a visitor there?"

"No, I'm all alone."

"Oh. I just thought maybe—"

Her cousin interrupted her. "You're sure everything is okay with you and Ben?"

It must have been the third time she had asked the question. And for the third time Cathryn reassured her. "Yes, we're getting along fine. Meredith, don't worry about it. It's all working out beautifully."

"Just wanted to be sure," she mumbled, "that I—we did the right thing."

Meredith seemed satisfied when they finally ended their conversation. But maybe reluctantly so, Cathryn thought, still wondering about her manner. Could Meredith be having second thoughts about the switch they had made? Wishing now that it was she who had come to Ben Adams and not her cousin? Cathryn hoped this wasn't the case, because at this point there wasn't much she could do about it. She turned her attention to her next call.

Minutes later, having learned that for the present everything was going smoothly in Louisiana, she left the alcove. She was wearing a smile of relief as she started out of the drugstore.

There was a heavyset man blocking the entrance when she came out the door. He was paying no attention to where he was going, and they almost collided.

Cathryn felt sorry for him as she stepped aside. The poor man, bent over almost double, was struggling to keep a pair of scuffs on his bare feet as he flapped along the pavement, muttering curses of frustration. He kept reaching down to pull the slippers back into place.

He murmured a brief thanks when she held the door for him, but he never looked up as he shuffled into the drugstore. He was still battling the strange scuffs.

She checked her watch as she strolled along the sidewalk of Lovejoy's main street. She had some time left before she met Ben at the Jeep parked behind the barbershop.

Pausing in front of a store that catered to the tourist trade, she admired the window display featuring a fascinating array of Alaskan products. Gold-nugget jewelry, canned salmon, fur mukluks, wild berry jellies, seal oil candles. They were all there.

Cathryn was trying to make out the price on an exquisite jade carving when a rough-edged voice raised a shout behind her. She swung around in faint alarm, scanning the sidewalk in both directions.

"Girlie! Here, over here!"

Across the street a burly figure in grubby pants and shirt stood by a battered pickup truck, arms waving to draw her attention.

FRANK SLID the two prescriptions across the counter. "What are the chances of getting these filled while I wait? Oh, and I'll take this package of gum. Also, have you got a phone in the place I can use?"

The young woman behind the pharmacy counter stared at him in silence. Frank scowled at her, thinking she was too mystified to answer him. He knew what he must look like slapping in here with these damn mules on his feet. Like a circus clown trying to get around in a pair of shoes miles too big for him. These were the closest to his size that Horner's Store could produce.

He was in no mood to assume the affable manner he used to keep strangers from being suspicious. His infected blisters were driving him crazy.

"There a problem?" he demanded.

The clerk was suddenly all apologies. "Sorry, I'm sorry. It's just that I was so surprised. *You've* got it, too."

What the hell— Did she think he had something catching? "What are you talking about?"

"Your accent. It's the same. Southern Louisiana. It is Louisiana, isn't it?"

Frank's scowl deepened. "So?"

"Well, the blond woman who was in here a minute ago buying cosmetics, she had a Louisiana accent, too. What are the odds for a coincidence like that in a place like this? I would have figured you were together except you hardly even glanced at each other when you passed in the doorway. It's too weird. Oh, you must be together."

Frank suddenly understood. Cathryn McLean! She was here. It *had* to have been her, and he had let her slip right by him without even being aware she was within his reach. All that had registered when she held the door for him was a pair of shapely legs below white shorts. He had been occupied with the miserable slippers.

"The blond woman. Where did she go?"

"I don't know. Just out. About the prescriptions—"

"Fill them," he barked. "I'll be back for them."

He was already on his way toward the entrance. She couldn't have gone far. If she was on foot, he could still catch up with her.

He burst onto the sidewalk, stumbling over the loose slippers, cursing the pain of the infected blisters that slowed him down.

IT WAS SOURDOUGH ANNIE. Cathryn would have recognized that ancient prospector's hat from two blocks away. She crossed the street to speak to her weather-beaten friend from the ghost town.

"How you doing, girl?" Annie seemed pleased to see her. She grinned a welcome when Cathryn reached her.

"Hot." The sun was glaring on this side of the street.

"Yeah, it can be murder in summer. Something newcomers to Alaska don't expect."

Annie drew her around the front of the pickup parked at the curb until they were standing close to the high cab that cast a welcome shade.

"Otherwise, I'm flourishing." Cathryn smiled at her. "How about you, Annie?"

"Me? I'm always good. You on your own in town?"

"No, Ben is visiting the barber. I'm exploring Lovejoy while I wait."

"Not much to see, but this is the closest we come to a metropolis in these parts." She cast a glance along the street, whose storefronts were mostly wooden, as well as old-fashioned. Then her beaming expression sobered. "So, how's it going with Adams? He treating you okay?"

"He couldn't be better, Annie," Cathryn said, anxious to assure the woman that her distrust of Ben was without foundation.

"No problems, then?"

"Nothing that we aren't working out." Not quite true, but she didn't think Annie was referring to their sex life.

"Good. That's good, then." Annie didn't looked convinced.

Cathryn was grateful when the conversation was curtailed by the arrival of a teenage boy. He emerged from the feed store where the pickup was parked, staggering under the weight of a cumbersome sack of flour.

"In the back," Annie directed him.

"Are you opening a bakery down in Percy?" Cathryn teased her.

"Always buy it in bulk. Cheaper that way. Hey, go easy with that," she barked at the teenager, who was getting ready to heave the load over the side of the truck. "Don't want my grub spilling out all over the street."

She charged to the rear of the pickup to lower the tailgate while Cathryn remained in the shade of the cab.

"Where are my apples?" Annie demanded.

"Coming up," the boy mumbled, depositing his load in the bed of the truck and heading back into the store for the apples.

"Buy those by the bulk, too," she explained. "Treats for Lulu."

The arrogant llama, Cathryn remembered.

Annie, leaning against the tailgate, chuckled. "Get a load of that."

Cathryn moved along the side of the truck in order to gain a view of the figure her friend indicated on the opposite side of the street. It was the heavyset man from the drugstore. He was slip-slopping from store to store just as furiously as the loose scuffs on his feet would permit, peering through the glass of each door before rushing on to the next.

"Looks like he lost something he's desperate to get back," Cathryn observed. "Probably his wife."

"And they call me a character. Well, it's Alaska. You see all kinds."

The teenager reappeared with the apples. Cathryn hastily got out of his way, retreating into the shelter of the cab.

Annie joined her there after the apples had been loaded and the tailgate closed. Her seamed face wore a solemn expression again.

"What I told you down in Percy that morning about coming to me if things don't work out . . . well, that invitation still holds."

Poor Ben, Cathryn thought. She just won't believe in him.

"I appreciate that, Annie, but I don't think it will ever be necessary."

She grunted. "You just remember it, girl."

The pickup departed a moment later. The man in the strange slippers had disappeared by then around the corner up the street. Cathryn moved off in the opposite direction, cutting through an alleyway that led to a gravel area where the Jeep was parked behind the shops.

HE WAS RELIEVED to get out of the barbershop. The place had been busy, and he'd had to wait his turn while suffering the fumes of someone's bad cigar. He stood on the sidewalk, filling his lungs with clean air. And that's when he saw it.

A Land Rover. A *green* Land Rover. It was cruising slowly along the street, its driver's gaze slewing from side to side. On the lookout for something. Or someone.

Land Rovers were expensive vehicles. They weren't common in Alaska. So he probably would have noticed it in any case. But this one held his interest as his eyes followed it up the block. It triggered something in his memory. Something he couldn't pin down at first. And then it came to him.

That rainy night when the Jeep had gone off the road and he'd been knocked unconscious, Cathryn had tried to flag down a passing car. A Land Rover, she had said. A green one.

It hadn't meant anything at the time. There had been too much else to think about. But now he wondered. What had an unfamiliar Land Rover been doing out there at that time of night on a seldom-traveled back road?

He was probably overreacting. There was no evidence that he had anything to worry about. But he continued to watch the vehicle as it reached the far end of the business district. It made a U-turn and came crawling back along the street.

He stood at the curb looking bored, as though he were waiting for a ride. But this time when the Land Rover swept by him, he made an effort to distinguish the driver's face as the man's restless gaze continued to probe both sides of the street.

He was passed over without interest but not before he caught a clear glimpse of a pudgy face and a balding head. It was not a face that he recognized, but there was something about the thin, determined mouth that made him uneasy.

That uneasiness escalated into a tight feeling in his gut when the vehicle, suddenly gathering speed, swung around the next corner into a side street. The street led to the area in back where the Jeep was parked. And Cathryn must be there by now waiting for him!

He didn't hesitate. Pivoting, he raced toward the mouth of the alley that was a shortcut through the block. He knew it. He knew he should have left her back at the cabin. But she would have been suspicious if he had refused her this time, and Lovejoy had seemed a harmless outing.

He heard the slam of a car door and the squeal of tires somewhere toward the rear of the buildings as he pounded through the alley. The warning in his gut was now making him sick with alarm.

He reached the parking area. The locked Jeep was there, but there was no sign of Cathryn. And no sign of the Land Rover. Convinced that the worst had happened, he charged toward the Jeep, searching his pockets for his keys.

He didn't find them. That's when he realized that he had given the keys to Cathryn, knowing she would return before he did and that she would want to let herself into the Jeep.

He was a damn fool, he thought as he skidded to an angry halt in the gravel. Why had he ever let her go off on her own?

The Land Rover! He had to go after the Land Rover, get her back before it was too late. He needed a fast car to follow them. The Jeep was alone in the parking lot. But there were other cars on the street out front. He would commandeer one, steal it if necessary. Whatever it took to find them and recover her.

He was halfway back through the alley before he remembered that he kept a spare ignition key in the glove box of the Jeep. All he had to do was pick up a rock and break through a window.

Time. He was losing valuable time.

Turning around, he sped toward the parking lot again. When he emerged from the alley this time, relief went through him like a flash fire. Cathryn, carrying a bag of ice, was coming toward him through a gap in the shrubbery at one end of the lot.

She looked cool and desirable in those white shorts and a tank top that had been gnawing at his self-control ever since they had left the cabin. He wanted to fold her in his arms, crush her against him protectively and thank the Almighty that she was safe. What he did instead as she reached him was rail at her like a scared parent.

"Where the hell have you been? I've been going crazy wondering where you got to. Are you all right?"

She stared at him, her aquamarine eyes wide with surprise. "What are you so excited about? I just went for more ice from the machine at the bait-and-tackle shop. And why shouldn't I be all right?"

"No reason," he mumbled. "Just ice, huh?"

"Just ice, Ben. I got worried when I checked the cooler after I got back to the car. With this weather, I thought maybe we didn't have enough cubes to keep our stuff cold until we got home." She tipped her head to one side, regarding him with puzzlement and a touch of mischief. "Are you sure they didn't do more than just barber your head?"

"Cute." He held out his hand for the keys. "Do I get trusted to drive us back, or are you going to leave me at the hospital here for observation?"

She laughed and tossed him the keys for the Jeep.

All right, he thought on the long drive back to the cabin, so maybe he *had* overreacted. And maybe he was being too cautious about the situation, but she was his responsibility. More than ever now, he realized. But he didn't dare to go into that.

Instead, he thought about the Land Rover and its driver. There was probably no threat there. The guy could have been looking for anybody or anything, and for any number of reasons. All the same, he wasn't comfortable with the presence of that car and its occupant in the area.

So why take a chance? he decided. Why not just make himself feel better about the whole thing by getting Cathryn out of the way for a few days?

Besides, he was fed up with restraining himself. She had indicated in a dozen subtle ways that she would welcome his lovemaking again. And with them alone together in the romantic setting he had in mind... Maybe he would just throw caution to the winds. Damn it, he wanted her. *Desperately* wanted her.

"Got an idea," he proposed enthusiastically. "What would you say to a camping trip for a couple of days? I've got all the necessary gear at the cabin."

"I've never been camping. Where would we go?"

"I was thinking the Athabascan River. The salmon should still be running there. It's quite a sight if you've never seen a salmon run."

"I'd like that. When?"

"Why not today? There's still plenty of daylight left, enough to get us over there and settled in before dark."

"Tempting. But what about Angel and her puppies?"

"We'll put out enough dry food. She'll be all right on her own for a couple of days. Remember, she knew how to survive when she ran away. Okay?"

"Okay."

He allowed himself to relax. It was going to be all right. There had been no sign of the Land Rover, either, since it had turned down that side street back in Lovejoy. They were alone on the road to the cabin.

Cathryn watched a little smile of satisfaction settle on his wide mouth. He concentrated on the winding road, permitting her to steal glimpses of him. She enjoyed the sight of him.

That visit to the barber had changed his appearance. His thick black hair, which had been much longer at the nape and grown shaggy around the ears, had made him seem tough sometimes. Cutting it made his face leaner and more vulnerable. Younger, too. There was much less evidence of the gray now at his temples.

Maybe it wasn't the haircut that was making her see him in a new way. Maybe it was other things. Like the way he had been worried about her when she wasn't there at the Jeep. As if she were precious to him.

That idea had been touching to her back at the parking lot. Now it excited her, as did his desire for them to go camping together. They would be alone in the wilderness in a special way that would be different from the cabin. Sharing a closeness that could create an incredible intimacy, an intimacy she had been longing to repeat since experiencing it with Ben that day at the hot springs.

She had never been so aware of her need for him.

IT HAD BEEN a wonderful day, Cathryn thought, her arms locked around one upraised knee as she watched Ben cook their supper over the open fire.

They were camped in a small clearing miles from any other human, surrounded by nothing but the beauty and peace of raw nature. The river was close by. She couldn't see it from her seat on the blanket, but she could hear its wild water through the thickening twilight.

Earlier, just after their arrival and while the light had still been strong, they had stood on a flat boulder at the river's edge and watched the spectacular activity just below them. Thousands of salmon were fighting their way upstream to their spawning grounds.

Cathryn had marveled at the swarms of fish, their bodies flashing in the sun as they executed impossible leaps up one high cascade after the other. Ben had told her over the roar of the river that this mass migration from the sea would have begun in late May or June. And here, weeks later on the upper reaches of the Athabascan, these salmon were still battling their way to the quiet pools from which they had originated.

They weren't the only creatures interested in the salmon. Across the river a trio of brown bears had waded into the tumbling waters. The bears had skillfully slapped fish onto the banks and feasted on their catches.

*As we're going to feast on ours tonight,* Cathryn thought. Or maybe not. Her anticipation was suddenly troubled by the odor of something burning.

"Uh, are you sure you know what you're doing in that frying pan?"

"You're going to love it," he assured her. "Blackened fish hot with pepper. It's my specialty."

She had her misgivings until he served them generous portions of the fresh salmon. It was a succulent dish, and she ate it with relish, even if its seasoning did leave her mouth on fire.

The heat of the day had fled, the evening air turning cool by the time they finished their meal. Cathryn shivered and drew her sweater around her shoulders.

"I can find a better way than that to keep you warm," he said. "Just let me take care of the cleanup, and I'll show you."

His husky promise made her weak with yearning. It was going to be all right. They were going to renew their magic.

Wanting him, she was impatient with the delay as he got to his feet and began to clear away the meal. He had insisted earlier on handling everything himself, telling her she could be responsible for their breakfast in the morning.

Resting her chin on her knees, she watched his rugged figure moving around the clearing by the light of the fire. There was a tenseness inside her that was nothing more than her eagerness for his embrace. That was what she told herself at first. But as the moment she longed for drew nearer and her gaze continued to follow him, this time with an unwanted sadness, she knew she could no longer deny the explanation for her tension.

Ben joined her at last on the blanket. His arms went around her without hesitation, drawing her close.

"Now, where were we?" he asked, his mouth moving tenderly toward hers.

It would have been so easy to melt into him. The easiest thing in the world. But she couldn't. Not this time. Not loving him now as she did so deeply. He didn't deserve her deceit. He deserved the truth. *No more lies, no more delays,* she challenged herself fiercely. *You will tell him everything, and you will tell him now.*

And if afterward it ended here, if he was outraged by her masquerade and unable to forgive her... That was the risk she had to take.

His mouth was settling on hers when, hands placed against his chest, she pushed him gently away. The glow of the fire revealed the immediate puzzlement on his face. She could hear it in his voice, as well.

"Meredith?"

"Oh, Ben—" There was a catch in her voice and anguish in the wry laugh that followed. "There—there's a truth you have to hear and I can't hide it any longer. I'm sorry, so sorry. I..." She faltered, then struggled onward. "Ben, Meredith isn't here with you. She never was. I'm Cathryn, Ben. I'm Meredith's cousin, Cathryn."

He said nothing, demanded no explanations. There was a blankness on his face that had to be hiding his complete bewilderment. The silence stretched on. She heard no sound but the rapids in the river.

She refused to let her nerve fail her. She had to get it out. All of it. She went on in a hoarse voice, telling him everything from the beginning back in New Orleans. Telling him how and why she and Meredith had switched places. There was only one thing she left out, and she hadn't the right to talk about that. Not yet.

And through it all, he listened without interruption, that old intenseness now in his expression. An intenseness that scared her.

He made no comment when she finished. She watched him get up and leave her there on the blanket. A wall of misery closed around her heart as her gaze followed his tall figure. He stood by the edge of the river, ignoring her as he studied the dark, powerful water.

Cathryn couldn't stand the suspense. Did he hate her now? Had she sacrificed everything by admitting the truth? Lost him forever?

Her fear was unbearable by the time he finally returned to where she waited. He hunkered down in front of her. She could see by the glow of the flickering fire that he wore an expression of decisiveness.

"You break my heart, Cathryn McLean," he told her in a slow, deep voice. "You break my heart with your courage."

The breath she had been holding came out in a rush of sweet relief. "Then you understand what I did and why I had to do it? You don't blame me?"

"I understand, and I don't blame you."

"But it must matter that I'm not Meredith when it's Meredith you wanted."

"I only know the woman who came to Alaska. And she's the one I care about now, the one I want to stay with me and be my mail-order-bride."

"Ben, are you sure? I need to know that you're sure."

"Then let me show you just how certain I am."

He reached for her, dragging her into his eager embrace. She lifted her mouth to his, welcoming his fierce kiss. Rocked by the urgency of his need for her. Taking joy and pleasure in the solid feel of him. Trusting the hands that lovingly stroked her breasts and hips.

They were ready for each other long before they shed their clothes with a feverish impatience. There was no cool night air now. There was only the heat of Ben's hard body covering hers on the blanket where they were stretched, and her own body strained against his as she drew him deep within herself.

The first stars blinked overhead. The fire crackled in the clearing. Cathryn wasn't there to see or hear them. She was in another place. A place where Ben took her with his wet kisses and whispered endearments. A place where they soared to a pinnacle even more incredible than their first time together.

BASTARD, HE THOUGHT as she lay sleeping in his arms.

He had taken advantage of her again. He had promised

himself he wouldn't touch her. At least not before she had learned the truth. She had given him her own truth, bared her soul. That should have been the moment when he shared his confession. Instead, standing by the river's edge, he had made a selfish decision.

He could no longer contain his need to have her again. But if he revealed himself, there was the strong possibility, perhaps even the certainty, that she would turn away from him. Cathryn herself had had the courage to take that same risk with her disclosure. But in the end he'd been a coward, wanting her too much to gamble on it.

"What have you done to me, Cathryn McLean?" he whispered into her soft, ash blond hair. "You make me weak just looking at you."

Weak when he needed all his strength for what lay ahead of him. He would have sworn just days ago that no woman could ever matter like this again. Not after the loss he had suffered. But Cathryn had brought him back to life, taught him with her spirit and warmth that he could care again. Care with a rich, deep meaning.

But a need like that was dangerous. It could make a man reckless with emotion.

He couldn't help himself, he thought, his arms tightening around her possessively. His defiant embrace made her stir in her sleep, brought a smile of contentment to her full mouth. He felt that smile deep in his gut. He couldn't resist brushing his lips across the slight, tantalizing cleft in her chin.

For tonight anyway she was completely his. But soon, very soon now, she would have to know about him before it all blew up in his face.

THE AIR WAS PURE and bracing when Cathryn crawled out of her sleeping bag early the next morning. She had a vague recollection of Ben rousing her sometime in the night. The temperature had dropped sharply by then, and he had insisted they needed the insulation of their clothes and the sleeping bags. She had stumbled through the process of getting into both like an exhausted child.

She was fully awake now and exhilarated by the freshness of the morning and the memory of their lovemaking last night. Kneeling by the sleeping bag close to her own, she checked on her companion. He was still asleep.

She bent over him, a tenderness swelling inside her at the sight of his face darkened by the shadow of an early-morning beard on his proud jaw. Her gaze traced the lines of his high cheekbones that sometimes gave him that enigmatic, brooding quality. She had once found that look tough, even dangerous. But there was nothing hard about him now. He was Ben, the man she trusted and loved.

He was also, she reminded herself sternly, the man who would expect to eat when he got up. And breakfast was her obligation.

Regretting the need to be practical when all she wanted to do was sit here and savor the sight of him, Cathryn got to her feet and busied herself with preparations. She soon had the camp fire going again and fresh water from the river heating.

Ben had stored all of their food in a chest, placing the container inside the Jeep to keep any wild animals from scenting it. The Jeep was parked on the other side of the clearing where a track emerged from the woods.

Cathryn headed for the vehicle. She had no warning. The bear was simply and suddenly there as she reached the back end of the Jeep.

## Chapter Nine

Cathryn's body went as rigid as ice. The bear, too, froze in surprise. For a moment that lasted forever, they stood there regarding each other in silence. There couldn't have been more than four yards separating them, a distance that the beast could have closed in one swift, vicious charge.

Trembling now, she tried to remember what Ben had told her yesterday about this species while they had watched the three bears on the other side of the river. He had said that Alaskan brown bears were the largest in the world, more powerful than the ferocious grizzly. They were dangerous if aroused, but they were also easily frightened and stayed clear of humans. This one didn't seem to know that.

There was nothing either useful or comforting in any of this information. If anything, she was even more terrified. And desperate. The animal was not lumbering away as she had hoped it would do.

Trying to quell her panic, Cathryn began to back off as slowly and carefully as she could manage. But even this cautious movement was a mistake. The bear began to growl, a threatening rumble deep in its throat.

Then another warning came from behind her. This time a welcome one.

"Cathryn, don't move. Not a muscle. Stay just where you are."

Ben! Thank God for Ben!

She obeyed him and remained perfectly still again. It was the hardest thing she had ever done. Every instinct inside her cried out for her to run into his arms. But she dared do nothing, not even turn her head to learn his intention.

She could hear him moving behind her, but it wasn't until he appeared in her peripheral vision off to the right that she understood his purpose. He was creeping along the perimeter of the small clearing, clutching the first weapon he had been able to lay his hand on. He had snatched a length of wood from the fire. One end of it was glowing and smoking with heat.

The bear was aware of his activity, too, and didn't like it. It was snarling now and stubbornly holding its ground as Ben advanced.

"I'm going to try to drive him off," he informed her softly. "Or at least distract him. When that happens, and he's paying more attention to me than you, I want you to dive into the Jeep and I want to hear the door slamming behind you."

She opened her mouth to object, but he silenced her with a fierce "No arguments! Just do it."

Cathryn waited, praying the bear would do the wise thing and retreat. It didn't care for the hot menace waving slowly in Ben's extended hand as he approached in a half crouch. The bear started to back away. She was sure it would turn and run.

But a second later its mood changed. The animal suddenly reared back with a challenging roar, growing to an immense size. And then it lunged.

Ben was ready for the attack. Just as one huge paw came flashing through the air, he dodged and thrust the flaming brand into the bear's sensitive snout. With a howl of pain, the animal dropped to all fours, whirled and took off through the trees.

Cathryn flew across the clearing, her relief turning to alarm when she saw that Ben had dropped the chunk of wood and was holding his right arm with his left. He hadn't escaped the attack. The bear's lightning-quick blow had connected with his forearm, its razor-sharp claws tearing a gaping wound several inches long. There was blood. A lot of blood. It was welling up from the wound, spilling onto the ground.

"I think this isn't so good," he said calmly. "I think maybe you're going to have to help me."

The first-aid kit, she thought, battling a threatening bout of hysteria. They had brought a first-aid kit with them. It was in the Jeep.

She was back with the kit in seconds. Ben was looking woozy by now, weaving on his feet. She was afraid he would pass out on her.

"Down," she instructed him. "Sit down on the ground."

He complied without argument. She knelt beside him, searching quickly through the contents of the kit. They had to stop the flow of blood. Sick with worry that a vein or an artery might have been punctured, she found a tourniquet and fixed it to his upper arm just above the elbow. He was silent and still as she tightened it with shaking fingers.

She was getting ready to dress the wound when he finally spoke, his voice sharp with anger. "You were supposed to get inside the Jeep before the bear went for me. Why didn't you get inside the Jeep?"

He was sitting here with his arm ripped open, the raw flesh exposed. She was scared out of her mind for him, and all he could do was complain about her disobedience.

"Don't talk," she ordered him. "And keep still."

Her own tone was tougher than his. He was meekly silent again. She didn't bother trying to clean the injury. That would have to wait. She applied a compress and began to wrap it with gauze. The blood soaked through. She kept on binding it until the flow seemed to ease.

"You'll have to keep it elevated," she said, releasing his arm. "Can you stand up?"

"Yeah."

She helped him to his feet. She didn't care for the way he looked. "How do you feel?"

"Like shi—" He broke off, sucking in air and then finishing lamely, "Not so great."

"Ben, we've got to get you to the nearest medical assistance."

When he nodded, raising no objection, she knew he must be in a bad way. He had lost a lot of blood. Too much, she was afraid.

She saw him settled on the passenger side of the Jeep before she took a moment to douse the camp fire and grab her purse. She wasted no time trying to gather their supplies, abandoning them in the clearing without a thought as she raced back to the Jeep.

It wasn't until she slid behind the wheel and reached for the keys that she remembered. She turned to him in horror.

"Ben, I can't drive! It's a stick shift. I've never driven anything but an automatic!"

"Cathryn, there's no way I can operate this vehicle myself. You'll have to manage it."

"But a clutch... I don't know how to handle a clutch."

He turned to her, his expression earnest. "You can do it," he promised her confidently. "It's not that difficult. I'll tell you how."

He was right. Hadn't she kept her wits when confronted with the bear? Played nurse when she knew next to nothing about proper first-aid treatment? She'd been cool and decisive in the emergency when she'd wanted to go to pieces. She could go on doing what was necessary.

"Show me," she said quickly.

He gave her a fast lesson in the use of the clutch and the gears, pausing every few seconds to take a steadying breath. She knew he must be in real pain, and she regretted the delay.

Taking her own deep breath, she started the engine, depressed the clutch and slid the stick into first. Her first efforts were hopeless ones. When she wasn't grinding the gears or jerking the car, she was killing the engine. Repeatedly.

"Cathryn, listen to me. Be patient with yourself, take it a little slower."

She concentrated, obeying his advice. Her progress was better after that, and though the Jeep lurched down the track, she was able to keep the engine from dying. She had gotten the hang of it by the time they reached the roadway and was able to shift gears with an acceptable smoothness.

She paused when they reached the turning. "Where do we go? Bearpaw? It's closer."

"No," he said sharply. "Not Bearpaw."

"Isn't there a doctor there? I thought you mentioned in one of your letters that Bearpaw has a doctor."

"Not a practicing one. He's retired, elderly."

"You're right. You should have a hospital. That means Lovejoy."

"No," he insisted, "not Lovejoy, either. There's a midwife that lives just off the main road about halfway between Bearpaw and Lovejoy. She can patch me up."

She stared at him. "Are you crazy? You're going to need stitches and God knows what else. I'm not taking you to any midwife. You're getting the professional treatment of a full staff. Hang on."

She swung the car onto the road, executed the shifts with the determined skill of a speedway driver and accelerated grimly. The Jeep leapt forward like a bull out of a chute.

"Cathryn—"

"No arguments about it. And, damn it, keep that arm elevated. Please."

He surrendered, slumping back against the seat. He must have finally realized that his condition could require a transfusion, and that with his blood type a hospital was absolutely necessary. They didn't talk about it, but she knew he had to be worried about this aspect of the situation.

Cathryn was worried, too. A pink patch on the surface of the bandage told her that blood was still seeping from the wound. She didn't like his color, either, or the way he sat there without any energy, eyes closed.

At intervals she pulled over to the side of the road. She hated the loss of these precious minutes, but the tourniquet had to be loosened periodically to prevent a failure of circulation. The rest of the time she drove like a fiend, amazing herself with her handling of the Jeep. But she was frantic. If anything happened to him... She didn't know what she would do. He meant everything to her now.

She blessed the Jeep for its performance. They ate up the long miles, covering the rough stretches without a problem. But the distance frustrated her. Her nerves were on fire with impatience before they finally arrived at the emergency entrance of Lovejoy's small brick hospital.

The Jeep ground to a halt, the engine cutting out when she released the clutch with a jerk. It was her first awkward maneuver since leaving the river behind them. It didn't matter now.

Cathryn turned to him. He had been absolutely silent on that last race down the valley. She was afraid he might have passed out on her.

"Ben," she informed him urgently, "we're here."

She was relieved when he opened his eyes and nodded.

"Should I have them bring out a chair for you?"

"Hell, no," he grumbled, favoring her then with a cocky grin. It was a weak grin, but it made her feel better. "If I survived that wild ride, I can certainly walk into an emergency room. You're a maniac at the wheel, McLean."

"All of us ambulance drivers are."

She went around the car to help him, but he waved her off with his good arm. His refusal to have her fuss over him made his sober request as they headed toward the hospital doors seem odd.

"You'll stick close to me, won't you? No matter how long I have to be in there, you'll be right there. You won't leave the building."

She promised, wondering why he was so anxious about that.

Lovejoy apparently had few medical emergencies. The only staff on duty was a young woman who received them with an enthusiasm that suggested she was inexperienced. But she did dispatch an immediate call for qualified personnel.

While they waited for the arrival of a doctor from elsewhere in the hospital, she got Ben prepared for treatment, taking down the essential details.

"Sounds like you might need blood," she said solemnly. "Do you know your blood type, Mr. Adams?"

"Uh, yeah, as a matter of fact I do. It's O positive."

"Sure?"

"I'm sure. I've never received blood, but I have given it."

Cathryn, hovering in the background, was astonished by his answer. It couldn't be right. It just *couldn't*. And yet Ben had been unhesitatingly confident in his claim. Then what was the explanation?

She never got the chance to ask. A stentorian voice from the doorway cut in on the scene. "It doesn't work that way, Ms. Dukowski. We don't ask patients their blood types or suggest they might need blood. That's for the doctor to determine, and only after the patient is tested for his type."

The head nurse, who looked every bit as tough as the bear that had attacked Ben and almost as large, had arrived in time to hear the last exchange. She marched across the room to the examining table where Ben was situated.

"I'll take over, Ms. Dukowski. Bear mauling, huh? Hardly ever happens, but when it does it can be a real stinker."

A lanky young doctor in jeans and a baseball cap appeared seconds later. Cathryn was asked to remove herself to a waiting area next door while they worked on Ben. His eyes met hers before she left the room. They wore a silent appeal for her not to forget her promise to stay close.

She went and stood by a window overlooking the parking lot, too shaken and confused to sit in one of the chairs. Was she wrong in her recollection? She didn't see how she possibly could be. She had read Ben's letters to Meredith over and over, practically memorizing them in her need to be as familiar as possible with the man she was coming to Alaska to meet.

And that long passage in one of his earlier letters . . . she could almost see it now. It was memorable because he'd made a big deal out of it. He had described an accident on the pipeline where he worked and how it had worried him. Because if he'd ended up needing blood, maybe his type wouldn't be so readily available in the wilderness. Ben Adams was a rare AB negative.

Oh, she must have it all wrong! Ben must have been talking about one of the other workers on the line.

But her uneasiness increased as she stood there waiting for them to come to tell her that Ben was going to be all right.

Her tension was unbearable by the time the young doctor joined her in the waiting room.

"Your boyfriend is one lucky son of a gun," he reported cheerfully. "Old bruin came that close to tearing an artery."

"There was so much blood."

"Always does seem to be more than there actually is."

"Then he didn't need to have blood?"

"Nope, thanks to your quick action. No surgery necessary, either. Just a lot of stitches he wasn't happy about, along with the appropriate shots. That arm is gonna be as sore as hell for a while, but it should heal without a problem."

"Can he go home?"

"I probably would have released him by the end of the day, but I understand it's a long ride back to your place. It's much safer if he stays here overnight for observation. I want to check him again in the morning to make sure everything in that arm is working like it should. He's none too happy about that, either." He glanced at his watch and grinned. "He's not going to be complaining much longer, though. I gave him something so he'd rest. He's asking for you. You'd better go see him before he drifts off to Happyland."

The doctor took her out in the hall and pointed to the room where Ben had been settled. He was already looking drowsy when she joined him seconds later. His gaze had been fixed on the doorway, waiting for her. He looked relieved when she appeared. Then he made a face.

"This is dumb. All I've got is an injured arm that will be as good as new in a couple of days. So what am I doing lying here like a helpless baby?"

"Mending. Go to sleep."

"Come here." He held out a hand.

Cathryn hung back in the doorway. Then, angry with herself for her hesitation, she crossed the room and seated herself on the chair beside his bed. His hand reached for hers, closing snugly around her fingers.

"You're an amazing lady," he told her warmly. "Thanks for playing paramedic."

"You're welcome."

His thumb lightly stroked her knuckles. "Don't get bored and decide to take a walk while you wait," he reminded her. "Be here for me when I wake up."

"I remember." Why was it so important to him?

"I'll try not to be too long."

His eyes closed, his features relaxing. She gazed at his lean face, hating the suspicions that were chasing through her mind. What was the matter with her? This was Ben, the man she loved. She could have cleared up the whole thing with one simple question. But she didn't. She didn't ask him about his blood type. Why? Because she was afraid he might not tell her the truth?

His hand no longer clung to hers. She thought he was asleep. But a moment later he whispered her name. She leaned toward him to hear his mumbled words.

"Couldn't bring myself to do that to you. I had a commitment. Still do. But I couldn't do it."

He was under the influence now of whatever the doctor had given him. He didn't know what he was saying, she told herself.

That's what she wanted to believe. *Desperately* wanted to believe. But as she sat there watching him finally sink into a peaceful sleep, she couldn't deny her mounting conviction that something wasn't right. Nor her fear that the man on the bed was suddenly a stranger.

Oh, this was insane! She couldn't go on waiting here all day with these ugly, disloyal doubts. She had to settle it. There was only one way to do that. She had to go back to the cabin, find that letter and learn exactly what Ben Adams had written about his blood type.

The head nurse satisfied her concern about leaving Ben when she found her at the nurse's station down the hall.

"He doesn't want to admit it, but his body suffered a trauma with that injury. He'll be out for hours. Best thing in the world for him."

"If he should wake up and ask, tell him I've gone home to check on our dogs and to bring him some things he'll need for the night."

With any luck, Cathryn thought, she could get to the cabin and back before he ever realized she had left. She didn't want to renege on her promise to him, but she had to *know*.

THERE WAS NO SIGN of Angel when she reached the cabin, but some of the dry food they had left for her in the dishes on the porch had been eaten. The dog was probably with her puppies.

Cathryn was sorry she wasn't around. She would have welcomed her company in this anxious moment. She hated going into the cabin by herself. The place that had been so warm and friendly suddenly seemed alien to her.

She knew what she really feared when she went inside. Not the silent, empty cabin itself but what she might learn here in the next few minutes.

Summoning her courage, she went into her bedroom and knelt on the floor. Her suitcase was under the bed. She hadn't touched it since the day she had arrived. She dragged it out and opened it. Its contents had been unpacked and placed in the closet and chest of drawers. All but the bundle of letters Meredith had given her that night in St. Louis.

Cathryn sorted through them, finding the particular letter she wanted. The others she returned to the suitcase, which she pushed back under the bed. Then she settled on the side of the bed, the letter in her lap.

How silly. Her hands were trembling, as if she were about to consult a document that would decide the rest of her life. An ordinary letter. She picked it up, removed the three pages inside the envelope and began to read.

A moment later, heartsick, she stuffed the sheets back in the envelope. It was true. The man who had written this letter had clearly described his blood type as AB negative. And the man in the hospital back in Lovejoy had insisted he was an O positive. There would have been no reason for him to lie about it.

But they were the same man. Weren't they? Then what did it mean?

All the way from Lovejoy, on that endless drive to the cabin, Cathryn had permitted herself to do nothing but pray that her memory was wrong. She could no longer do that. She had to deal with them now, all those suspicious little things she had chosen to overlook in her growing love for Ben.

They had been there from the start, those things. Hadn't Sourdough Annie sensed there was something not right about Ben and tried to tell her so? Even Angel in the beginning had distrusted him.

And lately... lately there had been other troubling signs. That day at the pool he told he had a Choctaw ancestor. Only afterward had she remembered that the Choctaw were a Louisiana tribe. Then just last night he had fixed blackened fish hot with pepper, boasting it was his specialty. A Cajun dish. Louisiana again, and Louisiana spelled danger for her.

Oh, this was ridiculous. These weren't reasons to condemn him. Or even reasons to suspect he might come from the New Orleans area. He didn't have an accent, did he?

*A lot of people from New Orleans don't have accents,* gibed a cruel little voice inside her head. *What's it going to take to convince you that he isn't what he pretends to be?*

"Evidence," she insisted out loud. "Hard evidence."

But from where?

*Maybe one of those places he was reluctant to have you go,* taunted the voice. *Like Lovejoy. He never wanted you out of his sight in Lovejoy. Even in the hospital he wanted you to stay close to him. Why? What was he worried about? That you might learn something you weren't supposed to learn? And Bearpaw. You never did get to Bearpaw. He had all kinds of excuses for you not going there.*

Bearpaw, Cathryn decided, shoving the letter carelessly into the drawer of the bedside table as she got to her feet. She would drive immediately into Bearpaw. There must be someone there who could answer her questions.

Her determination was strong. But there was no satisfaction in it, only a deepening misery.

BEARPAW WASN'T MUCH of a community—a small collection of clapboard buildings, some of them dilapidated, strung out along a narrow valley. The tiny wooden post office, with pots of flourishing geraniums out front and elk antlers mounted above the prominent zip code over the door, was the most presentable structure. Cathryn decided it was her best bet.

The frizzy-haired woman behind the counter inside looked bored and impatient. "Help you?"

Cathryn smiled at her guilelessly. "I'm trying to locate a friend somewhere in the area. I think his mail is delivered here. Ben Adams. Do you know him?"

For a moment she thought the woman wouldn't answer her. Her mouth had tightened in exasperation. She finally nodded, offering reluctantly, "I'll tell you the same thing I told the guy who stopped here a while back asking about Ben."

"Who?"

"I don't know. Somebody from the pipeline, I guess, wanting directions to Ben's cabin. Which I didn't give him, just like I won't give them to you."

"But why?"

"Because they wouldn't do you any good. The place is deserted. Ben is somewhere down in Anchorage for a few weeks while we hold his mail. And don't ask me where he's staying, because he didn't say."

"I see," Cathryn said in a small voice. So he had lied to her about the mailbox here being moved to Lovejoy. Everything had been a lie.

The woman leaned on the counter, grinning at her without humor. "With all these friends of his turning up, Ben is turning out to be a real surprise. I wouldn't have figured him as the popular type. Not the way he always kept to himself, hiding behind that beard of his, like it was just to cover the scar on his chin."

Cathryn didn't respond to that. She had learned all she needed to know. Everything she had prayed not to hear.

She thanked the woman, left the post office and drove numbly away in the Jeep. She didn't go far. She was too blind with pain to manage the road. Once Bearpaw was behind her, she pulled over on the shoulder and sat there behind the wheel in a swelling despair.

Fear soon invaded her wretchedness. A chilling truth she could no longer avoid. The evidence was too blatant. He was not Ben Adams. Then who was the man she had been intimately living with? How had he come to replace the real Ben Adams? And why?

But there was only one explanation for his presence here. He had to be one of Red Quinn's people. No one else would have a reason to keep his identity a secret from her. Her enemy had somehow traced her and placed his man here even before her arrival in Alaska. The false Ben had known all along exactly who she was. Ironic that she had convinced herself the wilderness would be safe for her, when all this time—

Wait a minute. If he was Red Quinn's hired assassin, then why hadn't he killed her immediately? Why had he continued his elaborate masquerade?

*Simple,* mocked the voice inside her head. *He fell for you. Remember what he told you in the hospital just a few hours ago?*

Cathryn did remember those mumbled words he had spoken under the influence of the sedative. *Couldn't bring myself to do that to you. I had a commitment. Still do. But I couldn't do it.* She hadn't understood those phrases then. Now they made perfect sense.

This was the reason for the demon that haunted him. The reason for that elusive quality of intenseness she had glimpsed in him from time to time. Even the reason why she had sensed a resentment in him that first day. It all fit.

*I had a commitment. Still do.*

Which meant that sooner or later he would have to kill her. No matter what she meant to him, he would do it. Red Quinn's kind never let anything stand in their way, not even love.

*But he never did actually say he loved you, did he, Cathryn? No matter what passion or tenderness the two of you shared, including that sweet promise last night about wanting you for his mail-order bride, he never once said it.*

She couldn't believe it. She couldn't believe that she was no more than a sexual infatuation to him. That there was no more meaning to their relationship than that. That when he'd tired of her, he would kill her.

*Can't believe it or don't want to believe it?*

In the end it didn't matter either way, she thought dismally. She couldn't take a chance on it. She couldn't risk her life, because if something happened to her, the only person who really mattered now would be alone in the world. She had to get out.

The need for urgent action helped her to put the anguish of her shattered faith behind her. Concentrating on the details of her escape, she swung the Jeep back on the road and sped toward the cabin.

It would take her only a few minutes to pack her things, and then she would return to Lovejoy. There was an airfield there. She would hire a plane to fly her to Anchorage. It didn't matter if she used one of her credit cards now. By evening she would be aboard a jet and on her way out of Alaska. Never mind her destination. She would figure that out on her way to Anchorage.

Whatever happened, she had to be gone from Lovejoy before he got suspicious waiting at the hospital and decided to come looking for her. It would all work out. She still had plenty of time.

But that time had already run out for Cathryn when she emerged from the Jeep in the clearing and hurried toward the cabin. A figure who had been sitting in the shadows on the porch stood and came down the steps to meet her. He wore a hard, demanding expression on his face, and his jet black eyes glittered dangerously. Her heart dropped at the sight of him.

# Chapter Ten

"Where the devil have you been?" he confronted her.

His appearance at the cabin was the last thing she expected. She was stunned by it. But it was imperative that she behave as though nothing was wrong, whatever massive effort it cost her. He mustn't guess she was on to him.

Cathryn thought fast and came up with a weak but acceptable excuse for her absence. "I ran down to Percy to see Annie. I wanted to ask her to look out for Angel and her puppies before I drove back to Lovejoy. You know, just in case there turned out to be complications with your arm, and we had to stay on there for a while."

To her relief, he bought her story and relaxed. "You and those mutts. You had me thinking the worst when you weren't here. What am I going to do with you, McLean?"

She had once been touched by his repeated concern for her. Now she knew it for what it was—a fear that she would get away from him. Before he could question her further, she quickly reversed their roles, playing out her own concern.

"Ben, what are you doing here? You're supposed to be in the hospital."

"And you were supposed to stick close. I woke up, and when they told me you'd come back here, I decided not to wait."

"You mean they released you?"

"Uh, let's just say I discharged myself."

"That was foolish of you. What if there *are* complications with the arm?"

"The arm is okay, but if there are problems with it, I'll go back. Hey, you're worse than that drill sergeant who calls herself a head nurse. Any more questions?"

"Yes," she said, stalling for time, knowing that she had to figure out some other way now to make her escape. "How did you get here?"

"Bought a lift from some kid in his jalopy. Come on inside."

The last thing she wanted to do was go inside the cabin with him, but if she refused, it would make him suspicious. Besides, he still looked a little shaky, as though he could use a chair. His condition might be useful to her.

"Yes," she agreed, leading the way into the house, "I think you need to sit down. Or better still, lie down."

But he was in no mood to do either. Once inside, he paced around the living room a few times and then came to stand in front of her. He was too close. She was suddenly afraid he would try to touch her, hold her with his good arm, kiss her. There was a perverse something inside her that actually wanted that. Still longed for it. A wiser side warned her to back away.

She held her position and waited tensely. His gaze, a little puzzled now, searched her face. "Cathryn, we have to talk."

A temptation, she thought. An opportunity to do what she yearned to do. Challenge him with her discovery, ask him his version of the truth. But she didn't dare. She reminded herself that he was dangerous.

She eyed his bandaged arm, noticed that he was weaving a little now on his feet. This was her chance.

"Fine," she said with a little smile. "But not until after you lie down and rest. You're in no shape to do anything but go back to sleep. It's either do that in your own bed, or I'm taking you back to the hospital."

He needed to talk to her, he thought. Needed to explain things. And he didn't want to wait, because there was a kind of remoteness about her that he didn't understand. It worried him. But he couldn't argue with her. Damn it, he was feeling dopey again with the lingering effects of whatever that doctor had given him.

"Maybe for a little while," he agreed. "Then we talk."

"Right," she promised.

She went with him into his room, made sure that he stretched out on the bed.

"Just one thing," he said before he closed his eyes. "What did I say to you in the hospital before I drifted off? I don't think I was making sense by then."

"I don't remember."

He nodded, satisfied. "Okay. So what are you going to do while I nap?"

"Maybe take a walk down to the lake, check on Angel and the puppies. Don't worry. Go to sleep."

She stayed by the bed for a few minutes, making sure that he did drift off. When his even breathing told her that he was asleep, she went into the living room. Her nerves were in a bad way by now, but she didn't dare to leave until she was sure he wouldn't wake up and stop her before she could escape.

She waited for a few tense moments, and then she slipped back into his room to check on him. He hadn't stirred. Trying not to look at that virile face, afraid she would weaken in her resolve, she backed carefully out of the room.

She never even glanced in the direction of her own room. She would have to abandon her things now. She couldn't risk rousing him with the activity of her packing. She had her purse and the car keys, and that was all that mattered.

Time, she thought as she crept out of the cabin. She was losing valuable time, and it was a long way to Lovejoy. Once off the porch, she hurried across the yard to the Jeep.

His bedroom was at the back of the cabin. Even so, she worried he might hear the sound of the engine. She couldn't take that chance. This edge of the yard, where the Jeep was parked, sloped away down the track and into the woods. Maybe if she released the brake and shifted into neutral, the Jeep would roll far enough along the lane that, when she started the engine, it wouldn't be heard at the house.

She climbed as silently as possible behind the wheel and tried it. It didn't work. The Jeep sat there. She got out and cast a swift glance in the direction of the cabin, fearing that she would see his face at the window. Nothing. But her heart was racing by now.

Putting her hands against the door frame, Cathryn summoned all her energy and began to shove. No use. She tried again. This time the Jeep began to move, gathering such surprising momentum on the incline that she almost lost her footing before she clambered inside and took control of the wheel.

Seconds later, with the woods swallowing the vehicle, she found it safe enough to close the door properly and start the engine. Then, with one fast look over her shoulder, she was off down the winding track.

She tried not to think about the man she was leaving behind her, tried to concentrate on nothing but her driving.

But by now she could feel the tears of sorrow and betrayal threatening to fall.

She was within a half mile of the main road when her luck failed her. The engine began to sputter and labor. She attempted to feed it more gas, but a second later it abruptly died. Her effort to restart it, as she furiously pumped the accelerator, proved useless. Then her eye cut to the fuel gauge. It registered empty.

Cathryn slapped the wheel in frustration. In all her frantic, long-distance chasing, she had neglected to stop and fill the tank. Had never even thought to check the gauge. How could she have been so stupid? Fear, of course. Fear had blocked out everything else.

She sat there for a long moment with the silence of the forest around her, appalled by her situation. She searched her mind for an answer to her dilemma. And then she remembered.

The foot trail to the ghost town. The shortcut that Sourdough Annie had described that first morning. It was within easy reach, just below the turnoff into the track. Annie had told her to come to her if she was ever in need, and Annie had a truck. A truck that could take Cathryn to Lovejoy.

She was out of the Jeep in a flash and rushing along the lane, purse in hand. As a precaution, she had snatched the keys from the ignition. She flung them off in the undergrowth before she reached the main road.

She found the path without delay. But as she trotted along its length through the thick evergreen forest, she worried. What if Annie wasn't there? What could she do then? Where could she hide from the man she had fled? Because there was no question about it. Once he learned she was gone, he would go to any lengths to overtake her and get her back.

HE SLEPT, but it was not a deep sleep. His mind was too restless for that, fighting the stuff they had given him. He had resisted the drug back at the hospital, too, wanting to stay alert and eventually losing the battle. But that had been in Lovejoy, where the man in the Land Rover might still be hanging around, a potential threat to Cathryn.

They were both safely back at the cabin now. No reason for his uneasiness here. He didn't understand it. Whatever the explanation, he was fully awake again less than a half hour later. His arm was aching, but he ignored that, grateful that the maddening drowsiness had finally faded.

He lay there on the bed, wishing Cathryn were here beside him. Preferably naked and with his arms wrapped around her, pressing her close. Well, one arm anyway. Maybe that could be arranged. But not until after he had talked to her as he had promised to do.

No more delays. The time had come to tell her everything. All he could hope was that she would forgive him and accept the situation. And if she didn't... He refused to think about that.

Aware now of the prolonged silence in the cabin, he roused himself and sat up on the edge of the bed. Cathryn must still be at the lake or with the dogs. He was impatient for her return. No, he thought with a frown, more than just impatient. Anxious. He hadn't liked her manner with him before his nap, had sensed that something wasn't right. Probably nothing at all. Still . . .

Restless again, he left his bedroom and went into her room across the hall. The window over her bedside table had a view of the path to the lake. Before he went out looking for her, he wanted to see if she was on her way back to the cabin. There was no sign of her on the path.

He was stepping back from the window when he noticed it—the corner of a letter sticking out from the table's single drawer. The drawer must have been hastily closed, catching the letter before it was completely inside.

There was enough of the corner showing to reveal most of its return address. It was the address of the post-office box Ben Adams kept in Bearpaw.

The letters to Meredith McLean, he thought. Cathryn must have brought them to Alaska with her. Must have been rereading this particular letter just recently. Why? A gut-level instinct told him that he'd better find out.

Snatching open the drawer, he scooped up the letter, perched on the edge of the bed and began to read. Seconds later he had the explanation for his nagging uneasiness.

She knew. She knew he couldn't be Ben Adams. This business of the blood types had given him away.

This would never have happened if he hadn't surrendered to her determination to bring him to the hospital in Lovejoy. But he had decided in the end that he'd better have reliable medical treatment, or he might not be in any shape to look out for her. He had risked Lovejoy, and it had been a big mistake.

Lovejoy meant a possible enemy in the form of the man in the Land Rover. That was why he had wanted her to stick close, why he had been alarmed when he'd awakened and learned she had left the hospital. And now—

Damn it, he should have told her everything instead of worrying that he might lose her with the truth. He shouldn't have let her find out this way. She must be thinking the worst about him.

And that's when it struck him like a fist in the stomach. Of course she was thinking the worst. And if she was convinced *he* was the enemy, she wouldn't hang around to ask questions. She would be running, just as she had run before.

*Cathryn! Where are you?*

Dropping the letter on the bed, he surged to his feet and sped toward the front door. He had already anticipated the grim result before he hit the open porch, his gaze sweeping the yard. The Jeep was gone!

He didn't hesitate, didn't even think about the impossibility of recovering her on foot. He pounded across the clearing and down the track with an impractical aim of reaching the main road and somehow catching another lift back into Lovejoy. Because that must be where she was headed. Lovejoy would offer her the fastest transportation out of here. And danger could be waiting for her in Lovejoy.

His lungs were on fire when he rounded a bend and spotted the stalled Jeep just ahead of him. He sprinted to the vehicle with the hope of finding Cathryn inside. She was gone, taking the keys with her. He grabbed the spare key from the glove box, but quickly realized that the gas tank was empty.

Taking a moment to recover his wind, he stared off into the forest. Where could she be headed now? Probably down to Annie's shack at the ghost town. The woman didn't like him, and she had a pickup. She would willingly help Cathryn to get away.

They would probably be on their way to Lovejoy before he could reach the shack. He realized the madness now of trying to overtake her on foot. And the Jeep was useless to him. Or maybe not. He suddenly remembered the can of gas for the boat on the lake, enough to get the Jeep to a service station. There was still a hope of intercepting her.

He took off up the lane, his long legs carrying him back to the clearing. He refused to think about the difficulty of managing the Jeep with an injured arm. All that mattered was Cathryn, who could be charging straight into death. He had to get her back. The loss that had driven him away from

New Orleans months ago would be nothing compared to his grief now if anything happened to her.

THE ANCIENT PICKUP truck was willing but maddeningly slow as it rattled toward Lovejoy. Cathryn, clinging to the passenger side of the shabby interior, tried not to be impatient with the delay. She had to remember that, without the Jeep, he couldn't possibly follow her. She was safe. But she knew she wouldn't feel easy until she was on a plane to Anchorage.

Annie, who was hunched over the wheel as if to coax more speed out of the old pickup, had been silent for some miles. Finally, without turning her head, she expressed her concern.

"Look, girlie, maybe instead of the airfield, you ought to be going to the cops."

Cathryn hadn't told her friend everything, just enough to make her understand the urgency of the situation. Annie didn't realize what her suggestion involved.

"No," she said sharply. She had trusted the police before, much to her regret. "Please, all I want to do is get away."

"Well, maybe you're right. Lovejoy's version of law enforcement isn't too great."

There was silence again in the cab as they bumped over the rough road. Cathryn leaned her head back against the seat, making an effort not to think about the man she was leaving behind. Impossible. His image was still strong in her mind. And if she was honest about it, in her heart, as well.

She couldn't help it. The tender moments they had shared were still vibrant, still very much a part of her. They were also a mockery, making her angry with herself for cherishing them. Because behind all the gentleness and passion were deceit and the treachery of a killer.

But no matter what he was, she couldn't simply stop loving him. Just turn off all her emotions like a faucet. That was the worst part of all this desolation that was clawing at her.

Her eyes were brimming now with the tears that had been threatening her since Bearpaw. She made an effort to squeeze them back, not wanting Annie to see how much she was hurting.

But Annie was no fool. "You went and fell for him, didn't you?" she growled softly.

Cathryn nodded miserably and dug in her purse for a tissue.

"Yeah, I could see that yesterday when we talked on the street. You had a glow that wasn't there the first time."

"I'll get over him," she said, mopping at her eyes.

She had to, she promised herself fiercely. She had to remember that he was the enemy now.

Annie didn't turn her head, but she removed one of her gnarled hands from the wheel and awkwardly patted Cathryn's knee. She appreciated her friend's comforting gesture.

THE YOUNG MAN with the ponytail, who stood behind the counter of the tiny building that was more shack than air terminal, shook his head in regret.

"Can't do it. Our twin engine already took off with a load for Fairbanks, and the Cessna out there is laid up for repairs. Won't be ready before tomorrow, if then."

Cathryn stared at him in dismay. She should have known it wouldn't be easy. "And that's it? No other plane?"

"Sorry."

She knew that Annie, standing beside her, could feel her desperation. "I'd take you to Anchorage myself, but I wouldn't trust that heap of mine to get us that far."

"A car rental?" Cathryn asked hopefully.

Annie shrugged helplessly. "Not in these parts, girl."

"But there must be some way out of here."

The young man leaned on the counter. "There's always the excursion train," he offered.

"What train?" Cathryn demanded. "Where?"

He explained it to her cheerfully. "It's a special they run for tourists on the old logging route. Comes down from Denali and lays over here for a couple of hours at the Love-joy station so the passengers can take in the local sights and shop for souvenirs. They've got all these cars from the fifties they restored, even play big-band music on board. Real retro stuff, and the scenery is great."

None of this was important to Cathryn. "Where does it go from here?"

"Valdez. No problem from there to Anchorage. You've got the ferry or all kinds of float planes to choose from."

"I take it," Annie said, "you wouldn't be suggesting this if you didn't know that the train is due at the station."

"I keep up with the schedule. We sometimes make connections for our own passengers." He glanced at the clock over the door. "Train's there now, should be there for another half hour. Plenty of time to make it."

It wasn't an ideal means of escape, but it appeared to be her only option. There was one advantage. She could lose herself among the tourists on the train and again at Valdez, making her trail that much harder to trace. She turned to Annie.

"Do you know how to get to the station?"

"Like it was home. Let's go."

Annie urged the maximum speed out of the old pickup as they left the airfield and headed for the center of town. Cathryn leaned forward in the seat, anxiously waiting for a glimpse of the depot and praying that the train was still there.

They swung at last into the station yard. To her relief, the gleaming silver cars, streamlined versions from another era, stood on the tracks. Annie braked the pickup just inside the lot.

"You hop out and get your ticket while I find a parking spot. I'll see you on the platform."

Cathryn climbed from the truck. A green Land Rover pulled in behind them as she hurried off to the old-fashioned station window.

The other passengers, noisy with talk and laughter, their arms loaded with their purchases from Lovejoy, began to return to the train when Cathryn joined Annie a moment later, her ticket in hand. The music of Glenn Miller poured from a loudspeaker, interrupted by the voice of a guide describing the spectacular scenery the tourists would see on the next portion of the trip.

On the platform there was a bustling holiday mood, to which Cathryn was oblivious. Her only thought was to get away. She had wanted the train to wait for her. Now she was nervously eager for it to depart, impatient with the delay. Annie, aware of her tenseness, tried to distract her.

"Look over there," she said, nudging Cathryn. "That character we saw chasing up and down the street yesterday and still wearing those dopey slippers. Wonder if he ever found what he was hunting for. Got himself a ticket, too, I see, so I guess he'll be joining the party on board."

Cathryn glanced without interest in the direction of the thick-waisted man down the platform. He was busy unwrapping a stick of gum. There was nothing harried about him today. He looked totally relaxed. She turned her attention back to Annie.

"I hate to ask this, Annie, when you've done so much for me. But the dogs, Angel and her puppies... If there's any way you could look out for them, because after this I don't know whether *he* will. But not," she added hastily, "if there's any risk to you about it."

"I'll manage to see to it somehow," Annie promised her.

"I'll try to write to you. That is, if it ever turns out to be safe to write."

"You're gonna be okay, girlie," Annie assured her. "Once this train pulls out, you'll be in the clear."

[Illegible faded text from previous page bleeding through]

# Chapter Eleven

Frank Tesler was careful to maintain an expression of boredom on his broad face. But underneath that bland mask, he was charged with excitement as he strolled down the platform.

Cathryn McLean at last! And this time there was no mistake about it. Her hair was shorter and a lighter blond than in the photograph they had given him, but it was her, all right. And the beauty of it was, she had fallen right into his lap.

Until mere minutes ago, an easy score had seemed an impossibility to him. Hanging around Lovejoy had driven him crazy, especially after he had lost her on the street yesterday. He had had enough of it by this afternoon. To hell with that doctor and his warnings.

Convinced that the infection in his blisters was beginning to clear up, that his feet would be all right, Frank had climbed into the rented Land Rover and headed out of town. He needed to get to that cabin. He needed to close in on his target.

He couldn't have driven more than three blocks when the pickup, on its way to the depot, had shot by him. He had immediately recognized her in the passenger seat. He didn't have to go after her. She had come to him. What a break!

Turning the Land Rover, he had chased the pickup, followed her into the station, bought his own ticket for the excursion. He didn't care where she was going or why. And he wasn't worried about the tough-looking old woman who had brought her here. Cathryn McLean had purchased a single ticket. She would be alone on the train. And vulnerable.

Frank stole another quick glance along the platform to make sure of his target. Pretty, he thought. Much prettier than her picture. A lot of that had to do with her smile. A pity he would have to end all of that. But business was business.

She was involved in a long goodbye with her friend. She wasn't going to disappear on him this time. He could safely leave her for a few minutes. He needed to check out the interior of the train before it got too crowded, try to decide just when and where it would be best to manage the hit.

Ticket in hand, Frank climbed aboard the end car. He was managing just fine now in the slippers, not drawing any particular attention to himself.

The other passengers were beginning to collect on the train, settling themselves with their packages. The big-band music continued to play. Murals and framed movie posters, all from the forties and fifties, decorated the walls.

It was not a long train, he discovered as he shuffled from one end to the other. No more than four cars. The two in front were dining cars. Waiters were already setting up for the supper that would be served shortly after they were underway.

Frank found himself back in the club car where he had started. He had one last place to investigate. The club car was also a dome car. A narrow stairway curved up to the observation level. No one seemed to be going up there. He found out why when he reached the top.

A meshed accordion gate had been mounted in the entrance to the deck. There was a padlock on the gate to secure it to a metal ring in the wall. For some reason they were sealing off this part of the car, though at the moment the padlock was open, the gate folded back.

Frank understood the situation as he moved up the aisle between the rows of seats. The glass in one of the great curving windows overhead had been shattered. A skinny teenager in coveralls was pulling the remaining shards of glass away from the metal framework. He paused when he became aware of Frank's presence.

"Dome is off limits for the rest of the trip, sir."

Frank smiled at him amiably. "Looks like somebody might have been partying a little too wildly."

"Naw. A rockfall along the side of the tracks down from Denali. Chunk went right through the glass. Now we gotta keep the dome closed off until we can get a replacement pane."

"Sorry. I didn't know. I'll get out of here, then."

"Yeah, I gotta finish clearing up the last of this so I can be off the train before it pulls out again."

Frank retreated. When he reached the gate, he made sure that the young maintenance man's attention was on his work. Then he snatched the key out of the bottom of the padlock, pocketed it and went down the curving stairway. At the bottom he stood against the wall, out of the way of the boarding passengers, and waited to see if any problem would result from his action. He didn't think so. The kid in the coveralls didn't look overly bright.

Ducking his head to a window, Frank checked the platform outside. Cathryn McLean was just parting from the old woman with an emotional hug. He pulled back from the glass and took a moment to deliberate.

Killing her on a crowded train was going to be one hell of a problem. But he didn't want to wait for Valdez. He didn't want to risk her slipping away from him again. It had to be here and now. Besides, the challenge in the situation pleased him.

Not the gun concealed in his jacket, he decided. Too noisy, even with the speakers blaring all that crap. He was wearing a fabric belt. It would make a perfect garrote. He had powerful hands. Came from those years when he had boxed. All he had to do was get close enough. The trick would be to lure her up into the dome, where they could be alone. He'd manage it somehow.

A second later he spotted the legs of the maintenance man as he started down the stairway. Frank leaned idly against the wall and pretended to be interested in the brochure that had accompanied his ticket. But he checked out the teenager with quick, stealthy glances.

The rest of the kid appeared, looking puzzled as he searched his pockets for the missing padlock key. His concern was only momentary. The speakers announced that the train was about to depart. Frank understood the young man's shrug. The gate had been safely closed behind him, the padlock snapped in place. No time to worry about the key.

The kid left the train, brushing by Cathryn McLean as she boarded. Frank was busy consulting the brochure when she passed him in the narrow corridor. Seconds later, with a single lurch, the train was underway. He wandered after her into the club car. He was already feeling elated.

THE JEEP HURTLED down the highway to Lovejoy, squealing around the curves at reckless speeds. He didn't care about the risk, ignored the painful stress to his injured arm that had to manage the gears while his left arm handled the wheel. All that mattered was reaching Cathryn.

The airfield, he thought. She would probably try for a plane out of here. He would go there first.

He was nearing the turning to the airfield when he saw it. A faded red pickup truck approaching in the other lane. He recognized the rusting vehicle. He had seen it parked behind the shack in the ghost town.

He knew Annie wouldn't stop. She would gun the pickup and sweep on by him. He made a lightning decision. He smacked the brake with his foot. Then, while the Jeep was still in the process of grinding to a halt, he whipped the wheel over to the left. The vehicle skidded sideways across the highway, blocking both lanes.

The pickup, within inches of a collision, screeched to a stop. Its driver stuck her gray head out of the window and blasted him with her curses. He wasn't surprised to see she was alone in the cab. But he was worried about Cathryn's whereabouts when he burst from the Jeep and raced around it to confront Annie on the other side.

"I'm not afraid of you, Adams!" she yelled at him defiantly from the cab. "Or whoever you are! And get your damn car out of my way before I plow it off the road!"

"Not before you answer a couple of urgent questions," he informed her grimly as he approached the window.

"I don't have to tell you anything! And you don't have a right to stop me like this!"

"Wanna bet?"

He reached for his wallet in his back pocket, aware that his arm was throbbing. He had wrenched it pretty severely when he'd shoved the wheel over like that. But it wasn't important. He found his identification and thrust it in under Annie's nose. She gazed at it suspiciously for a long minute, then at him, then back at the badge and card.

"You're a cop?" she muttered in disbelief.

"New Orleans PD on extended leave."

"Says you. How do I know this is genuine?"

"For now you trust your gut instinct. And if you care at all about Cathryn, you trust it fast and without an explanation. Where did you take her? To the airfield?"

Annie spent a few precious seconds coming to a decision. She finally shook her head. "No plane available. She's on the excursion train to Valdez. Pulled out just a couple of minutes ago."

Gone, he thought, his insides tightening with alarm. But just how bad was her departure?

"Now let's test your powers of observation," he said swiftly. "Let's see if you can tell me who might be on that train with her."

He briefly described the Land Rover and the man who had driven it. Even before she answered him, he could see by the expression on her face that the worst had happened.

"Yeah, he went aboard. But he wasn't interested in her."

"Annie, we're both going to have to believe my own instinct now when I tell you that this bastard is plenty interested in her. I think he's a professional assassin, and I think her life won't be worth anything if he manages to corner her."

"What are we going to do?"

Annie's news was a blow that left him feeling sick. But personal feelings were an obstacle to helping Cathryn. He thrust them aside, allowing his professionalism to take charge. "I'm going after that train."

"How?"

"The road south of town runs parallel with the rail tracks, doesn't it?"

"Yeah, for about twenty miles or so. Then they separate for good. But that train's got a head start. How can you hope to catch it before—wait a minute. There was someone on the platform saying that, on account of the scenery being so gorgeous in this next section, the train would be going slower so the passengers could enjoy the views. So, if that's true, maybe..."

He didn't let her finish. He was already backing away toward the Jeep. Every second now was critical. "Go back to the station, Annie," he shouted to her. "Do whatever you have to to get them to stop that train!"

Within minutes he was on the other side of Lovejoy, blessing the Jeep's reliability as it tore down the highway. There was no other traffic. He was alone on the road. That much was an advantage anyway, permitting him a maximum speed on the straightaways.

The railroad tracks were just off to his right, and on the other side of the tracks was a narrow river in a deep gorge. He checked the odometer on the dash. He must have traveled almost ten miles south of Lovejoy. No sign of the train yet. He refused to believe he wouldn't overtake it.

His service revolver. What he wouldn't give to have his service revolver with him. But he'd refused to carry a gun after New Orleans, couldn't bear even to touch one. Not that a weapon would do him much good if he didn't reach that train, managed somehow to board it.

He had driven this route only once before. He tried to remember just where the road and the tracks diverged. A bridge. That was it. Eventually the highway took a sharp right across a bridge that passed over both the railroad and the river. Then the highway continued west while the railroad disappeared straight into the wilderness of mountains and forest.

He had to intercept the train before that bridge, or he would lose it. And that meant losing Cathryn. But where the hell was it? He should have sighted it by now. He'd even expected to find it stopped on the tracks. Annie ought to have had plenty of time to reach someone in authority, convince them to halt the train. She must have encountered problems. He was on his own.

The train. Where was the—wait a minute. Was that silver flashing through the grove of aspen up ahead? He peered hopefully in the direction of the trees, but it wasn't until the Jeep cleared the grove that he knew for certain. The train at last!

The Jeep was already rocketing along the highway. He urged it to an even greater speed. The train was still on the move, but the Jeep surged forward, quickly closing the gap. He slowed when he came abreast of the cars, matching the leisurely pace of the train.

He wondered what his chances were for signaling someone on board, getting them to understand that this was an emergency and that they needed to stop. He laid on his horn, punching it repeatedly. And he prayed.

*Cathryn, be all right.*


THE MOURNFUL SOUND of Harry James's trumpet wailing through the speakers was a suitable counterpoint to Cathryn's mood. She was alone in the club car. The last of the passengers had drifted forward to the dining cars, where, according to the announcement, they would be served a supper as lavish as the views from the windows.

She had eaten nothing during this long day, but she was no more interested in food than she was in the scenery. The Alaskan landscape from her window had never been more breathtaking. A sinking sun gilded the snow fields capping the mountains and turned the countless waterfalls into liquid gold.

None of these sights made an impression on her. She scarcely noticed them. It was something else she saw in the glass of the window. The smiling face of the man who had called himself Ben Adams. He was the enemy, and she would never see him again. Then why did that sexy grin keep haunting her?

And why was the train crawling? Why couldn't it go faster? She needed to put distance between herself and the man she had fled, as much distance as possible. Hopefully, before this time tomorrow, thousands of miles of distance.

Harry James was interrupted by another announcement. Something about a certain glacier they would soon be passing. The big-band music resumed. This time it was something more cheerful. It did nothing to help Cathryn's mood. She continued to gaze absently at the view.

It must have been less than a minute later when she spotted it on the highway that paralleled the tracks. A familiar dark red vehicle. A Jeep Wrangler running with the train. It couldn't be real! She must have conjured it up along with his face.

Pulse racing, Cathryn strained toward the window. She couldn't catch a glimpse of the driver, couldn't even be sure it was the Jeep she knew. The growth between the road and the rail line kept interfering with her view. Dear God, what if it *was* him? She *had* to know.

"Frustrating, isn't it?"

Cathryn jumped, startled by the voice behind her. She swung around and met the affable gaze of the man in the slippers. Where had he come from? She could have sworn she was alone in the club car.

"I beg your pardon?"

"Trying to get an unobstructed view of the scenery," he said cheerfully. "It's impossible down here with all the trees in the way. That's why I've been in the dome. Perfect views from up there on both sides. You can see everything right over the tops of the trees."

"This is a dome car?"

"You must have missed the stairway on your way in. It's just off the far end back there."

He turned and moved a few steps along the aisle, pointing in the direction of the stairway. She could see his bare feet in the scuffs and now understood their necessity. Painful-looking blisters covered both of his heels.

He looked back at her. His round, friendly face was all smiles. "Great scenery at the top."

Cathryn didn't hesitate. This was her opportunity to get a clear look at the Jeep out there. She left her seat and started to scurry up the aisle. He moved aside for her.

"I'll excuse myself," he said. "Time I was putting on the feed bag in the dining car."

"Yes, thank you," she murmured.

She reached the curving stairway and quickly mounted the metal treads. She hesitated briefly at the entrance to the deck, aware of the cool air that was rushing in from overhead where one of the large panes was missing. It must be all right to be up here, though. The gate was open, and the man in the slippers had been here. All that mattered were the uninterrupted views he had promised.

She went far forward, away from the stream of air, and squeezed into one of the seats. She pressed toward the glass, her anxious gaze searching the highway below.

The Jeep was still out there, its speed matching that of the train's. She couldn't see the driver from this angle. She didn't have to. There was no mistaking the vehicle this time, nor the man who must be at its wheel. Never mind how he had managed to find and overtake her. He was here, and she was frantic, at a loss for action.

She heard it then. Over the noise of the train and the whistle of the wind invading the dome came the insistent blare of the Jeep's horn. He was trying to stop the train. He wanted her. What should she do?

In a panic, Cathryn started to rise from the seat with a vague aim of rushing below and finding someone in charge who would listen to her. Someone who would help. Her eyes were still on the Jeep, her feet feeling for the recessed aisle between the seating platforms when evil struck from an unexpected direction.

The lethal cord was looped over her head with such lightning violence that she had no chance to avoid it, much less understand it. Then, when she would have reacted to the vicious attack, it was too late. The twisted thing, whatever it was, was being tightened around her neck, cutting off her air.

Even as the lights exploded inside her head, followed by a blackness that started to swallow her, Cathryn was aware that she had made a terrible mistake. The man in the Jeep outside couldn't be her enemy, because her enemy, whoever he was, was right here.

Understanding brought an absurd relief. A relief that triggered her will to survive. Struggling against the fog of shock and fear, using anger as her weapon, she began to resist her assailant, body twisting, hands clawing at him.

So ferocious was her opposition that he momentarily lost his advantage. The garrote loosened, permitting her to gulp a fresh supply of oxygen. He began to drag her out into the aisle to a position where he could secure his powerful grip. She went on fighting, squirming so wildly that she finally glimpsed his face over her shoulder.

The ambush had occurred with such swiftness that she'd never detected a movement behind her, much less had the opportunity to identify her attacker. But now, even with his face contorted cruelly, the expression no longer genial, she recognized the man who had lured her to the dome. A relentless killer. But a killer with a weakness.

They were out in the aisle now, her back still to him. Finding her balance, Cathryn managed to hook one leg behind him and raised it as high as she could. She was blind to her target, but desperation made her aim true. The hard toe of her shoe came smashing down against the infected blisters on his heel, grinding against his sore, exposed flesh.

The blow was effective. Howling with anguish, he released her and staggered back against the seats. Catching herself on an armrest, she whirled to confront him. He would have recovered, come after her again. But the train, jolting over a rough stretch of track, destroyed his footing entirely. He toppled over backward, his head striking the edge of the seat platform. Then he was silent.

Cathryn, hanging on the armrest as she dragged in great mouthfuls of air, saw that he was still clutching the belt he had tried to strangle her with. He would use it on her again if she didn't get out of here. She was sure he was only stunned. He would be back on his feet within seconds.

Swinging herself upright, she tore down the aisle, scrambling over his sprawled body without a pause. Hope turned to despair when she neared the stairway. He had closed the gate, fastened it with a padlock. She was trapped with him in the dome!

Shouting through the mesh would be a useless endeavor. There was no one on the level below, no one who could hear her over the music on the speakers. The key to the padlock. He must have it on him.

Cathryn whipped around. Too late to search him. He was already regaining his senses, groping for a support to pull himself to his feet. He was strong, much stronger than her, and she had no weapon. But she wasn't simply going to give up and let him kill her. There must be some—

The missing glass in the dome! If she could pull herself up through the window overhead, reach the roof of the train, maybe he would be unable to follow her. Even if he did manage to force his much heavier body through the opening, it was a chance to avoid him. She would do anything in her desperation. It was probably suicidal crawling out there on a moving train, but she didn't let that stop her.

Cathryn was up on the seat in a flash. Climbing onto its back put her so close to the bowed glass ceiling that when she stood erect, hands gripping the edges of the metal frame to steady herself, she found her head and shoulders already through the opening.

The wind blasted her, making her hesitate. Then she heard his furious curse from somewhere close below, and it fueled her with new determination. Arms out on the roof to lever herself, she summoned all her strength and heaved herself through the opening.

One of her legs still dangled in midair. She glimpsed him up on the seat just beneath her, grabbing for her ankle to haul her back. For a second he had her, her foot clutched in his hand. She kicked wildly, and he came away with her shoe. Her leg free, she drew it quickly up through the gap.

She was fully on the roof now, body flat and clinging like a scared insect. It was a precarious position with the wind tearing at her and the train swaying drunkenly. It would have been impossible to hang on at all if she hadn't managed to emerge on the flat spine of the dome, from which the windows descended on either side like curving ribs.

She had to get off the dome, reach the almost level roofs of the other cars and work her way toward the engine. And that meant wriggling forward on her stomach foot by foot. Even crawling on hands and knees was something she didn't dare to try. The spine was too narrow.

Like a swimmer paddling in heavy seas, she pulled herself along the spine. Her breath was coming in labored gasps by the time she was finally able to lower herself from the dome to the less treacherous roof of the next car.

Only then, steadying herself against the rocking train, did Cathryn permit herself to look back across the dome. What she saw through the strands of her blond hair whipping across her face added another degree to her terror. Her enemy hadn't abandoned the pursuit. He was squeezing through the opening behind her.

HE KEPT THE JEEP level with the train and went on blaring the horn. He feared it was a wasted effort, but he had yet to think of something else to try. Damn it, where was Annie? Why wasn't she getting the train stopped so he could board it?

Ducking his head, he checked again on the train to see if his clamor might have alerted anyone on board. What he discovered with that glance made the blood go cold in his veins.

God in heaven, there was a figure out there on the roof of one of the cars. Not just any someone. It was Cathryn up there! How had she—?

He almost lost control of the Jeep then, almost ran off the road with another chilling discovery. He'd sighted a second figure emerging on the roof of the last car. There was no mistaking who it was and what he was after.

Gripping the wheel, he steadied the Jeep along with his nerves. Cathryn would die unless he could reach her. She needed him and she needed him now. A new urgency provided him with a possibility. Wild as it was, it was the only solution available.

His foot plunged the accelerator to the floor. The Jeep leapt forward, racing ahead of the train. The bridge that crossed the tracks and the river couldn't be more than a few miles down the road now. He had to beat the train to the bridge.

*Hang on, sweetheart. I'm coming.*

He had already outdistanced the train. It was behind him now. The bridge. Where was the bridge? There was a wooded bend in the road. He took it at a dangerous speed. Cleared the woods. And there was the steel span just ahead, arching over the tracks and the river gorge.

The Jeep barreled toward the sharp turn to the bridge. He slowed it just enough to make the swing. Then he was on the approach and climbing. Only yards to go, and here was the bridge itself.

He brought the Jeep to a halt, left the engine running and flung himself from the car. The train was already thundering down the tracks beside the gorge as he reached the rail. No time to consider his action, to calculate the risk. It was almost here.

He climbed over the rail, positioned himself on the lip of the bridge. Mere seconds to take a measure of the drop. It was an easy distance in feet. But a leap onto a moving train made it seem like an impossible task. Where Cathryn was concerned, he would manage the impossible.

He tensed in a half crouch, timing himself as the engine roared under him. Then, as the first car started to roll by, he launched himself into space.

He hit the roof on hands and knees, the impact sending a jolt of pain through his injured arm. But he couldn't worry about that, couldn't even grab a second to congratulate himself on the success of a landing that a stuntman would have envied. A startled Cathryn, gaping at him in disbelief, had managed to work her way to the car just behind his. But her pursuer was closing on her from the roof of the third car.

Scrambling to his feet, he found his balance against the yawing train and executed what amounted to a fast tight-rope walk from the first car to the second one. All right, he was on the same roof with Cathryn now, but how did he protect her? Because if that bastard had a gun—

He did! With the threat of interference, the hired killer had produced a semiautomatic pistol from inside his jacket. He was creeping toward them now, a vicious grin on his fleshy face.

"Cathryn, get down," her rescuer commanded as he reached her. "We may have to take our chances and go over the side of the train."

She dropped to her hands and knees, staring in terror at the trees and boulders flashing by. "It's too fast! We'd never make it!"

He crouched beside her. "It's either risk a jump or die up here."

And that seemed to be a certainty, because their enemy was now on the same roof with them. He already had the gun leveled at them in triumph. He had only to cover a few more feet to be sure he wouldn't miss.

"Cathryn, go!"

She tensed but she couldn't do it. She couldn't willingly spring to her death. She didn't have to. At that second a head poked through the gap back in the dome. It was someone from the train, shocked to see that there were people on the roofs. He shouted a challenge, his words lost in the wind.

But the unexpected yell behind their enemy was enough to alarm him. His head swiveled in surprise. And the man Cathryn knew only as Ben instantly seized advantage of the situation, diving at their adversary.

Clinging to the roof, she watched the two men locked in a raging struggle. In spite of his bulk, the killer was agile.

Ben, weakened by his injury, was exerting a tremendous effort to overcome him. Cathryn never knew how he managed it, but the gun suddenly spun into the air and came bouncing down on the edge of the roof.

She went for it, crawling rapidly across the width of the car. She never reached it. The killer, desperate to reclaim his weapon, delivered a powerful blow to his attacker's vulnerable arm. Ben, slammed aside, lost his footing and went down. In one swift rush the enemy pounced on the semi-automatic. Recovering his balance on the treacherous brink of the roof, he raised the gun toward Cathryn, his face livid with hate.

She would have died in that second if it hadn't been for the river. It turned at this point. The rail tracks did not. Without warning, the train jounced onto a trestle that crossed the gorge. The jarring motion destroyed the restored balance of the man on the edge of the roof. He teetered there for an instant, fighting to save himself. Then, with a whimper escalating into an angry howl, he went over the side, plummeting to the rocky water below.

The next thing Cathryn knew, she was up on her knees. And *he* was there, also on his knees and holding her tightly. Covering her face with kisses and asking her between those kisses if she was all right. She wasn't all right. She was still shuddering over the horror of that man's death, even if he had been determined to kill her.

"Your arm," she kept muttering foolishly. "Is it open again? Bleeding?"

He didn't answer her. The train was in the forest again on the other side of the river. It was slowing, stopping. She was dimly conscious of people below pouring from the cars, of raised shouts along the embankment.

He lifted his head. There was a grin on his lean face. "Oh, sure," he said, "*now* Annie manages to get the train stopped."

She stared at him. "Would you answer just one question for me?"

"Anything."

"Who are you?"

## Chapter Twelve

"Nick Gillette."

Cathryn had been repeating the name to herself all the way back to Lovejoy. This time she said it aloud, trying to accustom herself to the sound of it. Trying to get used to his real identity. Not easy when all these weeks she had been thinking of him as Ben Adams. But she liked his name. Nick Gillette. It had a strength that suited him.

"French," he said. "Cajun French. Probably Creole, too. And Italian. Definitely Italian in there somewhere. And who knows what else. My ancestors liked to mix it up."

"Choctaw," she reminded him.

He grinned at her. "Slipped up with that one, didn't I?"

"Only after I began to put everything else together."

They were outside the hospital where Ben's arm—no, *Nick's* arm, she prompted herself—had been treated again and pronounced no worse for his ordeal. The body of their attacker was being recovered from the gorge by the local authorities, and then Nick would meet with them to present his statement.

There was a stream behind the building that meandered through the alpine meadows. Nick had asked her to stroll with him on the path along its edge. He wanted a quiet place away from interruptions to offer his explanation. And Cathryn needed that explanation.

"So tell me, Officer Gillette," she asked him. "Just how did I wind up with you instead of Ben Adams?"

"I could claim something like authorized surveillance, but it was much sneakier than that. Blame it on Gary Bolling, and just be glad that devious mind of his is on the side of the good guys."

Cathryn knew he was referring to the assistant district attorney in New Orleans. "Gary Bolling can also be very persuasive. Like he was with me when I first agreed to testify against Red Quinn."

"And with your cousin, too. Eventually, that is. Gary showed up at Meredith's place just hours after she saw you off on that bus. She refused to tell him anything, even denied that she'd had any contact whatever with you."

"But in the end . . ."

"What else could she do when Gary had the best argument in the world? He promised her that, no matter where you were hiding, Red Quinn and his people would find you. But if he could get to you first, he would move heaven and earth this time to make sure you were kept safe."

"So Meredith told him everything." No wonder her cousin had sounded so guilty and uncertain when she'd phoned her the other day.

"Leaving Gary with one hell of a situation when he flew back to New Orleans. He couldn't reach you because Meredith didn't know where you were holed up for the week before you were scheduled to leave for Alaska. And he had no legal right to hold you at the airport. Figured, too, that after what you'd been through, you would refuse protection and just vanish again."

"But there was a way not to lose me," Cathryn said, realizing the scheme the assistant D.A. must have devised.

"Correct. He'd let you go on to Alaska, and he would see to it that you had professional protection when you got there. Only you couldn't know about it because you'd run again."

"Enter Nick Gillette," she said softly.

"Yeah," he admitted with a gruff reluctance. "Nick Gillette."

His fingers had been threaded through hers as they moved along the bank of the bubbling stream. A never-let-you-go kind of connection that gave her a warm glow. But the pressure he exerted now on her hand was another form of communication. An appeal for forgiveness.

"Go on," she said, squeezing back with her own message of reassurance.

He didn't respond for a moment. He stared off into the endless Alaskan twilight that cloaked the mountains. There was regret in his deep voice when he continued. And that recurrent pain she had yet to understand.

"I was the perfect candidate," he said. "Been living in Anchorage for almost a year, so I was already in place, and Gary knew and trusted my work from New Orleans. He also knew I was low on funds and probably wouldn't need much convincing to accept the job. He was right, damn him."

"And Ben Adams?"

"Also caved in for a reasonable price," Nick admitted with a trace of bitterness. "So there we were, the three of us engaged in this conspiracy that had to be kept secret. Gary realized by then that the information leaking to Quinn and his crowd must be coming through his offices. He told no one down there about the setup or my involvement in it."

"But they must have immediately learned somehow about my coming to Ben Adams in Alaska. The man on the train had to have been sent by Quinn."

Nick frowned. "You're right, of course. That much did get out, and as soon as everything is settled here, I intend calling Bolling on it."

They paused on the edge of the stream. A cold wind blew down from the mountains, rustling the leaves on the willows nearby. Cathryn shivered. Nick turned to her, sliding his arms around her and drawing her into his warmth.

"Better?"

She nodded, then shook her head.

"Make up your mind, McLean."

"Can't. Not until you tell me what you did with the real Ben Adams."

"Tucked away in my Anchorage apartment. You wouldn't like him. He never mourned a bit over the loss of your cousin. Unfaithful, too. Already found himself a new girlfriend somewhere."

"What a pity. I was hoping to look him up, satisfy my curiosity about how the original compares with the replacement."

His arms tightened around her. "I wouldn't advise it."

"No?"

"Definitely no."

"Maybe you're not being fair. Maybe you never gave him a chance."

"A week holed up with him in that cabin was more than a chance. It was a sentence. We drove each other crazy, but I had to learn everything I could about him and the area before you arrived."

"We were holed up in that same cabin," she countered.

His teeth gleamed through the dusk in a wicked smile. "Not the same kind of intimacy, was it?"

Cathryn pressed against his solid warmth, savoring his familiar male scent, the way his body was molded to hers, arms cherishing her. "I think you're right," she said weakly.

"I think this is a case where the replacement is much superior to the original."

Head lowered, he tenderly nuzzled the mole high on her cheek. "I hope so," he muttered. "I was half out of my mind the whole time I was with you."

"Why?"

"Because you were supposed to be just an assignment. You know, getting you to trust me so that eventually you'd confide in me, and maybe then I could persuade you to go back and testify, which was a commitment I had real trouble with." This explained his drugged mumbling in the hospital earlier. "I wasn't supposed to fall for you. That wasn't in the plan. You'll never know how many kinds of bastard I called myself and how many times I came close to telling you the truth. I couldn't. I was afraid you'd vanish on me."

"Awful thing to have a mail-order bride walk out on you," she said. "Especially after you've gone and paid for her ticket."

"True. There should be a fair return on the investment."

"Consider this the first dividend, then." She locked her hands behind his head, drew his face down close to her own and kissed him slowly and thoroughly.

"Sweet profit," he murmured when her mouth finally released his.

"Count it as the first of many."

He chuckled deeply, his beard-roughened cheek slowly caressing her smooth one. They stood there holding each other for a long moment, listening to the sounds of the water in the stream and the wind searching through the willows.

"Nick?"

"Mmm?"

"Why did you leave New Orleans and come to Alaska?"

Her question was a mistake. His mood altered immediately, becoming dark and strained. She felt his body go rigid against hers. Then he pulled away from her abruptly, left the path and moved down to the close edge of the stream. He stood by the willow thicket, his back to her.

Cathryn followed him, determined to understand whatever it was that made him so intense at times. He was like that now, she thought, gazing at his profile in the murky light. A strong profile with its Roman nose, but a brooding one.

"You were a runaway like me, weren't you?" she pressed him gently.

"You see too much, Cathryn McLean."

"I was a research librarian, remember? We never give up until we've gathered all the data."

He was silent. She waited for him patiently, hoping he would tell her. When he realized she wasn't going to give up on him, he began to share his secret.

"I had to get away from New Orleans. I had to go just as far as I could, and Alaska seemed as far off as any place."

"Why, Nick? Why did you have to leave your work and your life down there?"

"Because I was coming apart." He went on in a mechanical voice, and as he spoke, his hand steadily and systematically stripped away the leaves on a willow bough hanging beside him.

"There was this woman I was involved with. Karen Justice. Not smart having an affair with your partner, especially when you're both cops. But since when does smart have anything to do with it when it comes to attraction? Old story, huh?"

"Were you in love with her?"

"I don't know. I never had the chance to find out. She was gone before we ever got to that stage."

There was a harsh edge in his tone, telling Cathryn what she'd already guessed. That Karen Justice was no longer alive.

"We were on a routine drug bust," he continued. "Not that any of them is ever really routine, but this one was supposed to be a straight operation. They have to be selling the stuff to you before you can collar them. I was all set to meet with the dealer, but Karen wanted to do the trade. Said her cover would be much less suspicious. Our superior agreed with her."

"And you objected to that?"

"Not enough. Karen was good but not all that experienced. And I had a bad feeling about the scene. I should have listened to my instinct. I should have fought the decision."

"It all went wrong?"

"Very wrong. She went in wearing a wire. We were outside as backup, ready to storm the place as soon as the exchange was made. The dealer was supposed to be alone. He wasn't. His friend fingered Karen as the cop that had arrested him two months before. I don't think I'll ever stop hearing her screams over that wire. Before we could get to her, the scum had executed her."

Nick tugged viciously at the willow bough, released it with a snap and then added woodenly, "It was a situation as familiar as an old TV movie, but when it's real and you're involved in it... Believe me there's nothing that feels familiar about it."

"You blamed yourself for her death."

"Yeah, I guess so. Maybe. I just know they kept telling me the pain would go away, and it didn't. In the end I had to get out."

Cathryn ached for him, knowing how haunted by grief and guilt he must have been. And still was, she feared.

"How you must have resented me," she said softly.

He turned to her, wearing a little smile that tugged at her insides. "You were an assignment I didn't want, but I was trying to start a security service in Anchorage and I needed the money. You involved me again with life, and I was afraid of that. I didn't want to feel, didn't want to know all the old emotions. But they were there from the minute you stepped off that plane."

"Regrets?"

"That much of a fool, I'm not. As for what happened in New Orleans..." His arms slid around her, drawing her close. "Someday I'll make peace with it for good, put it all behind me."

She hoped so. There could be no future for them together otherwise.

"I've got shadows back in New Orleans to put behind me, too, don't I?" she said. "The murder of Francis Menard, the senator's brother. It must have been something vital for Red Quinn to have risked killing him like that himself, for not waiting for one of his goons to handle it. There's just something strange about that, Nick."

"Maybe, but that's for New Orleans to deal with. Because after today you're out of it."

"Am I?"

"Damn right you are."

His arms tightened, holding her safely. She enjoyed that sense of total security. For a moment. In the end there was no way to avoid reality.

"It's not over, is it, Nick?" she whispered. "We both know what I have to do."

"You're staying right here with me in Alaska," he insisted, hanging on to her so fiercely she thought her bones would snap.

She understood his sudden anger. It was motivated by fear. The fear that if he let her go, he would lose again, as he had lost so tragically in New Orleans. She understood, but it didn't change anything.

She shook her head. "I have to go back and testify. I see that now."

"To hell with Bolling and what he wants. It isn't his life that's on the line. Quinn's hit man is dead. That gives us the chance to get you away, and this time no one will know where except you and me. Alaska is a big place."

"The death of Red Quinn's hit man may already have been picked up by the media and be all over the news. If it has, he'll immediately send someone else after me. Nick, there's nowhere left to hide. I realize that now. The only way I can ever be free of him is to help put him behind bars where he belongs. Because once I go on that stand, there's no longer a reason for him to—"

"No! It's too risky. I won't let you do it. Not after what almost happened on that train. The assistant D.A.'s got to understand that now—"

He had no chance to continue his argument. They were interrupted by a sturdy figure hurrying along the path from the hospital.

"Hey, you two," Annie called to them. "They're back from the gorge with the body and waiting to talk to you. Gonna be a long session, so I'll leave you with one piece of advice. Avoid the coffee in those machines. Tastes like something that head nurse might've brewed in a mean mood."

RED QUINN'S THICK, freckled hand squeezed the remote control as if it were flesh and bones he wanted to crush. He stared for a few seconds at the blank television screen he had just switched off. Then he cast his savage gaze in the direction of the man who shared the richly paneled office with him.

"Been all over the news since late last night," the mobster growled. "Haven't identified him yet, but I don't kid myself it wasn't Tesler who ended up on those rocks. Which means the McLean bitch is still on the loose. How long, Morgan? How long is she gonna stay lucky?"

The lawyer, immaculate in an expensive business suit, smiled confidently at his friend and employer. "Her luck has already run out, Red."

"Yeah? What is it this time? Another lead on her through our connection with the D.A.'s office? They're not stupid over there, Morgan. They've got to realize by now there's a leak. Bolling's not gonna let any more information get passed to our source. How many hit men can we keep sending anyway, even if one could get near her again?"

Morgan Hurley shook his head. "We don't have to go after her anymore. This time she'll come to us. *Willingly.*"

Quinn leaned forward in his chair, his brutal face flushed with eagerness. "Let's hear, and it better be good."

"Since when am I not dependable, Red? And thorough. I've been digging into her life all this time, trying to find something useful. Something that could provide us with the means of an alternative, just in case Tesler failed. Knowledge is power, Red. You know that."

"And?"

"Nothing. Not at first. Then I went back to her days at the university in Baton Rouge, ended up calling in a favor before I was through. I struck the mother lode, Red. You're going to like this."

The lawyer went on to explain what he had learned about Cathryn McLean and how they were going to turn her secret against her.

When he was through, Quinn chuckled. "Yeah, it's good. It's real good. You taking care of it?"

"Everything is already in place, Red. You don't have to worry. The boys were careful."

Quinn turned his gaze in the direction of the wide windows overlooking Lake Pontchartrain, cruel eyes squinting against the brilliance of the early-morning sun on the expansive water.

"So now we just sit back and wait, huh? You sure this'll work?"

"It will work. And I don't think we'll have to wait long. She cares too much not to make regular contact."

"Which means she'll end up just where I want her," Quinn snarled. "Mouth shut forever."

THERE WAS A CHILL in the early-morning air that felt more like autumn than summer at its peak. Cathryn, shivering, hurried into the fresh clothes that Annie had managed to obtain for her last night from one of Lovejoy's stores. She dressed quietly, careful not to disturb Nick, sprawled on the bed in a deep sleep.

He needed to rest. Yesterday had been long and arduous, robbing him of his strength after the injury to his arm. There had been no question of returning to the cabin after that late meeting with the local authorities. Both of them had been exhausted and gratefully accepted the hospital's offer of a room for the night.

Cathryn wouldn't have minded another hour or two of sleep herself. But she had a phone call to make, and she didn't want Nick knowing about it. Not yet. She needed first to reassure herself that everything was still all right back in Louisiana, and then . . .

She paused to draw a steadying breath, her gaze softening as it lingered for a moment on his sensual face and sleep-tousled black hair.

And then, she promised herself with a nervous smile, she was going to tell Nick about the other man in her life. She was already praying that he would forgive her silence and understand. That he would accept Zachary.

Their conflict over her testifying had also to be settled, she thought as she slipped out of the room, purse in hand. They hadn't returned to the subject last night, too tired to do anything but tumble into bed. But it could no more be avoided today than the matter of Zachary.

It was too early for any activity in the hospital corridor. There was no one around as she made her way to a public phone at the other end. But it would be hours later in Baton Rouge, a reasonable time to reach her party.

Cathryn was startled when the phone at the other end was snatched up on the first ring. The frail grandmother usually needed a moment to get to the telephone. She must have been right there by the instrument.

"Hilda? It's Cathryn. Is everything—?"

"Thank God, thank God," the elderly woman babbled. "He said I wasn't to do anything but wait for your call. *Nothing.* But it could have been days before you phoned again. Even waiting hours was unbearable. I didn't know what to do. What should I do?"

There was a pitiful pleading in her voice that made Cathryn instantly sick with alarm. "Hilda, what's wrong? It's Zachary, isn't it?"

"I couldn't keep him indoors. Not all the time. The house is so small. He had to go out and play sometimes. Just into the backyard. Never any farther than that. And I would check on him from the window. Every few minutes I checked."

She was hysterical, not making sense. Cathryn fought for self-control, an essential calmness. "Hilda, slow down. Tell me clearly exactly what happened."

"I am telling you. Zachary went into the yard just after breakfast. One minute he was there in his sandbox, and in the next minute he was gone. I went out to the garage to look for him. He goes into the garage to find bits of wood for his buildings. So I went into the garage after him. He wasn't there, and that's when—"

Her voice broke on a sob.

"The rest," Cathryn urged her. "Hilda, you have to tell me the rest of it."

"There was a man," she continued. "I didn't see his face. He wouldn't let me turn around to see his face. He stood behind me and spoke in this rough voice. He said they took Zachary, that he would be all right if I kept my mouth shut. But if I called the police, told anyone but you, we'd never see him again."

"What else?" Cathryn demanded. "What else did he say?"

"That you were to come back at once and alone. Wait with me at the house. They would contact you here, tell you what you had to do to get Zachary back."

"Hilda, you didn't call the police, did you?"

"I was scared," she wailed. "Too scared to do anything but sit right here by the phone and pray you would call."

"You did the right thing. These people mean what they say. Hilda, sit tight now and wait. I'll be there as soon as I can."

"You'll hurry. Please hurry."

"As fast as I can. Remember, not a word to anyone."

Cathryn's hand was shaking as she hooked the phone back on its cradle. Her worst fear had been realized, the very thing she had been making every effort to avoid.

Quinn and his people must have learned immediately of their assassin's death, and this was their response. But how had they discovered Zachary's existence when she'd been so careful? Not that it mattered now. Her escape to Alaska, using herself as a decoy, had failed.

She had to believe they wouldn't hurt Zachary if she obeyed them. She would go out of her mind otherwise. It was her they wanted. She had no illusions about what would happen to her when they got her. But she was prepared for that as long as she won his freedom and safety.

*Don't think about what Zachary must be feeling right now, how terrified he must be. You won't be able to bear it if you think about it. You can only help him by holding yourself together. You have to act.*

She picked up the phone again and called the airfield. She learned that the plane had returned from Fairbanks and would fly her to Anchorage as soon as she reached the field.

Her next action was harder. *Much* harder, but necessary.

Mercifully Nick was still asleep when she slipped back into their room. She had never hated anything so much in her life as having to walk out on him like this without a word of explanation. Knowing how much she would hurt him, especially after what he had shared with her about Karen Justice.

But she couldn't. She couldn't tell Nick about what she must do. He would try to stop her. He was a cop, would insist she involve the police. Would want to accompany her to Baton Rouge, placing himself at risk along with Zachary. There was nothing he could do that would guarantee results. Only she could do it. Protect both him and Zachary.

She had come to get the key to the Jeep, which had been retrieved and brought to the hospital the night before. She found the key on the table beside the bed, along with the other contents of his pockets he had emptied there last night.

Pausing beside the bed, key in hand, she stole one brief moment to search his sleeping face. To impress its wonderful image on her brain. She didn't deceive herself that she would ever see it again. She wanted to do more than just look. She longed to touch him. She didn't dare.

*Forgive me, Nick.*

Turning, she crept from the room, closing the door silently behind her. The Jeep was waiting out front in the parking lot. She would arrange at the airfield to have it returned to him. Have whoever brought it back let him know that she hadn't been snatched, that she had left by choice. He deserved that much. No note. What could she say?

The image of his face was with her as she sped toward the airfield. Would be with her all the way back to Louisiana. But his face wasn't the comfort she had sought. She was leaving him, and it was tearing her up inside. She didn't know how she could stand it.

# Chapter Thirteen

"Take it easy, Nick. You sound like a guy on the verge of hyperventilation, and I'm not there to help you breathe into a paper bag."

As always the assistant district attorney was composed and reasonable. Nick was in a mood to appreciate neither of those qualities. He was frantic.

"I want answers, Gary," he barked into the telephone. "I *need* answers."

"Nick, I told you. She hasn't contacted me or my office. You sure you got her message right?"

"She wasn't snatched. She walked out. I'm telling you, she changed her mind. She's determined now to testify, and she knew I was against it. Why else would she take off on me?"

"Okay, but it seems funny. Why the sudden haste? If it *is* her intention to testify, why risk trying to rush back here all on her own after what she's just been through?"

"Because she knew I would try to stop her, and you can forget any lectures about that. Look, we've been through all this. We're wasting time. Every minute we talk, she's getting farther away."

"Nick, I can relate to your desperation."

*No, you can't. You're not in love with Cathryn McLean.*

"I'm as worried about her as you are," Bolling continued, "but maybe this isn't the explanation. Maybe she's just plain scared and in the end simply decided on another disappearing act."

"You don't know her. She wouldn't do that. Not this time."

"All right. I'll start making inquiries, get out an alert for her. Let's hope in the meantime she gets in touch with me."

"It's not good enough, Gary. I want her back. *Safely* back. I'm going after her myself, whatever it takes. And don't try to take me off the case."

"You do what you have to, Nick. Just watch yourself. You know what Quinn and his crowd are like. Keep me posted. And no heroics. You need backup, you call for it. Anything else?"

"Yeah. Clean your house and discover who that informer is. Cathryn wouldn't be in this fix if Quinn hadn't had a pipeline."

"I'm working on it, buddy. Trust me, I'm working on it."

NICK'S MIND WAS TRAVELING as fast as the Jeep that carried him toward Percy.

Where was she? Where the hell was she? On her way to New Orleans? He had been certain this was her destination before talking to the assistant D.A. Now he wasn't so sure. Much as he hated to admit it, Bolling was right. Her sudden departure without a word of explanation just didn't make sense.

So why had she run out on him this time? Fear? A failure to trust him after his admission last night that he had been hired to persuade her to go back to testify? Had she ultimately viewed that as a betrayal? Convinced herself he had only made love to her in order to win her cooperation?

How could she think he would deliberately seduce her? He was furious with her if she thought that. Didn't she know by now that he was in love with her?

How could she know? He hadn't told her he loved her. He should have told her he loved her. But there had been no time, and now—

No! He refused to think it was too late.

But he was scared. Angry and scared. Angry that she had left him. Scared that maybe she didn't feel the same about him, that this might even be an explanation for her flight.

More than anything else, he was anxious about her safety. She was out there somewhere, vulnerable to an enemy who would do anything to locate and destroy her. He had to find her.

Calls to the airlines out of Lovejoy and Anchorage had gained him nothing. They would divulge no information about their passengers, not without official intervention. No time to secure that. That was why he was on his way to Percy.

He hated the necessity of this trip to the ghost town, the frustrating delay that was involved. But he couldn't just go off blindly searching for Cathryn. He had to begin with a direction of some kind. He was praying Sourdough Annie could provide that.

Cathryn must have told the old woman something about her plans in order to enlist her help yesterday. Maybe she had confided a destination on the long road into Lovejoy. A destination that was still her intention. It was his one hope.

Nick was relieved when he rounded the last turn on the rough track descending into Percy and saw smoke curling from the chimney of Annie's shack. There had been the chance she hadn't gone back to the ghost town after parting from them at the hospital last night.

Annie had just stepped into the yard to feed her llama when Nick arrived. She stared at him in surprise as he climbed from the Jeep and approached her. Then her gaze went back to the vehicle, looking for another passenger.

"No, Annie, Cathryn isn't with me. I don't know where she is, but maybe you do. I need your help."

He went on in an earnest voice to explain what had happened and just why he had come. She listened with no expression on her seamed face but what he feared was a lingering suspicion of him in her rheumy eyes. And all the while he pleaded with her, the damn llama kept nudging his shoulder. Looking for a handout, he supposed.

Annie's only comment when he finished was addressed to the animal, "Lulu, back off. He doesn't have any apples, and you already had your quota for the day."

The disdainful llama trotted away in the direction of the river. Annie regarded him blankly for a minute. Then she shook her head.

"I think you're all right. I think you do love her. That's why I wish I could help. Can't. She never said where she was going. Not a hint about it. And that's the truth, I promise you."

Nick nodded dismally. This was it, then. A dead end.

Annie considered him for another moment, face sympathetic this time. "Did mention her cousin back in Missouri, but I guess you've already taken her into account."

*Meredith.*

He was a fool. About as complete a fool as you could get. He should have remembered Meredith straight off. Cathryn's cousin was the only person she had trusted and turned to when she'd escaped from New Orleans. So why wouldn't she go to her again? And if she wasn't with her cousin, there was the strong possibility that Meredith had heard from her. Would know where to find her.

"Annie, I could kiss you."

"Better rethink that. The last man who tried ended up sore for a week in a spot I won't mention."

"Will you settle for a large thank-you? And, uh, doing me another favor maybe?"

"Like?"

"I'm going to be on the next plane to Missouri. Would you look after Angel and the puppies while I'm away? I'm not sure when Adams will return to the cabin or if he can be counted on to take care of the dogs when he does come back."

"Already promised Cathryn I'd be checking on them regularly. What are you waiting for? Go find her."

Nick obeyed her command, folding himself behind the wheel of the Jeep and racing up the track that took him out of Percy. Once back on the main road, he turned in the direction of the cabin.

He regretted the need for this quick detour before he headed back to Lovejoy and the airfield, but he had to have the letters from Meredith to Ben Adams. They bore her address in Missouri, something that Gary Bolling could provide him, except he didn't care to waste time on another call to New Orleans. Besides, he wanted to study those letters on the long flight. They just might offer some clue that could lead him to Cathryn.

The letters that Adams had loaned him were still there in the drawer of the bedroom bureau when he reached the cabin. He scooped them out and tossed them into a bag along with a few clothes and essential toiletries.

He was on his way out of the cabin when he remembered that Cathryn had abandoned her own clothes. He went into the room she had occupied, found her suitcase under the bed and flung her things inside.

He shouldn't have taken the time. Seconds counted. But he needed to do this. Packing her clothes was an act of faith. It made him confident that he would be able to bring them to her.

*Be there for me, sweetheart. Wherever you are, be there for me.*

NICK'S PATIENCE WAS at its lowest level as he sat behind the wheel of the rental car, anxiously searching the numbers of the houses along the residential street of the rural Missouri town.

Getting this far had cost him exasperating delays at two airports, three exhausting flights over an indirect route and disappointment in St. Louis when he'd checked with Gary Bolling again by phone. There had been no contact from Cathryn, no word on her whereabouts. She had been missing now for more than thirty hours, and the strain was almost more than he could bear.

He crawled past a brick building surrounded by a playground. It was summer. No kids in evidence. Probably the school where Meredith McLean taught. There were more houses shaded by maple trees.

Meredith's house was the last one on the street, located in the open where the town turned into a countryside of farm fields and rolling hills. It was a small, neat ranch house with a picture window and black shutters.

Nick parked in the driveway. A blast of afternoon heat struck him as he climbed from the car. This wasn't Alaska. He had forgotten just how hot July could be in this part of the country.

He was on his way to the front door when he heard a radio playing somewhere from the vicinity of the backyard. Altering his direction, he followed a flower-bordered path that took him around the side of the house. There was a deck attached to the back of the building. A portable radio on a redwood table filled the air with a country-and-western tune. There was no one on the deck.

And then he saw her. She was wearing cutoffs and an old T-shirt, her familiar blond hair like a halo in the sunlight. The sight of her casually weeding a vegetable garden at the edge of the lawn made his insides go soft with sweet relief.

"Cathryn!"

Startled, she lifted her head from the tomato vines over which she was bending. Shading her eyes against the glare, she turned to stare at him with a nervous smile. The relief immediately drained away from him, leaving a dull ache in its place.

It wasn't Cathryn, though the resemblance was remarkable. They shared the same slim figure, cap of ash blond hair and pleasing features. But there were distinct differences. Even from here, Nick could tell that Cathryn's cousin lacked the radiance of her smile, the warmth of her eyes, the mole high on her cheek that he loved.

She put down the plastic bucket into which she had been thrusting the uprooted weeds and came toward him across the narrow lawn, her manner plainly guarded.

"You've made a mistake," she informed him. "There's no one here by that name."

Her voice was husky, without Cathryn's lilting quality. Maybe because she was rightfully suspicious of him. Or maybe just because his feelings for Cathryn made any other woman seem ordinary to him.

"Sorry for the mistake," he said. "You're Meredith, of course. I'm Nick Gillette, the guy who's been looking out for her in Alaska."

Her blue eyes widened as she sensed a reason to be alarmed. But she kept her face blank and admitted nothing. Even after he displayed his identification and quickly filled her in on all that had happened, she was reluctant to trust him.

"This sun is murder," she said. "If we're going to talk, we'd better move into the shade."

She led the way up onto the deck, where the back of the house cast cool shadows. She didn't offer him a chair. Neither of them was in any mood to sit down. She turned off the radio and faced him. She looked as worried now as he felt. She was hesitant for another moment as she measured him. Then she made up her mind.

"I don't know where Cat is. She didn't come to me this time, and I don't blame her. Not after the way I betrayed her to your assistant district attorney."

"She'd be dead by now if you hadn't helped him to arrange protection for her. Ben Adams wouldn't have prevented that assassin from getting to her. You did the smart thing, Meredith."

"And now you want me to help you again." There was a bitter note in her voice as she leaned back against the deck's rail. "Not this time, even if I could."

"Why?"

"Because Cat doesn't trust you, or she would have let you know herself where she was going. And why should she trust any of you? This is twice now Quinn almost got to her because information was leaked on her whereabouts. First with that safe house in New Orleans, and then Alaska."

"I'm not the district attorney's office, Meredith. Anything you tell me goes no further."

Her shoulders lifted in a small shrug. "But I don't have anything to tell you. I haven't heard a word from her. I don't know where she could have gone or why."

She was lying. He could tell by the way her eyes evaded his. He remembered something he had read on the plane in one of Meredith's last letters to Ben Adams. Something he'd regarded as potentially useful. She had mentioned accompanying her cousin to Baton Rouge over the weekend. No explanation for the trip, but her tone had suggested something secretive and unpleasant about it.

"What's in Baton Rouge?" Nick demanded.

She cast her gaze around the deck, searching for something. Then she laughed, her hands spread in a gesture of helplessness. "I was looking for a cigarette. I gave them up ages ago, but I suddenly had this urge for a cigarette. Silly."

He refused to be sidetracked. "What's in Baton Rouge, Meredith?"

"The state capitol. You want a cold beer? I have some in the refrigerator."

"Meredith, help me," he pleaded. "I'm trying to save her, not hurt her. She's out there on her own somewhere, and I've got to get to her before Quinn does. If I don't get to her..." He couldn't finish. All he could do was shake his head in desperation.

She surveyed him in silence for a moment. "Oh, hell, you're in love with her."

"Yes."

"Then you'd better deserve her. And I'd better not be making a mistake by telling you something she might kill me for revealing. It's true I don't know where she went, but it could be Baton Rouge."

"Why?"

"Because Zachary is there. Someone she cares about more than herself. He was her biggest reason for hiding out in Alaska. She was using herself as a decoy to keep Quinn away from Zachary."

"Who is Zachary?"

There was a roughness in his voice that must have betrayed the sudden jealousy he couldn't help. She smiled at him wryly. "Her six-year-old son."

Nick was astonished. "She has a kid, and no one knew anything about him?"

His face had to be an open book to Meredith. The emotion she read this time was resentment because Cathryn hadn't trusted him to know something so major about herself.

"Don't judge her, Nick. There are good reasons why Cat kept his existence a secret from everyone, even you. It's complicated, and I'm not going to say any more. It's up to her to explain it, if and when she wants you to know."

"All right, it isn't important now. Getting to Baton Rouge, and hoping Cathryn is there, is all that counts. But where in Baton Rouge?"

"Hilda's. Zachary is with Hilda now. His grandmother."

"Your—?"

"No, no relation to Cat and me. Nor to Zachary's biological father, may he rot in hell. I told you it was complicated."

This was something else for Nick to ignore momentarily, though he was even more mystified now. "So, have you got a phone number for this Hilda?"

Meredith shook her head. "Wouldn't do you any good. Even if she bothered to answer the phone, she'd only deny Cathryn was there."

"You're right. Much better if I go there directly."

"*We,*" she corrected him. And before he could object to her intention, she added quickly, "The woman would probably be too scared to open the door to you. She's elderly and not in the best of health. On top of which, she suffered a terrible loss not long ago. But I'm someone she knows and trusts."

Another mystery, Nick thought. "Can you leave right now?"

"Give me five minutes to change and toss a few things into an overnight bag."

"You've got them. Meanwhile where's your phone? I'll check with the airport in St. Louis. With any luck we should be on a flight to Louisiana this afternoon."

Even better, he prayed, they would find Cathryn at the other end.

THE HOUSE WAS in a blue-collar section of the city where most of the properties were small but decently maintained. It was a narrow, old-fashioned bungalow that sat well above the perpetually damp Louisiana earth. Two ancient pecan trees graced the front yard.

Twilight was settling on Baton Rouge, but the air was still heavy with the humid heat of the day when Nick parked the rental at the crumbling curb. He left the car, accompanied by Meredith, and led the way along the overgrown walk and up onto the porch.

He rang the bell, waiting anxiously as the seconds crawled by. There were no lights in any of the windows. "What if she's not at home?"

"Hilda almost never leaves the house," Meredith answered him confidently. "She's arthritic. Give her time."

Nick was tense with impatience before the curtain at the window of the front door was parted slightly. He glimpsed a lined face in the opening and a pair of nervous eyes peering at them through the glass. He wisely moved to one side so that the old woman would have a full view of his companion. He let Meredith do the talking.

"Hilda, it's all right. It's Cathryn's cousin, Meredith. Remember? And the gentleman with me is a friend."

There was a long, uncertain moment of hesitation, and then came the sound of a lock being turned. The door opened on a chain, revealing a small, frail woman in the crack.

"What do you want?" The nervousness was in her voice, as well as in her eyes.

"Can we come inside?" Meredith coaxed.

"I don't know...."

"Please, Hilda, it's very important. We'll only stay a few minutes."

There was another long pause. Nick could scarcely control his frustration. It was Meredith's pleading smile that finally persuaded the woman to admit them. She nodded reluctantly, closed the door and released the chain.

Seconds later they were in a dim parlor that smelled of mildew and furniture polish. There was no air-conditioning in the house. The room was sweltering. A window fan did a poor job of circulating the air.

Hilda, moving slowly, lowered herself onto a sofa. Meredith settled beside her and introduced Nick, who perched tensely on the edge of a chair facing the two women.

"This is Nick Gillette. He was with Cathryn in Alaska. They became very close."

Hilda glanced at him, then looked away. "Why are you here?"

"We've come looking for Cathryn," Meredith explained.

"She isn't here. Why should you think she should be here? I haven't seen her or heard from her."

"Where is Zachary, Hilda? Can we talk to Zachary?"

"I shouldn't have let you in. It was a mistake. You'll have to go now."

Nick noticed how her voice trembled. Her hands were shaking, too. The woman had fear written all over her. He leaned forward in the chair, forcing himself to speak to her gently.

"We're here to help Cathryn, Hilda," he appealed to her. "The boy, too, if he needs it. You do know where they are, don't you?"

"No."

"Look at me, Hilda, and tell me you don't see how much I care about Cathryn and how scared I am for her and her son."

She gazed at him through the shadows of the room. "I—I can't," she said, her voice quavering. "They'll kill Zachary if I tell anyone."

Her admission was a blow. Nick, preserving his self-control, struggled to win her confidence. "They have the boy. That's it, isn't it? That's what brought Cathryn back from Alaska. Hilda, they may kill him anyway if you don't help us to get to them. Tell us, Hilda. If you value either of them at all, tell us."

There was silence in the room except for the lazy whir of the fan. A taut silence. And then the old woman began to speak in rapid, broken phrases. The whole story came pouring out in a rush. She was weeping by the time she finished.

Meredith squeezed close to her on the sofa and held her, trying to comfort her. Her eyes met Nick's, exchanging their mutual horror. Cathryn was going to exchange her life for her son's.

It couldn't happen. He *refused* to let it happen. It wasn't too late to save both of them. He wouldn't let it be too late.

"How long ago did they make the contact?" he demanded.

The woman shook her head.

"Hilda, answer me."

"Just before you arrived, they phoned. And then Cathryn left in a taxi like they instructed."

"Where? Where is the switch to be made?"

"Riverbend."

"Where—?"

"I know it," Meredith explained. "Cat and I used to go there as kids. It's an amusement park south of town. No longer open. Scheduled for demolition, I think."

"You remember the way?"

"I can find it."

"Let's go."

He surged to his feet, putting his emotions on hold as he headed for the door. The only thing that could serve him now was a brain like ice, and maybe his training as a cop. Along with a fast car. He trusted the rental out front to be that.

## Chapter Fourteen

The taxi pulled away and vanished around a corner, leaving Cathryn all alone in the rapidly fading light. She crossed the deserted street toward the fanciful Moorish-style entrance to Riverbend. The sight of those twin plaster towers, now tarnished and crumbling, had thrilled her as a child with the promise of all the magic that lay behind them. The only feeling they evoked now was anxiety for the welfare of her son.

The iron-grille gates were padlocked, barring her entry into the park. But, as she had been instructed to do, she stood in front of them for a minute, a streetlight clearly revealing her. They wanted to be sure she was unaccompanied and bearing no visible weapon.

The evening air was sultry and still. The only sound was the drone of a dredging operation in the Mississippi off the levee at the far end of the park. The noisy crowds that had once thronged to Riverbend were gone forever. There was no one in evidence now. But Cathryn knew that the thugs who wanted her were hidden somewhere in the shadows watching her.

The required minute of waiting seemed like a lifetime. When it ended, she turned to the right and followed the high wall surrounding the park. A few yards along she reached a narrow service door. It had been left unlocked for her.

Slipping inside, she closed the door behind her as directed and retraced her route to the main gates. The broad avenue that was the midway stretched out in front of her. She began to walk slowly up its length, careful to remain in the center of the street and to display no action that might be defined as threatening. She didn't dare to look back toward the freedom of the street.

She knew that her progress was being monitored, knew what would soon happen to her. She was prepared for that moment and refused to let it unnerve her. She had to stay calm in order to negotiate Zachary's release. Keeping her mind numb, she distracted herself with memories.

She and Meredith had come here years ago. Even then, Riverbend had been a little seedy. They hadn't noticed that. Their young eyes had seen only excitement and the lure of pleasure. Not now. Now the games and concession stands along both sides of the midway were shuttered and pathetic looking in the weak glow of the few security lamps.

She was nearing the webs of steel that formed the double Ferris wheels when a voice barked at her from the darkness.

"Far enough! Get your hands up and keep them up!"

She obeyed, coming to a standstill and raising her arms. A figure emerged from the side of the penny arcade. She ordered herself to betray no fear as he approached her, gun in hand.

"Where's my son?" she demanded.

"Shut up," he growled.

He circled her cautiously at a safe distance, then moved in to frisk her. Her skin crawled at the intimacy of his hands examining her. She could smell a cologne on him. Strong and overly spicy.

"She's clean," he reported.

Two other shapes appeared from the depths of the arcade. One of them was dark and burly and gripping a much smaller figure by the hand. Zachary. They moved toward her as she held her breath.

When they were close enough for her to see the blindfold on Zachary, she exhaled in relief. There had been the awful risk that, once they had her, they would refuse to free Zachary. But the blindfold was their safeguard against any future identification of them by the boy. At least they drew the line at murdering a child. That was the only thing in their favor. It was all she asked for.

They reached them, and Cathryn started to go to her son. But the younger one who had searched her grabbed her by the arm. She dared to defy him. "Stop that!" She twisted free and crouched down in front of Zachary.

He was thin and small for his age, and she knew he must be terrified. She spoke to him gently.

"Sweetheart, it's Cathryn. Are you okay?"

He had been told recently that she was his biological mother, but she was still a stranger to him. Someone he called Cathryn and had yet to fully understand and accept.

"Cathryn?" he whispered in a small, uncertain voice. He started to remove the blindfold, but she caught his hand.

"No, not yet. In a minute. Everything is going to be fine in just a minute." There was so much she wanted to say. So much she wanted him to know, but she wasn't given the opportunity.

"That's enough," the older one ordered in a rough voice. "Tell him goodbye and let him go."

She got to her feet. "He'll need the money I brought him. All right to take it out of my pocket?"

"Make it quick."

She extracted the folded bills from the pocket of her jeans and placed them in Zachary's hand. "Listen to me carefully, sweetheart," she instructed him, praying he wasn't too scared and confused to follow her instructions. "I'm turning you around now. When the blindfold is off, you'll see some gates straight in front of you at the end of the street. I know you can climb over them. I've seen you climb the trees at your grandma's. When you're on the other side, you go as fast as you can toward the bright lights down the block. There's a store not too far. Ask someone to call a cab for you, and when it comes, tell the driver to take you home. Do you remember your address?"

"Yes. Why can't you come with me?"

"This isn't smart," interrupted the younger one. "We're taking a chance letting him go."

"Can it," his companion muttered. He stood behind Zachary and leaned over him with a sharp warning. "All right, kid, I'm taking off the blindfold. But you don't turn your head and look back. You run for those gates without a peep behind you. Understand?"

Seconds later, choking on her emotions, Cathryn watched her son clamber over the iron gates and disappear into the darkness. It wasn't fair. She hadn't gotten to tell him goodbye or how much she loved him. She would never see him again. Never watch him grow up. But he was safe. That much she had managed for him.

"Let's go," the one in charge commanded.

They were impatient now to get it over with, the younger one uneasy about the delay. Red Quinn's two goons closed in on either side of her and began to lead her into the depths

of the park. She didn't ask them where they were taking her
or what was going to happen when they got there. She knew.

She tried to keep her mind a blank as she walked between
them, thinking it would be easier that way. Impossible. She
kept seeing Zachary's small face, frightened and bewildered. She saw another face, as well. The face of the man
she loved. She was stricken by its image.

*I don't want to lose you, Nick. I mind that the most, but
there was no other way.*

They passed the merry-go-round under the Victorian-style
pavilion. The dismantling of the park had already begun.
The valuable hand-carved horses were gone. The pavilion
looked forlorn and ghostly without them.

The thinner, younger one snapped his head to the right.
"What the hell was that?" he muttered.

His companion glanced at him without interest. "What
was what?"

"Thought I saw something moving out there."

The older one chuckled. "Yeah, the Phantom of Riverbend. Don't be an ass. Nothing there. If there was, it'd be
the night watchman, and he's been too well paid to interfere."

"Place gives me the creeps," grumbled the younger one.

Cathryn was silent as they moved on. Imagination, or had
she also glimpsed a flitting shadow? *Wanted* to glimpse it,
because hope in any form refused to be extinguished? No
point in deceiving herself. She would seize any opportunity
to survive, but no chance would present itself. Better if she
prepared herself for the inevitable.

They crossed the tracks of the kiddie train, passed the tilt-
a-whirl. A giant skeleton loomed above them, pale against
the evening sky. Cathryn recognized the structure. The
Thunderbolt. The park's most breathtaking roller coaster.

There was a jagged gap at the bottom of the coaster's first steep hill where timbers and track had been removed. The tall fence against the levee close on the other side had also been torn open. The hole must have been created to permit the loading of demolished materials onto barges.

Apparently the easy access to the river was just as convenient for her two escorts. When they turned into the opening, she knew this was the place they had chosen for her execution. The ground was uneven. She stumbled, and one of them jerked at her savagely.

There was the sound of heavy machinery somewhere nearby, the clanking of chains lifting a load. Her younger captor started nervously.

"What's spooking you now?" the older one challenged him. "It's just the dredging across the levee. Gonna cover the shots, remember?"

"Then let's do it and get out of here."

They had come to a stop now in what had been the coaster's first valley. They faced Cathryn, guns drawn. The plunging, broken tracks ending abruptly at their backs.

"Relax. Another two minutes, we're gone, and she's floating downriver."

Cathryn shut her eyes, waiting for the impact of the bullets that would end her life. She heard a roaring in her ears and thought it must be the sound of her own terror inside her head. It was followed by wild yells. She couldn't be responsible for those.

Her eyes flashed open, gaping in astonishment at the sight above her. She understood it immediately. The earlier noise hadn't been the dredging operation. Someone at the Thunderbolt's loading platform had raised the coaster's cars to that first lofty peak. And now those empty cars were dropping over the incline, hurtling straight toward them like a rocket out of control.

For a fraction of a second, like her shouting captors, she was too paralyzed to move. Then all three of them scrambled to safety. The two men dived toward the levee. Cathryn instinctively flung herself in the other direction.

What followed were images so rapid and explosive that they barely registered on her brain. The Thunderbolt's cars leaping into the vacuum where the tracks ended. The screaming of rending metal. Sparks flying from the wreckage.

The shadow that they'd imagined minutes before suddenly became a reality. Sprinting from under the lacework of the coaster's timbers, he snatched her by the hand. And before the confusion had time to subside, she was running with him toward the midway, away from the howls and gunfire behind them.

The park's security lamps were too scattered and dim to permit recognition. But she would have known her rescuer anywhere, even in absolute darkness. He couldn't be here. *Shouldn't* be here. But he was, and her heart soared.

"Nick!"

"Surprise!"

"I like your surprises. Even when they're runaway roller coasters."

"Yeah, well, without a gun I had to point something at them. Look, save your breath until we get out of here because—uh-oh."

They had reached the midway, where they came to a halt. Charging toward them through a pool of light from the other end of the street several hundred yards away was the uniformed figure of the night watchman. The gun in his hand cut off their escape.

"He's one of them, Nick," she warned him.

"Time to duck out of sight."

They turned and fled into the deepest shadows at the side of the street, keeping their voices to the level of urgent whispers as they ran.

"One of them, huh? And with those other two bastards behind us— Any other way out of here besides the front exit?"

"Not without making us clear targets on top of the levee. Loops right around the park. Riverbend, remember?"

"Trapped. Then we evade them until help arrives. Only which way?"

She tried to think as they hugged the darkness, feeling their way.

"Make it fast, Cathryn. Can't see the watchman now, but he must be closing on us."

Decide, she ordered herself. Decide *now.* "I know this place like you probably know the back alleys of New Orleans. This way!"

She took off at a fast trot, cutting to the right between the bumper cars and the moon ride. Nick was close behind her. They spoke in breathless undertones.

"Hung out here a lot, did you?"

"Every chance I got."

"Where you taking us?"

"Not sure yet. I'll know it when we get there. The watchman—"

"No sign of him behind us. Looks like we lost him."

"But he's out there somewhere, along with the others, and they—"

"Yeah, they won't give up until they find us."

"I have to get us to a safe hiding place, then."

They were in a landscaped area now where the light was very poor. They slowed their tense pace briefly in order for Cathryn to make sure of her direction.

"Nick?"

"Right here."

"What you said back there about help arriving. Is *it* on the way?"

"Let's hope so. With any luck Meredith will find a way to send in the cavalry."

"Meredith?"

"Long story. All you have to know right now is that Zachary is with her. I waited until they were safely in the car before I climbed the wall."

She was grateful for that. Grateful that he was with her now.

"So all we have to do," he said, "is hang on long enough. Where are we?"

"Center of the park. We should be— Yes, there it is."

In front of them was the gleam of softly lapping water.

"What is this place?"

"A series of connected lagoons. This is the largest one. There were boats for riding on them. Like Venetian gondolas."

"Romantic. Can't say the same for that."

He indicated the dark bulk of a structure occupying an island in the middle of the lagoon. The sinister Gothic pile, complete with turrets, was reached by a drawbridge from the other side.

"The Devil's Castle," she said. "My favorite. It was the park's—"

Her explanation was interrupted by the frantic shouts of their pursuers not far behind them.

"If you're going to get inspired," Nick urged, "this is the time for it."

"Think I have."

She caught him by the hand, drawing him swiftly along the edge of the lagoon in the direction of the island. It was when they rounded a large concession stand that she found what she was seeking. There, just visible in the thick shadows, was the fleet of gondolas stretching in an arc toward the island. The craft had been lashed together to keep them from drifting.

"How are you at boat-hopping?"

"Thought you were the one who wasn't crazy about them."

"No choice. The gondolas are deep. If we can get out to that farthest one and lie flat—"

"Let's do it."

Keeping low, they scrambled silently from one rocking gondola to another. Reaching the last one, they dropped over the side and stretched themselves along the bottom. Seconds later came the sound of feet pounding along the pavement that circled the main lagoon. The searchers called to each other as they spread out along the waterways.

Cathryn and Nick were squeezed together face-to-face on the floor of the gondola. His arms were around her, holding her securely. Neither of them moved or dared to speak. They waited. The footsteps finally retreated, the cries faded. Mercifully the gondolas hadn't been investigated. Their pursuers had moved on.

For the moment they were safe, but they stayed where they were on the floor of the craft, clinging to each other. Slowly lifting her hands, she began to touch Nick's face. She couldn't see him in the warm darkness of the night. She suddenly needed to be sure he was real.

"I thought I'd never see you again," she whispered in awe, her fingers stroking his beloved features.

He pressed a kiss against the palm of her hand. Then he groaned softly in what she hoped was frustrated passion.

"Nick, I know this is an awful time for confessions. But I want you to know about Zachary and me. Just in case..."

"We *will* make it," he promised her fiercely.

"Yes, but I want you to know now. I wanted to tell you about him long ago, but I didn't dare. I was too afraid for him. Then, when I finally did trust you to know, it was too late."

She paused, permitting them to check for any sound that might be their searchers returning. But the heavy, humid air was silent except for the faint stirring of the water in the lagoon.

Cathryn made herself go on. This was the hard part, but she could bear no more secrets between them. "I was nineteen and going to college here in Baton Rouge. I had never dated much and was terribly naive, no real experience at all. This boy I met . . . I thought we were in love, that he genuinely cared. I found out just how wrong I was when I got pregnant, and he simply disappeared."

"Sweetheart," he whispered, his arms tightening around her lovingly, "you don't have to relive this for me."

"Yes, I want you to know how it was. How vulnerable I was after that, thinking I'd never again have a real relationship with a man because I was just plain scared of another disaster, of repeating all my mistakes. But then you came along, Nick, and everything changed."

"I know, love," he murmured. "I know."

"Not about Zachary," she went on softly. "You have to hear about Zachary. I—I gave him up for adoption right after he was born. There was no way I could keep him. The pregnancy was a difficult one, and I wasn't well afterward. And with no funds to speak of and no family left by then, except for Meredith...well, I just wasn't in any state to raise a child. I did what I thought was best for him. I gave him up to a couple who would love him and make sure he had all the advantages I couldn't provide.''

"And you regretted it afterward," he guessed.

"There wasn't a day that went by that I didn't regret it. But I made myself stay out of his life. I thought he would grow up never knowing me. Then just weeks ago his adoptive mother and father were killed in a car accident. Zachary went to his only surviving adoptive relative, his grandmother, Hilda.''

"I met her," Nick said.

"Yes, of course. That would be how you found me. You must have noticed then that Hilda's health is poor. She's in no position to bring him up. She was able to contact me, ask me if I would take Zachary. Did I *want* him? There was nothing that could keep me from having my son.''

"Except Red Quinn," he said.

"That's right. Before I could make the arrangements to have Zachary with me in New Orleans, Francis Menard was killed, and I was suddenly a hunted woman. Hilda had to keep Zachary safe here in Baton Rouge, and I had to keep his existence a secret by going away from him as far as I could.''

"Alaska."

"Yes, Alaska. I thought under another identity I could build a new life, and that when I was settled, Zachary could—''

She was interrupted by the sound of voices. The killers looking for them had returned. Cathryn could feel Nick tensing. They kept silent now, listening.

"They're somewhere around here," one of them called insistently. "I can almost smell them."

"Did you check those boats before?" the other answered from farther away.

"Thought you did."

"Jerk! Do it now."

"We've got to get out of here," Nick whispered.

"How, without running straight into him?" She could already hear the clatter of the gunman boarding the first gondola.

"How deep is the lagoon?"

"If you're thinking about our going over the side, it isn't a good idea. They used to say when I was a kid that they couldn't keep the water moccasins out of the lagoons. I'm not too eager to test those rumors."

Nick shuddered. "Me, either. Then let's go to Plan B."

She understood his intention when he lifted his hands to the ropes that connected them to the other gondolas and began to work rapidly at the knots. If they could free their craft and get the gondolier's pole into the water, they could shove themselves to cover on the nearby island. Cathryn joined him in attacking the knots.

It was no easy job. They had to huddle below the level of the gunwale or betray their presence. And all the while, as they fought the knots, they could hear the enemy moving closer as he climbed from gondola to gondola.

"That does it," Nick breathed when the last rope slid loose. Snatching up the pole, he started to get to his feet.

"Nick, he'll see you!"

"Don't know any other way to push us out of here. Keep down."

The second the pole dipped into the water, there came a volley of yells and curses. Cathryn, crouching below the side of the gondola, was terrified for Nick, who was exposed to the barrage of bullets that immediately followed. At least two of them struck the gondola.

The bullets were still flying a moment later when their craft reached the island, but at this distance they were ineffective. Cathryn, looking over her shoulder as she followed Nick ashore, glimpsed the shadowy form of the younger gunman already rushing back to the embankment on his side. There was no sign of his friend.

"You weren't hit, were you?" she anxiously questioned Nick as they fled through the shrubbery. "Tell me you weren't hit."

"Never touched me," he assured her. "Handguns like his aren't reliable except at close range. Let's keep it that way."

"Meaning we'd better get off the island before they cut us off on the other side."

The gloomy, massive castle loomed above them on the right as they worked their way rapidly in the direction of the drawbridge.

"Cheerful," Nick remarked. "What's the Devil's Castle doing in an amusement park?"

She was too busy finding a path for them through the azalea bushes to answer him. How long now had they been evading their enemy? And how much longer must they try to conceal themselves before help arrived? Had something prevented Meredith from contacting the police?

Rounding the island, they gained the approach to the drawbridge. They had wasted no time, but they were already too late. The heavier man was racing toward the bridge on the other side, his companion not far behind him. They would be caught on the bridge before they could cross it. They were trapped on the island.

Nick swore violently. Cathryn had a more useful reaction. She was on familiar ground here. Neither of those two gorillas chasing them could possibly know this place as she did. Hopefully she still remembered all the surprises.

"Come on," she said, grabbing Nick by the hand and pulling him around.

"Where to now?"

"Inside," she insisted, dragging him through an archway.

"What are we getting into with this Devil's Castle of yours?" he demanded as she led him swiftly up a brick ramp.

She supposed it was time he knew. "The fun house, of course."

His only answer was a strangled noise deep in his throat.

"Don't worry, Nick. I know all the devil's tricks, even in the dark. And this is the first of them."

They had reached a screened porch that was the way into the fun house. But it was a screened porch like no other. It consisted of wall upon wall of floor-to-ceiling screen doors.

Nick came to a startled halt. "What the—?"

"It's a maze. The challenge is to discover which door will let you into the next row, because most of them are fixed and won't open."

"I hope you've got the answer to all of them. *Now,* Cathryn."

She understood his urgency. There were footsteps pounding through the archway behind them.

"This way."

Hurrying to the center of the outer wall, she thrust against a screen door. It swung open, admitting them into the first passageway.

Thereafter, they twisted and turned rapidly through the labyrinth. Her accuracy was remarkable. They were just two rows away from the doorway into the solid wall of the castle now. Her judgment failed her at this point, trapping them in a stubborn dead end. By then the first of their pursuers was banging away at the screen doors of the outer wall, trying to force his way inside. Seconds later, bullets came winging through the layers of wire mesh.

"Uh, it's getting a little crucial here, Cathryn."

"I'm trying, Nick. I think they changed some of these doors. Wait, here we go."

Two screen doors later they were plunging into the castle itself, leaving the enemy slapping viciously at the walls of strong mesh behind them.

"Ought to keep them occupied for a bit," Nick chortled. "Whoa, where are we?"

Blackness, total and bewildering, had swallowed them.

"Stay close and hang on to me," she hissed, "or you'll find out the hard way."

They were traveling through a winding corridor. The air was damp and stale. The sound of their footsteps echoed and then changed in tone a moment later, telling Nick that they had reached an open space.

"We're in the crooked room," she informed him. "There are railings here, but they're not much good in the dark. You've got to be careful because—"

A loud thump told her he hadn't been listening and had landed in a heap at her feet. "The damn floor is slanted!"

"Told you to hang on to me. The whole room is built at crazy angles."

"Devil's Castle is right," he grumbled, pulling himself erect. "It *is* hell in here."

"You okay?"

"Dandy. Just get us out of this place."

"I'm afraid the next room isn't much better, Nick."

He found that out. There were disks embedded in the floor of the chamber. It was like finding your way through a field of land mines. Step on a disk, and it whirled you off your feet.

He lost count of the corridors and the hazards. Somewhere along the way he heard thuds and howls of rage and frustration a safe distance behind them.

"Sounds like they got to the crooked room," he observed with a grim smile. "Hope they break their butts in there."

There was no answer. He suddenly felt all alone, and he panicked like a kid. "Hey, where are you, Cathryn? I'm up against a wall here, and something about it feels treacherous. If it's another one of your sur— Holy smoke!"

The whole wall had abruptly come alive with a blinding light. Nick found himself face-to-face with the fiery, leering figure of Satan himself. Even if the castle's mechanical host was safely behind glass, he was sure his blood pressure suffered a blow.

He quickly backed away from the display, discovering that he was in a Hades-style torture chamber. Phony or not, the place was damn eerie.

Cathryn suddenly appeared from around a corner looking worried. Not by any of the devices in the chamber, he realized. She was staring at the red lanterns on the walls, which hadn't been glowing a minute ago. There was more light streaming through a small, pointed window in one of the castle's turrets located at the side of the room. She rushed to the window.

"The whole park is blazing with light! The watchman must have turned on the power for them everywhere, including here."

This was bad, she thought. They had been able to keep well ahead of the two hoodlums in the dark because she had the advantage of knowing her way through every obstacle in the fun house. But now, with the lights, she and Nick could be overtaken or cut off at the exit.

He appreciated the situation himself. "I wouldn't be opposed to a fast way out of here."

He hadn't meant that plea quite so literally, he thought a moment later when he found himself launched into a chute behind Cathryn on what had to be the longest, steepest, swiftest slide anywhere.

"Great!" he croaked as they whizzed down to the lower depths of the fun house. "What's waiting for us at the bottom? Old Lucifer himself with a flaming pitchfork?"

He wasn't. What did receive them was a kind of giant whoopee cushion over which they had to wallow to gain the solid floor of another corridor.

"This is nearly the last of it," she promised as they turned a corner to confront an enormous, open-ended barrel.

Looks harmless enough, he decided, eyeing the shoulder-high, horizontal drum. But in this place nothing was what it seemed. Ducking his head, he followed her through the short tunnel. They emerged in a chamber of mirrors. Their distorted images leapt out at them from every side.

"Exit," he implored. "Where's the door out of here?"

Cathryn wasn't listening to him. She had moved to the back of a tall mirror situated at an angle just outside the barrel. She was in no hurry now. She should have been in a rush. Couldn't she hear it? The clatter of footsteps rapidly approaching the barrel on the other side. The first gunman was almost here.

"It's a two-way mirror," she explained, resting her hand on a lever high on the wall.

"He groaned over the delay. "And guns shoot, and we don't have one. They do, remember?"

"What I remember," she said, "is a fun-house attendant lurking behind the mirror here to surprise unsuspecting victims."

It was too late to make her understand their desperate need to run. The younger hood, well in advance of his heavier friend, was already entering the barrel, revolver waving in his hand. Nick was prepared to shove Cathryn behind him. She had her own agenda, choosing that instant to throw the lever.

The great cylinder immediately began to revolve. With an oath of fury and surprise, the gunman was tumbled off his feet. Nick was impressed. He also knew an opportunity when it was so readily offered to him. Issuing a battle cry that would have made his rebel ancestors proud, he dived into the rumbling barrel on top of the sprawled and screaming enemy.

Slipping, sliding, cursing, the two men slugged it out on the floor of the rolling drum. Cathryn tensely followed the struggle, watching for a chance to help. It wasn't necessary. Nick managed to wrest the revolver out of his opponent's grip. By the time she got the barrel stopped, he had the brute pinned under him and the weapon ready to face their next pursuer.

It wasn't the second gunman who appeared in the opening moments later. This arrival was wearing the uniform of a Baton Rouge police officer, as were the other figures who swarmed into the chamber of mirrors from the opposite direction.

Cathryn didn't pause to welcome them. She was too busy speeding joyfully into the barrel to fling herself into Nick's arms.

## *Chapter Fifteen*

"Your son all right, Cathryn?"

"He seems fine," she answered the assistant district attorney. "Meredith took him back to his grandmother's and promised to stay with him until he fell asleep."

Gary Bolling nodded, his earnest manner in contrast with his boyish appearance. "That's a blessing. Had to have been a tough experience for him, but children Zachary's age are pretty resilient."

Cathryn, aware of Nick's prolonged silence, glanced at him. He was seated close beside her on the sofa of the amusement park's front office, where they were meeting with Bolling, who had arrived just minutes ago. She wondered what was bothering Nick. He was glowering at the assistant D.A.

"It's all getting sorted out," Gary assured them, leaning against the edge of the desk from where he faced them. "They've got the night watchman now, too. He'll face charges along with Quinn's two goons."

Small talk, Nick thought impatiently. He didn't like it. He didn't like the fact that Bolling was suddenly here in Baton Rouge.

Gary eyed him insightfully. "Something wrong, Nick?"

"You tell me. You didn't have to race up here by chopper to deal with any of this in person. Another phone call could have assured you that we're all right now and that Cathryn is ready to go back to New Orleans and testify. So what is it you want?"

"All right, I'll get to the point. I need Cathryn to help us. Tonight. Before anyone back in New Orleans has a chance to learn what happened up here or how it turned out. We're going after that informer."

Nick's response was immediate and emphatic. "No way. It's enough that she's willing to testify against Quinn. You're not going to ask more than that, not after all she's been through. I don't want to even hear what you're proposing."

"I do," Cathryn said in a low, solemn voice.

He swung his head, staring at her. She didn't like it that he was making decisions for her. What could he do? It was her choice to listen. He could only fume in helpless silence while Bolling briskly pressed his advantage.

"We think we know now who's been passing knowledge of your whereabouts on to Quinn and his crowd. In fact, I'm certain of his identity, but without real evidence I can't act on it."

"Someone inside your office?"

He shook his head. "That seemed the obvious explanation for the leaks, even though I trusted the handful of people who had to be involved in your situation. There was only one outsider who shared in any of the secrets, and that was because, not only did he have a right to know, he was above suspicion. That was before I put an investigator to work. Interesting results."

"Who?"

"Senator Hugh Menard," Bolling informed them quietly.

Cathryn stared at him in disbelief. "That's impossible! It just can't be! The senator has always been a sworn enemy of Red Quinn. He hated everything he stood for, and his brother... He took Francis's death very hard and wanted Quinn to pay for his murder."

"I'm sorry, Cathryn. I know how much you admire Menard, but it all points to him."

"It's crazy. It would mean he and Quinn are somehow in collusion."

"That's right. And incredible as it seems, there is an explanation for such a complicity. My investigator found it among Francis Menard's notes, a jotting that was either overlooked or considered not important when the examiners went in after the murder. Francis had scrawled a question on the back of an envelope about a large, unexplained contribution to his brother's campaign fund. You were a volunteer for the senator's reelection, Cathryn. You tell me what the biggest concern was at his campaign headquarters."

"Money," she admitted reluctantly. "Everyone knew what a close race it was going to be and that his opponent had no problem with funds. But the senator..."

"Exactly. Know what I think the scenario was? I think Red Quinn went to the senator and offered him a whopping sum in exchange for future favors, and a desperate Menard caved in and agreed. I imagine that sum got buried somehow, but the senator's campaign manager, Francis, eventually found evidence of it and was outraged over his discovery."

"And that night at the campaign headquarters," Cathryn said in a small, disillusioned voice, "Francis must have been threatening to expose Quinn and his brother."

"So Quinn shot him." Bolling nodded slowly. "Yeah, I think that's just how it was. And the senator is protecting himself now by helping Quinn. Only I can't prove it. I need to prove it, Cathryn. I need to bring both of them down."

There was silence in the office. Nick glared at the assistant D.A., hating and fearing what was about to happen and feeling helpless to stop it.

"What do I have to do?" Cathryn asked, her expression already decisive.

"With your cooperation we can move quickly on this. We *have* to move quickly before Quinn learns his two goons failed tonight and warns the senator. The chopper is waiting. We can be in New Orleans in minutes."

"And then?"

"The senator will be shocked when you turn up at his house and tell him you're through running and ready to testify. That you've gone straight to him because he's the only one you trust now to secure the protection you didn't get before. He'll be alarmed and, if Quinn told him about tonight, he'll wonder how you got away. The one thing he won't fail to do immediately is alert Quinn you're there. When he does, we've got him, because my people will be close outside. The phones will be covered. I've already obtained a court order to monitor all calls there. You won't be alone, Cathryn. We'll be ready for action because we'll hear every word. We're going to fit you with a wire."

A wire, Nick thought. Cathryn would wear a wire. As Karen Justice had worn a wire on that drug bust and gone to her death.

It was the casual mention of the wire that sent him over the edge. He surged to his feet. "You bastard! You'd use her as bait, sacrifice her just to get a resolution of your lousy case!"

Gary stood away from the front of the desk and tried to deal reasonably with his violent opposition. "Take it easy, Nick. It's not going to be that way. Cathryn will be removed from the scene, well out of danger before Quinn or any of his people arrive to collect her."

"It's a risk. You can't be positive Menard will phone Quinn. That he won't try something himself."

Cathryn got to her feet and stood close beside him, her hand on his arm. "Please, Nick." Her voice was calm. It was also frighteningly determined. "I need to do this. I need to see all the loose ends tied up. I don't want to live with any more shadows or uncertainties. Besides, Francis Menard was a good man. I'd like to help expose the brother who betrayed him."

Nick stared at her, knowing that no anger or argument was going to change her mind. He turned his head, facing the assistant D.A. with a savage expression, "I'm going to be there when she goes in. Right there, just as close to the action as I can get. And I wouldn't advise you to object to that."

CATHRYN EMERGED from the deep shadows of the live oak where she had been left to wait. A nearby streetlight allowed her to check her watch. It was time.

She moved a short distance down the block and started up the brick walk of the Menard home. It was a handsome, Georgian-style residence in the upscale suburb of Metairie. Most of the windows were dark. It was late.

Nothing stirred in the warm darkness. Cathryn, suddenly nervous, felt as if she were all alone in the night. Only an illusion, of course. She realized that, though they were well hidden, Bolling's officers were now in place everywhere on the grounds, covering all the doors and windows. And Nick. She knew that Nick was somewhere out there close by.

The certainty of his presence renewed her courage as she mounted the front stoop and rang the bell. A dog in the neighborhood barked and then was silent. Seconds later the porch light came on over her head. She waited, feeling certain she was being checked from the peephole in the door.

She must have been recognized, because the door was quickly opened. It was the senator's wife who stood there in the foyer, a stunned expression on her face.

"Cathryn! It *is* you, isn't it? I could hardly believe my eyes."

"I'm sorry to come to you like this out of the blue," she apologized, "but in the end it seemed the safest thing to do."

Vivian Menard, still bewildered, glanced out into the night. "You didn't come here all alone, did you?"

"It's all right. I was very careful. I left the taxi two blocks down and walked the rest of the way. Mrs. Menard, I know it's late, but I need the senator's help."

Vivian didn't hesitate. She drew her into the foyer, closed the door behind her and faced her with a concerned expression. "Are you all right, Cathryn? You must have had a terrible time out there on your own."

"It was pretty rough, yes."

"And, of course, you're in no state to go into any of that right now. Never mind, it's enough that you're here. And thank heaven you made it."

"I had to. I'm ready to turn myself in as a witness, but I don't trust anyone now except the senator to help me do that."

"I don't blame you. You did the right thing in coming to him. I know how relieved he'll be to see you. Let's get you comfortable, and then I'll tell him you're here."

Cathryn, following her out of the foyer, could see why Vivian Menard was such a famous hostess on the Washington scene. She was small and elegant and immensely likable. The living room into which she led her reflected her cultured tastes.

She insisted on settling Cathryn in an easy chair. "Can I get you anything? The housekeeper is in bed, but—"

"No, I'm fine."

"Forgive me. You're anxious to see Hugh, and I'm prattling. He's still in his office. I'll just be a minute. You try to relax, dear."

It was a kind but impossible invitation Cathryn realized as Vivian hurried away. Left suddenly alone, she was tense over the prospect of facing Senator Menard. She had to remind herself that she wasn't alone at all, that help was just outside listening to everything.

The reassurance did nothing to ease her doubts that were triggered by the presence of what must be cherished family heirlooms everywhere in the room. They seemed so wholesome, making her wonder if Gary Bolling could be mistaken about the senator. His contention was still more theory than fact. Maybe...

A smiling Vivian reappeared. "He's waiting for you in his office, Cathryn."

This was it. She got to her feet and followed the senator's wife. They went down a long hallway toward the back of the house, passing the darkened kitchen. Turning a corner, they reached a closed door. Vivian stepped aside.

"No need to knock. Go right on in."

Cathryn thanked her and opened the door. She found herself looking, not into an office, but into a garage occupied by two cars. Astonished, she wheeled around. Vivian Menard stood there still smiling. A pistol was now in her hand.

"Go on," she said in a silky voice. "Into the garage. And don't try anything because I'm not afraid to use this gun on you myself if I have to."

"What—?"

"Not 'what,' Cathryn. *Who.* We're going to take a little drive over to Lake Pontchartrain to meet him. Did you know that's where Red Quinn lives? Lovely property right on the water. He'll be so glad to see you."

"The senator—"

"Oh, he's been in bed for the past hour, so I don't think we should disturb him. In any case, he wouldn't approve. Or understand." She gestured with the pistol in the direction of the garage. "Let's move now. You can tell me on the way just how you managed to survive Baton Rouge."

Cathryn started to turn toward the garage. In that instant the door directly behind Vivian opened on a back stairway to the second floor. The silver-haired figure of Senator Menard, clad in robe and pajamas, emerged into the passage.

He was clearly startled by the presence of the two women. And equally staggered by the sight of the gun in his wife's hand. "Dear God, Vivian, what have you done?"

"What you should have done yourself," she answered him, her voice laced with contempt. "I got the funds that are going to make it possible to return you to office and me to Washington, where I belong. And now I intend to see to it that we don't lose those funds.''

"Vivian, give me the gun."

"Don't interfere, Hugh. Go back upstairs. Forget—''

Her head swung around in alarm at the sound of glass and wood shattering from the front of the house. It was followed by other crashes from the side and back, along with the pounding of feet.

Senator Menard used that opportunity, while his wife was distracted, to snatch the pistol from her hand. He was holding it when Nick, the first to reach the scene, dropped in a rigid crouch, his own weapon raised toward the senator. There was a murderous expression on his face.

"Nick, no!" Cathryn cried out to him, realizing he must have entered the house before hearing over the wire the last part of the exchange. "It was his wife! *He* never knew!"

There were other officers then crowding into the area to take charge of the situation. Their bodies blocked the way, preventing her from going to Nick. He hadn't moved. Though he had lowered his gun, he remained in that frozen crouch, a shaken expression on his face that scared her. What was wrong? Now that she was safe and it was all over, why was he suddenly unable to deal with the scene?

The area was cramped with too many people. As soon as the questions and confusion eased, she struggled through the sea of figures to reach Nick. He wasn't there. He had dropped his gun on the floor and walked away, disappearing without a word.

THERE WAS very little traffic in the streets at this late hour. Gary Bolling was able to talk freely while he drove Cathryn to her apartment.

"She didn't argue about it," he said, referring to Vivian Menard. "She knew it was either cut a deal with us or face charges that wouldn't be mitigating. She told us everything."

Cathryn nodded, pretending an interest she didn't feel. She could barely concentrate on Gary's explanation. All she could think about, worry about, was Nick. He was still missing.

"The senator always shared everything with his wife," the assistant D.A. continued. "Even the sort of information he had no business telling her. But it was that kind of relationship. She was a part of him. And, of course, she had enormous influence with him. We turn left at this light?"

"Yes," Cathryn murmured.

"And that was what she was able to sell to Quinn—her influence and her useful knowledge. She proved how valuable they were when she could pass on to him the secrets of your whereabouts."

Gary was trying to be kind. Trying to relieve her anguish over Nick. The least she could do was summon a spark of concern about the case. "It's hard to believe her life-style in Washington mattered that much to her.

"But it did. She loved the power and politics as much as the social scene. It was how Vivian Menard defined herself, and she was ready to do anything to keep from losing it."

"Macbeth's wife," Cathryn said. "I don't suppose the senator will go on with his campaign now."

"Probably not."

"I'm sorry about that and what he must be suffering over this."

"And I," Gary said, pulling into the street where her apartment was located, "am unhappy that you insist on going back to your place."

"I told you, I'm through running and hiding. There aren't going to be any more attempts on my life now that they're all in custody and their confessions already on record. You admitted as much yourself. It's that building there."

"All right," he relented, drawing to the curb in front of the three-story, converted Victorian that overlooked City Park and Bayou St. John. "I know you want to be alone in your own surroundings while you wait for Nick. I guess I can appreciate that. But remember the deal. You don't stir out of this car until the officer I arranged for arrives."

He'd left her no choice. She had agreed to the posting of an officer at her door, at least for the time being.

Gary turned off the engine while they waited. There was silence in the car. It lasted for several minutes. It lasted until Cathryn could no longer stand it.

"Maybe he's not going to come. Maybe I'm just kidding myself that he will."

She was not referring to the officer Gary had called for, and he knew that. "Trust him," he advised.

"I'm trying to do just that, but I keep remembering how he looked tonight. There was such torment in his eyes. I didn't understand it then, but I think I do now."

"Tell me."

"It was because of his partner who was killed in that drug bust. I didn't remember about Karen Justice and what she meant to him when I insisted on going alone into the Menard house wearing the wire. It was the same scene all over again. Don't you see what I did to him? I made him relive that hell, and now..."

"You think he can't forgive you."

"Why else would he have vanished once he knew I was in the clear? Gary, I'm afraid I've lost him, and I—I just don't think I can stand that."

"Don't do this to yourself, Cathryn. Give him a chance."

"I hope he'll let me." She was silent for a moment, staring out at the night. Then she turned to him again. "Tell me something, Gary. You know him probably better than anyone. Is a part of Nick, maybe even a big part, still in love with Karen Justice?"

She shouldn't have asked. She could see that Gary was uneasy with her question. He was saved from answering her by the appearance of the patrol car bearing the young officer who had been dispatched to look out for her.

Gary accompanied them to the front door of her building. "Look," he said before parting from her, "I think I have an idea where Nick might have gone. I'll do my best to hunt him up and bring him back to you. In the meantime try not to worry. And get some rest."

He departed without further explanation. The officer escorted Cathryn to the second floor, checking out her apartment before stationing himself on a chair outside her door.

Left alone, Cathryn gazed around her tiny apartment, wondering now whether it had been wise of her to insist on returning here. She had made it a pleasant, cozy retreat, which hadn't been difficult since many of the original Victorian embellishments were preserved in the conversion, including a marble fireplace in what had been the master bedroom and was now her living room. But it was a lifetime ago she had left these rooms. The place seemed strange and unfamiliar to her, not the comfort she had counted on. Her spirit was still in Alaska, and her heart with the man who had shared the wilderness with her.

She made herself a cup of tea, which she didn't want, but it gave her something to do. Then she settled in her favorite spot, the window seat that overlooked the street. It was impossible to obey Gary's advice. She could neither rest nor keep from worrying.

She thought about Zachary and how eager she was to have him with her as soon as the matter could be arranged. But mostly she thought about Nick. Where did the assistant district attorney think he had gone? She wished she had made Gary tell her. This waiting was torture.

It was almost an hour later, and she was anxiously watching the street, when a car arrived out front. She pressed to the glass of the window, her breath quickening with hope. Then she realized it was just one of the other tenants in the building arriving home after a late night. Disappointed, she went on waiting. A few minutes later the phone rang. She rushed across the room to answer it.

"It's Meredith, Cat," her cousin identified herself. "I'm at Hilda's. They told me when I called the police department that you'd gone home."

"Zachary. Is something—"?

"He's fine, Cat. Both he and Hilda are just fine, the two of them in bed long ago. But I couldn't go to sleep until I knew what happened."

Cathryn was instantly contrite. "I'm sorry. I should have phoned, but it was so late I was afraid I'd wake everyone in the house. Besides, I've been . . . pretty distracted."

She filled her cousin in on the night's events.

"So, no word on Nick yet, huh?"

"Not yet."

They talked for another few minutes, Meredith offering her comfort along with her opinion of Nick. Her cousin's closing observation of him made Cathryn smile even in her misery.

She was alone again when their conversation ended, her only companion the monotonous hum of the air conditioner. She curled up in an easy chair, but there was no question of sleep for her.

Gary had no luck finding him, she thought. If he had found him, she would have heard by now. They would have been here after all this time. He wasn't coming. She had to face that now. Nick wasn't coming.

But a spark of hope refused to be extinguished. She went on clinging to it.

The first streaks of daybreak were lighting the sky when she heard the slam of a car door out front. She raced to the window and looked down into the street. Her heart missed a beat at the sight of the two men standing by the car shaking hands. Gary and Nick.

The assistant district attorney climbed back into his car and drove away. Nick turned and started for the front door. She buzzed him into the building and then waited for him in the open doorway of her apartment. The alert young officer asked no questions. He could see by the joy and anticipation on her face that there was no cause for concern.

*Thank you, God. Thank you for bringing him to me.*

They met in her doorway, where he gathered her into his arms. They stood there for an emotional moment. Saying nothing. Just holding each other tightly.

In the end she had to know. She pulled away from him and searched his face. He looked terrible. Unshaved, face haggard with exhaustion. As though he'd been through a grueling ordeal. But there was one encouraging sign. Bloodshot though his eyes were, there was a peacefulness in them. The haunted shadows were gone.

He favored her with a tired little smile. "I've put you through hell, haven't I?"

"It doesn't matter. Not now." She took him by the hand and drew him into the apartment, shutting the door behind them. "All that counts is you're here now."

"Yeah, it does matter," he insisted. "You didn't deserve my running out on you like that. I lost control, Cathryn. I'd been holding it all in since Baton Rouge, sick over the possibility of something happening to you. And then when it was all over and you were safe... I just suddenly went to pieces."

"Because of Karen Justice, you mean. Because you'd lost her like that."

He didn't answer her. He gazed around the apartment. Then he asked quickly, "Everything okay in Baton Rouge?"

She told him it was, that Meredith had called and they had talked. He nodded wearily and went and settled on the window seat. She joined him there, watching as he collected his thoughts.

"I want to tell you where I've been."

"You don't have to tell me," she said, clinging to his hand. She didn't want to know. She was afraid to know.

"It's important," he said. "I went to Karen."

"Oh."

The unhappy expression on her face moved him to remorse. "No, you don't understand. I went to the cemetery, Cathryn. See, I didn't attend her funeral or her burial. I couldn't bring myself to do it. But I realized last night that I had to go there now and tell her what I should have told her when she died. And that's where Gary found me and where we talked it out."

Removing his hand, he turned on the window seat to face her. He framed her face, his hands on either side. "I had to tell Karen goodbye. Let her go. Closure. Isn't that what people call it?"

"Yes."

"That's what I did, then. Closure. No more ghosts, Cathryn. Not for us."

Her eyes had misted with tears. He saw them and was anxious about them.

"Don't cry, sweetheart. There's nothing to cry about now. We should be celebrating. You brought me back. I'm alive again because of you."

"No tears, then," she promised him.

"That's right. Just smiles. For people in love it should always be smiles."

"Are you in love?"

"You want evidence?"

"It would help."

He kissed her then. A long, deep, provocative kiss.

"Sufficient?" he whispered.

"Uh-uh."

"What do you want? Words, too? Oh, hell, I haven't, have I? I've never said it. We've never stopped running long enough for me to tell you how much I love you. So, anyway, I do."

"And I do. Love you, that is. And now it's sufficient."

"Or will be when . . ."

"What?"

"When you tell me what Meredith said about me when you two talked on the phone."

"Now, why would you imagine she had anything at all to say about you?"

"Because women compare notes about guys."

"They do, huh?"

"It's a fact."

"Well, I don't think I will."

"Why not?"

"Because it'll just swell your male ego."

"That good, huh? Come on, it deserves a little swelling after the beating it's taken these last couple of days."

She considered him, head tipped to one side. "I'm going to regret this, but all right. What she said was, 'Keep him. He's not only a hunk, he's one of the worthwhile ones.'"

Nick beamed. "*Are* you keeping me?"

"That depends. Do I still get to be your mail-order bride?"

"Only if I can take you back to Alaska with me. You think Zachary will like Alaska?"

"Sure to. All that wildlife to chase, all those mountains to climb."

He grabbed her by the hand and pulled her to her feet, his body recharged by excitement. "Let's find out."

She laughed. "Now?"

"Why not? You've got a car, haven't you? And the distance to Baton Rouge is nothing. Let's go get our son and tell him he's moving to Alaska."

*Our son.*

"I like that," she said softly. "I like that very much."

# HARLEQUIN®

# INTRIGUE®

# COMING NEXT MONTH

**#385 BULLETPROOF HEART by Sheryl Lynn**
*Lawman*
Reb Tremaine appeared on the Double Bar R, his sexy lips saying
he could handle horses and his eyes saying maybe he could love a
widow like Emily Farraday. But Emily was in trouble. And the
danger didn't stop when she realized that everything Reb had told
her about himself was lies....

**#386 TELL ME NO LIES by Patricia Rosemoor**
*The McKenna Legacy*
Rosalind Van Straatan needed to know the truth about the night her
legendary grandmother confessed to a murder she probably didn't
commit. The irreverent and disturbingly sexy Skelly McKenna wasn't
exactly her first choice of investigative partners; unfortunately, he was
her only choice.

**#387 SPENCER'S SHADOW by Laura Gordon**
*The Spencer Brothers*
Anne Osborne desperately needed a hero, but Cole Spencer didn't
agree with his brother that he was the best man for the job. But then he
gazed into Anne's trusting eyes, and he knew he'd go to the ends of
the earth to protect this classy lady from a ruthless killer who thought
Anne knew too much.

**#388 A BABY'S CRY by Amanda Stevens**
Ten years after Dillon Reeves walked out on her, Taylor Robinson had
reason to believe that their child was not stillborn, as she'd been told.
Dillon had never known about the pregnancy, but would he agree to
help Taylor find their child?

---

# AVAILABLE THIS MONTH:

**#381 RULE BREAKER**
Cassie Miles

**#382 SEE ME IN YOUR
DREAMS**
Patricia Rosemoor

**#383 EDEN'S BABY**
Adrianne Lee

**#384 MAN OF THE MIDNIGHT
SUN**
Jean Barrett

Look for us on-line at: http://www.romance.net

# REBECCA
## 43 LIGHT STREET
# YORK
## FACE TO FACE

*Bestselling author Rebecca York returns to "43 Light Street" for an original story of past secrets, deadly deceptions—and the most intimate betrayal.*

She woke in a hospital—with amnesia…and with child. According to her rescuer, whose striking face is the last image she remembers, she's Justine Hollingsworth. But nothing about her life seems to fit, except for the baby inside her and Mike Lancer's arms around her. Consumed by forbidden passion and racked by nameless fear, she must discover if she is Justine…or the victim of some mind game. Her life—and her unborn child's—depends on it….

Don't miss *Face To Face*—Available in October, wherever Harlequin books are sold.

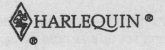

HARLEQUIN ®

43FTF

## HARLEQUIN®

# I N T R I G U E®

*The Spencer Brothers—Cole and Drew...*
*two tough hombres.*

### Meet

*Cole Spencer*
Somehow this cowboy found himself playing bodyguard.
But the stunningly lovely, maddeningly independent
Anne Osborne would just as soon string him up as let
him get near her body.

### #387 SPENCER'S SHADOW
### September 1996

*Drew Spencer*
He was a P.I. on a mission. When Joanna Caldwell-
Galbraith sought his help in finding her missing
husband—dead or alive—Drew knew this was his
chance. He'd lost Joanna once to that scoundrel...he
wouldn't lose her again.

### #396 SPENCER'S BRIDE
### November 1996

*The Spencer Brothers—they're just what you need to
warm you up on a crisp fall night!*

TSB

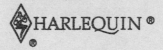

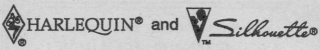

## HARLEQUIN® and 🅥 Silhouette®

### are proud to present...

# HERE COME THE GROOMS™

Four marriage-minded stories written by top Harlequin and Silhouette authors!

Next month, you'll find:

| | |
|---|---|
| *A Practical Marriage* | by Dallas Schulze |
| *Marry Sunshine* | by Anne McAllister |
| *The Cowboy and the Chauffeur* | by Elizabeth August |
| *McConnell's Bride* | by Naomi Horton |

**ADDED BONUS!** In every edition of *Here Come the Grooms* you'll find $5.00 worth of coupons good for Harlequin and Silhouette products.

On sale at your favorite Harlequin and Silhouette retail outlet.

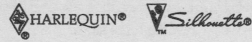 

HCTG896